W9-BMZ-850

From One Place to Another

A NOVEL BY

CAROL WHITE

Published by TriMark Press, Inc.
800.889.0693
www.TriMarkPress.com

PUBLISHED BY TRIMARK PRESS, INC., DEERFIELD BEACH, FLORIDA.

LIBRARY OF CONGRESS CATALOGING-IN-PUBLICATION DATA

FROM ONE PLACE TO ANOTHER BY CAROL WHITE

THIS BOOK IS A WORK OF FICTION. NAMES, CHARACTERS, PLACES AND INCIDENTS EITHER ARE PRODUCTS OF THE AUTHOR'S IMAGINATION OR ARE USED FICTITIOUSLY. ANY RESEMBLANCE TO ACTUAL EVENTS OR LOCALES OR PERSONS, LIVING OR DEAD, IS ENTIRELY COINCIDENTAL.

ISBN: 978-0-9849568-2-1

10 9 8 7 6 5 4 3 2 1
FIRST EDITION, FICTION
PRINTED AND BOUND IN THE UNITED STATES OF AMERICA.

A PUBLICATION OF TRIMARK PRESS, INC.
368 SOUTH MILITARY TRAIL
DEERFIELD BEACH, FL 33442
800.889.0693
WWW.TRIMARKPRESS.COM

To my dear friend
Wendy
Love Carol

Also by Carol White

Hidden Choices

Dedication

For Deborah Briggs, my BFF, best reader
and biggest fan.

Acknowledgments

Deepest gratitude to my friends at Gilda's Club and the National League of American Pen Women, Florida Writers Association and the IWWG. I am thankful for the wonderfully supportive libraries throughout Palm Beach and Broward counties, and eternally grateful to Murder on the Beach Bookstore for their sponsorship.

Thanks also to my friends at CBI and the Gift Shop where I spent many hours writing and rewriting this book.

I'm indebted to the wonderful establishments mentioned in the book that I frequent in Boca Raton, Delray Beach, Coconut Creek and Winston-Salem.

I owe so much to my editor, Penelope Love, my publicist, Ashley Ford, and Barry Chesler, all of whom made my life and lists easy.

Thanks, family and readers, for liking the chapters I sent early on and encouraging me to hurry up and finish.

The List

Part One

Part Two

Part One

From
One Place...

Chapter 1

June

News at Seven

On the evening of my thirty-sixth birthday, my husband, Mark, announced our marriage was over. We were squeezed into a booth only an anorexic could love at Winners Circle, an upscale restaurant of our Boca Raton country club, Boca Forest, when Mark delivered his pink slip version of a break-up notice.

"Dina," he said, "we've had almost fifteen years of a pretty damn good marriage, but you know as well as I that we were never truly meant to be together."

I knew no such thing, but at least he didn't say that we'd never been soul mates. As two of the many transplanted Manhattanites now living in Boca Raton, Mark and I shied away from the terms du jour we mocked throughout our marriage – such as "soul mates" and most currently, "baby night," which actually was supposed to be my birthday present. Then, in an assuaging tone he added, "at least we're doing this before we had kids."

Although Mark meant it as a good thing, whatever composure I was clinging to took a nosedive and I lost it. It's not that I gave up my self-control or calm; I mean I literally lost most of the poached oyster appetizer I'd just ingested.

Catching the bulk of it in an oversized black napkin that Winners Circle courteously provides to prevent renegade white-napkin lint from sticking to the basic black many women still wore, a stray, slimy clump remained lodged in my throat. My last thought before almost passing out was if someone doesn't do a Heimlich on me in the next thirty seconds, my husband's going to be a widower and won't even have to pay alimony. In a last-ditch effort I coughed up the offending mollusk and added it to the mess in the napkin, averting a stain on my consignment shop St. John black knit outfit.

"Madam is fine?" said a nearby server with a slight unidentifiable foreign accent, possibly from south Jersey.

"Yes, my wife is fine," said Mark, using that term without the ex in front of it for perhaps the last time.

The waiter bowed his head and retreated, hands held in the popular Praying Mantis fashion, until reaching his corner where he visually connected with Leo, our pit bull of a maître d', nodding that the crisis had passed.

"Why?" I said, croaking it out.

"I've met someone. She's my soul mate."

Chapter 2

June

Signs

Mark practically sprinted to the valet as I raced to keep up with him. Appearances were important at Boca Forest and I wasn't about to give up the perfect couple image before knowing the rest of the story. Living less than a quarter-mile from the clubhouse, my husband and I always walked the short distance for dinner, even in the sultry June weather. As we waited for our politically incorrect, gas-guzzling glossy black Hummer to be valeted to us, I realized why Mark insisted upon driving this particular evening.

I was in a daze when he pulled into our circular driveway and landed at the front door of our Mizner-inspired (poor Addison was probably turning over in his grave) house instead of using the two-and-a-half car garage. He sat in the driver's seat for a minute, his head turned downward listing toward his left shoulder like a nesting flamingo. I thought he was going to apologize for the very bad joke or at least for ruining my birthday, but all Mark said was, "can you toss me out a bottle of vitamin water?"

"Aren't you coming in?" I said, still not comprehending the situation.

"No, it's better this way. My bags are in the trunk. I'll be in touch to explain everything, but right now I just can't stay. Forget the water," he said, while reaching across my body to open the door for me. A gentleman to the end.

"You can't be serious," I said, "we have to talk about this. You, yourself, just said we had a pretty damn good marriage – and where did you come up with that expression anyway? We've had a great marriage and you know it."

"You had to have seen this coming. Couldn't you tell I wasn't happy? Please don't make a scene."

"Actually I thought regurgitating the twenty-four dollar appetizer was enough of a scene," I said in my iciest tone.

"There you go again with the sarcasm."

"Oh, so after fifteen years of what you called my rapier wit, it's finally gotten to you?" I said, trying to defrost.

"Dina, please. It's not that. We probably never should have gotten married."

I could hear the vibration of Mark's phone from his pocket. Although his first instinct was to answer it, he didn't.

"Is that your soul mate?" I said.

"Does it matter?"

"I guess not."

"Listen, Dina, I'm sorry. Really, I am. It just happened so fast – it's like I had no control over things. It was love at first sight, for both of us," he said with a sigh so long and loud I thought about vomiting again.

"Okay, I don't need to hear that. We're a married couple and no, I didn't see it coming and how was I supposed to know you weren't happy? What I do realize is that your business has slacked off, and you haven't been yourself, and if this is about money we can tighten our belts. Honey, I love you. Please don't do this."

"I have to. You wouldn't understand."

"Try me because what I see is a married man with big responsibilities, so you better think hard before you leave," I said, trying to be heavy handed. "And how could you just drop it at dinner and make your exit. This isn't like you," I said, trying to expand the conversation so that Mark would stay put.

"I just apologized for that. I realize it's new for you, but Taffie and I have been discussing it for weeks. I've even spoken to Ted and he's drawing up the divorce papers. I'll be as fair as possible, but like you said, my business is off and not just slightly. You might have to get a job. The house is paid for, but I don't know if I'll be able to keep up with all the expenses. The club just raised the dues and who knows if there'll be an assessment coming up for hurricane damage or road repairs. I'll be by later in the week to pick up the rest of my stuff. In the meanwhile, get yourself a lawyer. Ted can't represent both of us."

I only heard three words out of that entire conversation:

1. Divorce

2. Job

3. Taffie

None of them appealed to me on any level.

"I can't believe you're doing this," I said, not sure if I should come on strong or do the damsel in distress bit. What I was sure about was keeping my husband.

"Dina, you should know me by now – once I make a decision, it's a done deal, and when you get used to the idea you're going to see it's for the best. You'll have to move on and get passed it. Part of our problem is that we've been stuck in this fishbowl existence for years trying to keep up, blowing through our money just so we can make the right impression on our so-called friends."

"I agree and that's an easy fix. Let's find another place to live. What about downtown Delray? I know we've never really fit in with the crowd here, but what if we bought a great loft or a townhouse, right in the heart of the village…we could walk everywhere, just like in New York. We don't need a house this big."

"Dina, no."

He didn't have to explain further. I was grasping at straws that didn't exist. It was over as far as Mark was concerned, but I had no intention of giving up so easily. I had to stretch it out until he came to his senses and returned to me and our pretty damn good marriage.

"Yes, I will have to move on" is what I said to my husband while devising a plan to keep things exactly as they were. "Let me know when you'll be stopping by to pick up your things; I don't want to be here."

"I understand. Taffie and I can come over when you're at your bridge game this Thursday."

"Mark, this is still my house and I would appreciate it if you would leave Taffie out of it. Literally."

"Dina, this is still our house, and I'll need help. I'm leaving all the furniture for the time being so I don't want to have to hire a moving van just for my clothing and personal things. You won't be here anyway. Don't worry, she's not going to steal anything. She could buy and sell ten of these houses."

"Then let her buy and sell over at the Polo Club and stay the hell out of Boca Forest and my house," I said to my

6

prick of a husband whom I was beginning to dislike.

I got out of the Hummer and walked up the fake cobblestone path to our front door, trying in vain to hold back an avalanche of tears.

"Dina, wait!" yelled Mark.

I brightened as Mark hurried to where I was standing. He'd see my tears, gather me in his arms and forget all about Taffie. We'd make a baby as planned and I wouldn't have to devise a scheme to win back my husband.

"You don't have your keys," he said, as he opened the door for me and departed.

Chapter 3

June

Going Nowhere

In the midst of a full-blown sob, I entered the black-granite-floored foyer of our house, the Bella Vue model, the name being a mismatched French/Italian combination, and my cruise control forwarded me toward the kitchen where I called my BFF, Wanda Blake. My sister and her husband, who lived in North Carolina, and our parents, who were summering in Asheville, could wait.

I also needed something to eat. Aside from a solitary breadstick that preceded the oyster calamity, breakfast had been my only meal of the day as I'd skipped lunch in anticipation of our big celebratory dinner. After putting on the tea kettle, I grabbed two frozen cranberry-walnut scones and popped them into the microwave. A minute later, my snack was laid out on the breakfast room table, a granite and wrought iron monstrosity that was featured in every furniture store a decade ago. All the stone and stucco that Mark and I were first enamored with now seemed over-bearing and so heavy it was a wonder the house didn't sink. Nibbling a bite of the pastry, I decided to go whole hog and pulled out a crock of Danish butter and some black cherry jam, and poured the tea. With sustenance I was able to call

Wanda, and prayed her husband wouldn't answer. He did.

"Linz, hi, it's me, is she there? What? Oh, yes, I'm fine. Allergies, you know," I said, not wanting to explain my weepy voice to her therapist husband who'd start analyzing anyone who sounded an iota off to him, which was everyone.

"Hey, Dina," said Wanda, "happy birthday, again, sweetie. We still on for lunch at Seasons tomorrow? Can't wait to see you because I have mucho surprises for you!"

"Mark's gone."

"Gone? What happened? He's not…" she said.

"No, he's not dead. He left me."

"Oh," said my friend with only a mild trace of surprise in her voice.

"What the fuck does that mean? You couldn't have known about this, did you?"

"I'm sorry, sweetie, but I suspected," Wanda said.

"And you didn't tell me because…?"

"I was going to, but I thought maybe it was a passing fancy – you know, a mid-life crisis."

"That might be true if everyone in his family didn't live to be over a hundred. Just tell me what you know."

"Dina, let's wait till we sit down for lunch and a couple of martinis."

"Just tell me, Wanda. I need to know now," I said, punctuating every word.

"Well, okay then. Hold it a minute…no, Linz, she doesn't need to speak to you, I've got it," she called out to her husband who, no doubt, was lingering within arm's reach. "A couple of weeks ago I saw Mark and some young blonde with Crest-Whitestrip teeth and a French pedi sticking out of her Jimmy Choos, sharing a monster burger and sipping one giant soda through two straws over at Top-Burger. It wasn't the first time I'd seen them, and I'm not the only one."

"Top-Burger? Mark wouldn't be caught dead eating there."

"He was there. I almost had a corollary when I saw them."

Did I mention that my friend was the queen of malaprops?

"I still can't believe you didn't tell me. You're my best friend – we tell each other everything. I am severely pissed at you," I said.

"Hey, don't shoot the messiah. I told you I didn't think it was serious. I'm sorry Dina. I just thought it would be better to wait and see if it ran its course."

"It's don't shoot the messenger," I said, well, actually screamed into the phone. It was one of the few times I just couldn't help myself.

"Messenger? Whatever. Anyway, let's talk it out at lunch tomorrow, okay? My treat."

"Of course it's your treat! It's my fucking birthday and my husband just left me!"

"Honey, stop cursing and let me come over. You shouldn't be alone," said my friend who was probably feeling guilty about the cover-up.

"No, Wanda, I'm still absorbing it. I can't believe he dropped the bomb on my birthday. Sorry I yelled at you, just venting. Let me go now, because I need to think and make a couple of lists of what I'm going to do to get him back."

"Oh, you and your lists. Okay, sweetie, I'll see you tomorrow, but put this on the top of your list: the name of a good lawyer. I'll bring you the number for Millie Rise; she's a crackerback."

"Crackerjack," her husband yelled out to tone-deaf

10

ears. I rarely corrected my friend's mistakes; Linz had been doing it for years to no avail.

"See you tomorrow, Wan. One o'clock."

I hung up before she had a chance to say anything else, or, God forbid, put her husband, who must have been panting to pontificate, back on the phone.

Now I was beyond furious. Mark's eating junk food at Top-Burger with his little Barbie doll was worse than screwing her.

You see, the one thing I did really well was cook.

Chapter 4

June

Lunch at Seasons '52

Wanda was already seated at a primo lakeside table when I arrived. To describe Wanda as anything other than kooky just wouldn't do her justice. Her lanky frame was topped with a nest of red curls that fell into a v-formation tumbling halfway down her back. She wore a ton of pale makeup accented by black mascara layered on so thick that it seemed as if huge spiders were crowding in and around her eyes. Her signature Orange Flame lip gloss completed the half-Kabuki/half-hooker look, and she pulled it off without a hitch. Yes, that was Wanda Blake, my BFF since the third grade.

"Nice table, Wan," I said, greeting her with a hug, any previous animosity from last night's phone call behind us.

"Happy birthday, Dina. Come on, sit down," she said while signaling a nearby waiter to order cocktails.

Neither of us were big drinkers, except for the occasional glass of wine, but it had been our tradition for years to celebrate our birthdays with a martini or margarita.

"Good afternoon, ladies, I'm your server, Jared. May I offer you ladies a cocktail?"

I always left the martini ordering to Wanda because

12

she worked for a big-time caterer, and was up on the latest combinations. Today's selection was a pomegranate martini with fresh lemon juice.

"Very cold, straight up and big," Wanda told the waiter who was standing there at attention. "And, bring us the dirty ice on the side."

"Coming right up, ladies," said the server who appeared to be no older than twelve.

"Did you see how he looked at you, Dina? You know, men aren't the only species who can go younger."

"Sweetie, he wasn't looking at me and even if he were, do you seriously think he'd be interested in anything more than getting directions? Did you notice he called us 'ladies' several times and not 'girls?' When did that happen?"

"Oh, so what, that's how they train them. But it wouldn't hurt you to start flirting a little – you know, get back into practice, I mean in case Mark doesn't come back."

"I'm not going to flirt with any boy whose name begins with a J and that includes all the Jasons, Joshes, Justins, Jakes, Jadens, and especially Jareds. They're all too young. And I won't need to practice anything. What I need is for Mark to come back, and I think there's a good chance he will," I said in my wonder-woman voice.

"Really? I mean, yeah, that could happen. But, keep your options open…dating one younger man doesn't make you a kruger."

I knew she meant cougar and not an abbreviated term for a gold piece, but I let it pass.

Jared arrived with our two cocktails.

"The bartender made too much, so here's the rest of it," Jared said as he placed the martinis in front of us. Depositing a bowl of ice in the middle of the table he twisted in a small glass carafe holding several ounces more of the crimson colored drink – just enough to fill half again our glasses. This time he looked directly at me. "Enjoy, ladies."

"Jesus, look at that butt," Wanda said as soon as he turned back to the bar area. "And don't tell me he's not interested in you. Come on, girlfriend, don't look a gift shop in the mouth."

"Wanda, didn't we agree never to call each other 'girl-friend?' BFF I can handle, but that's about it. And, hon, it's a gift horse," I said, once again correcting her.

1. Why was I doing something I'd always shied away from?

2. Was she beginning to annoy me?

3. Did she know more than she was spilling about my situation?

"You're killing me today! That can't possibly be right. What the hell is a gift horse? Come on. Let's have a toast. To my BFF, with the emphasis on forever, happy birthday and a happy rest of your life."

I took a gulp of the cocktail while Wanda barely touched hers, and just as I was wondering how much alcohol I could consume and still drive home, Jared appeared with one of Seasons' famous flatbreads.

"Here you go, ladies, and it's on me today. I don't always take care of such nice and beautiful ladies. I know you're going to like this; it's the chef's special. It's got sliced tomatoes, zucchini and melted goat cheese with fresh basil. I mean, like who would ever make that at home?" said Jared, of course unaware that Wanda and I could have turned out the flatbread with our eyes closed.

"Thanks, Jared," I said, this time lowering my lashes before meeting his gaze. He actually could have been around twenty-four or five, putting him at a mere dozen years my junior.

"Any time and remember, you can always ask for me as your server when you call for reservations. I only work the lunch shift 'cause I'm going to school at night," our attentive waiter said, hanging around obviously wanting to tell us more.

Jared was getting more interesting even if he was one of the zillions of young J-guys around town. At least he didn't tell us he was an out-of-work actor.

"Oh?" said Wanda, ready to pimp me out. "I knew you must have your sights set on something more than waiting tables. Uh, what are you studying?"

"Acting. They make a fortune. I'm gonna be a millionaire by the time I'm twenty-one, just like that Facebook guy," said my would-be boy toy.

"Well, good luck with that and thanks for the flatbread," I said without much gumption.

"Yeah – no problem – I'll be right back to take your orders."

Off he went with a slight swagger thinking that perhaps he'd scored. He hadn't.

"Any more fix-ups for me?" I said, starting to laugh.

Wanda joined in with her staccato-style giggle and told me I should be flattered.

"Okay, now that we've gotten Jared out of the way, I need to know more about Mark's girlfriend, Taffie."

"Sweetie, it's your birthday. Can't we just celebrate? I love that outfit on you, consignment?"

15

"Where else?"

"You should wear more khaki, looks good with your hair. I like it short on you, and if you wore gold hoops you'd look amazing."

"Please don't try changing the subject; I need to know everything if I'm going to win him back."

"It's just that I don't want to bring you down. It's bad enough Mark laid all this on you on your birthday; you don't need to hear more."

"Not only on my birthday, but we were also going to start trying for a baby last night. I'll celebrate with you after we get this crap out of the way. Fill me in. What does she look like for starters?"

"Just remember, curiosity cured the cat, so you better be sure you want details."

"I'm sure," I said, holding back from correcting her once again.

"Well, the easiest way to describe her is that she looks a lot like Taylor Swiss."

"The singer?" I asked, wanting to be sure she was referring to Taylor Swift, the flawless and talented twenty-something songstress.

"Of course, the singer! How many Taylor Swisses do you think there are?"

"Apparently two now that Taffie's in the picture. I already know that she's young and now I know she's beautiful. What else?"

"She's filthy rich," said Wanda, confirming Mark's remark about her ability to purchase multiple dwellings.

I poured the remainder of the martini from the small carafe into my empty glass, and raised it toward Jared, who'd been lurking nearby, indicating that I was ready for another.

"Wan, you're not drinking your martini? Don't you like it?" I asked my friend.

"I'm pregnant."

I dumped her drink into my glass and chugged it. My BFF could drive me home.

Chapter 5

June

Surgery

Two weeks before Mark's departure I was a surgical outpatient at one of Boca's hospitals for a minor procedure to remove a couple of throat polyps. The doctor said that after a short recovery my speech might take on a deeper tone with no other side effects. I was thrilled because I always wanted to sound like an adult. Telemarketers would no longer ask for my mother, and the golf shop staff had better stop addressing me as honey. I couldn't wait to try out my sexy new voice, which had to be perfected by birthday/baby night.

Mark's leaving me had nothing to do with the surgery except that I should have been more aware that he'd begun to distance himself from me. The surgeon decided to keep me overnight after I developed a slight fever.

When I called Mark to update him on my condition he seemed annoyed.

"Dina, I thought it was all arranged. I was going to pick you up in a little while. I have a golf game with the guys in the morning. I was just about to leave for the hospital."

"They won't release me with a fever. The doctor said it should pass by tomorrow morning. Can't you make it then?"

"No way. How many golf games do you think I can give up? Can't you call Wanda or one of the girls?"

"Wanda said she was going to be over at Boca Grove in the morning for a client meeting, and the Forest girls will be playing tennis, golf or bridge."

"What about your mother or father? Aren't they here for the week? Boynton's not that far – they can hop on 95 at Woolbright, and it wouldn't take them more than twenty minutes to get to the hospital."

"I didn't tell them about the surgery."

"They don't know?" said my husband in a semi-concerned tone.

"No, I didn't want to worry them. It wasn't a big deal. I'll tell them after I'm home."

"Have the nurse call a cab."

"Okay," I said, trying to conceal my disappointment. Wasn't I more important than a golf game? "Can you at least visit me tonight?"

"I don't think that's such a good idea. Didn't the doctor tell you not to use your voice the first 24 to 48 hours? You sound like a frog. We shouldn't even be having this conversation. Now get off the phone and take a nap or read a book."

"I forgot my Kindle," I said, trying anything to keep Mark on the line even though my throat was a little sore.

"Well, ask one of those candy-stripers for a magazine. For God sakes, Dina, it was two lousy polyps, not a heart transplant. I gotta go because there's nothing in the house to eat."

"Mark, there's tons of food in the fridge and there's a portion of baked ziti in the freezer. Nuke it for six minutes and you'll have dinner."

"I don't feel like bothering. I'll just eat at the club."

"Dinner by yourself at the club? You've never done that."

"Dina, who the hell are you now, the FBI? Just get some rest and I'll see you tomorrow after golf and lunch."

Realizing he'd been harsh, Mark tempered his goodbye with a quick "feel better, I love you" before hanging up.

So I stayed overnight in my double room listening to my roommate, Candy or Cookie Gooch or something that sounded like that, snore like a steam engine. At least she had a husband who visited even though he munched on a half-eaten cigar the entire time and called me Dinah.

"Come on, Dinah," said Duke, my roommate's loving husband, "help us out over here and have some of this gooey chocolate. It's Godiva, nothing's too good for my gal," he said while patting his beloved's hand, which had an I.V. inserted, but to her credit, she didn't complain.

"Thanks, anyway," I said, almost moved to tears by his compassion, "but I'm only on liquids and Jello for the next day or two."

"Hah! I knew I shoulda brought the bourbon for ya!" he said, with a heavy southern drawl. "But I can see you're hurtin'; you don't have to hide those tears from us."

Cookie or Candy, who'd heard the earlier phone conversation with my absentee husband, picked up on my discomfort and suggested that Duke accompany her down the hall to the lounge area.

"You get some rest now, Dinah, and I'm gonna leave a few pieces of chocolate for you. Just take 'em home so you'll have something to remember us by. They pack 'em wrapped in foil so they'll stay fresh. You take care now."

"Thanks, Duke, and you take real good care of my gal pal there."

I tried not to cry after they left; first because it hurt my throat, but mainly I wanted to believe that it was much more important for Mark to be on the golf course where he discussed business than to visit with me. After all, it wasn't a heart transplant, although I was beginning to think that maybe my husband could have used one.

My temperature returned to normal by the morning and my doctor released me. Hailing a taxi in Boca Raton isn't the same deal as it is in Manhattan. You have to call ahead, and usually someone shows up around the requested time. The nurse wheeled me out to the curb and smoked a cigarette while we waited for the guy to arrive.

"Why do you smoke if you're a nurse?" I said in my new Lauren Bacall voice, "is that even allowed?"

"Honey, nurses in this hospital can do whatever the hell they want," she said, "this is Boca, or haven't you heard?"

Although I was a little miffed that she called me honey I let it go. I was excited about getting home. I knew Mark had business troubles and was probably concerned about our plan to start a family, but that would work itself out once I was pregnant.

I had another plan for tonight:

1. Prepare an elegant dinner for Mark.

2. Soft foods for me.

3. Start going over baby names.

Chapter 6

Backstory

For most of our fifteen-year marriage Mark and I, Dina Marshall, lived at the Boca Forest Country Club in Boca Raton, Florida. "Forest," as it was affectionately called, attracted a wealthy and relatively youthful crowd due to the recent construction of a two-story fitness center and spa. Along with three golf courses and numerous tennis courts it was a perfect home for young successful professionals, like Mark, as well as retired executives.

We also had our share of members of The Lucky Sperm Club: residents, who through major inheritances and family businesses that paid them to stay away, could afford an enviable lifestyle and never work a day in their lives for it. It was a perfect spot for Mark to engage new clients in what he did best, financial planning. Before our move to Boca, he was able to transfer to a local branch and brought in enough business to keep them satisfied.

Since my husband wasn't the only game in town, he needed a hook. What occurred to him was food, more specifically, invitations to our house for my gourmet dinners. This might not have been enough of an attraction throughout other parts of the country where meals are prepared and eaten at home six nights a week, but Forest was a major Boca Raton country club where no one cooked, or even had to.

Breakfast was available in the club's Bagel Oasis every morning before golf and tennis games; lunch was a buffet that could have fed the inhabitants of Noah's Ark; and dinner, in addition to the hundreds of restaurants around town, was served in one of Forest's three dining rooms, seven nights a week.

Our head chef, André, held a contest to rename the club's dining rooms and the winners were given a free dinner in one of the three. Winners Circle, The Bridle Grille, and Crop & Saddle were chosen by the staff from over five hundred entries. Boca Forest wasn't an equestrian club, but the judges felt the horsey names lent an air of sophistication to Forest.

Those residents on a budget simply chose to gorge themselves on free and plentiful goodies available during the club's happy hour held at the lower level bar. Bar None opened at five, and for two hours an entire family, with their guests, could be nourished for the price of a soda or a glass of wine. Although there was no charge for the food, this gracious feast was certainly part of our dues, but those who frequented the early evening supper rationalized that it was complimentary.

Some of Bar None's patrons were legitimately watching their pennies; others were just cheap.

The restaurants at Forest opened for dinner at six, and diners had to pass by Bar None to get to any of the three, sometimes making rude comments loud enough for all to hear about the freeloaders, and at other times a passive-aggressive joke.

"Hey, Fanucci! You lose at poker this week?" or "Come

on, Herbie, treat your wife to a real meal."

The remarks might have embarrassed some, but most took it good-naturedly and continued to pile their plates high with wings, potstickers, crudité, crackers and cheese while asking for free refills on soft drinks for their kids, and shoveling in ice to stretch their own cocktails.

Most of the ovens in our homeowner's kitchens still had the instruction pamphlets inside.

It was easy for Mark to drum up dinner guests as he was a scratch golfer, which guaranteed his inclusion in all the prestigious games and tournaments. Everyone wanted my husband in their foursome.

It was during those eighteen holes of golf followed by lunch at the clubhouse that Mark enthralled the men with stories of my Rack of Veal with Sun-Dried Tomato Sauce, Stuffed Meat Loaf, or Turbot with Maple Glaze; and because I was health conscious, my low-fat desserts were as good as the real thing. One of the men jokingly asked when the next dinner party was, and Mark extended the first invitation.

Our house became known as the in-place to dine, leaving the club and local restaurants to those who could endure the clamor that season brought with mediocre food at sky-high prices. Our club imposed a modest monthly dining minimum, but that was easily filled by lunches or cocktails.

After a few slices of Breast of Capon au Cassis, and heaps of Green Beans Almandine, along with my special Spring Salad (made with five kinds of fresh lettuce, not the bagged stuff) Mark would slide into his pitch, accompanied by dessert and coffee. One bite of my Blackout Pudding Cake or Vanilla Pear Trifle quashed any resistance our dinner guests might have had. The hook worked.

As Mark's business picked up, I cooked more and more meals and eventually fell from the social loop at our club. In order to keep up with the dinner parties, I also had to drop out of the golf and tennis leagues, and was forced to give up my card games, except for one bridge game on Thursday afternoons. I cooked for clients at least three or four evenings a week, and that was about all I had time for.

Mark also began promising deliveries, such as my Lemon-Raspberry Loaf Cake for Gail Avery's Garden Club Tea (to which I was not invited) and assorted fat-free muffins to his golf buddies so they could stay away from the caloric breakfast of bagels and cream cheese served at the Bagel Oasis.

The only time I sat down and relaxed was when Dex Ryder, the PPS man, arrived with shipments of cooking supplies and fancy grocery items that I couldn't find locally, or no longer had time to shop for.

PPS was short for Premium Package Service, which all residents of Forest and neighboring country clubs were entitled to. The clubs had their own credit card that included membership in this prestigious delivery service.

When the real estate market was booming, brokers made overnight fortunes selling country club homes to snowbirds eager to spend winters in Florida, and to where they'd eventually retire, as well as to young Turks. Dex had made some sort of an arrangement with local stores and businesses to have his private trucking company service many top clubs in the Boca area. I'd never heard of this practice anywhere else in the country, but that was only one of Boca's peculiarities.

Of course, we could still use a regular credit card and

have packages shipped via UPS, but belonging to PPS was another exclusive privilege that residents fell into like a vat of dark chocolate.

Dex's prices were a little higher than normal delivery fees, but he also provided in-house service, which included opening and unwrapping large cartons and removing all packaging. Changing a light bulb or putting up a rack of hooks was part of the unwritten job description for PPS drivers, and the upcharge more than covered the time spent doing those little chores. The men who worked for him were schooled in what was expected of them, with courtesy being a priority.

Dex was the exclusive driver for Forest, the largest club in the area, and because he had an interest in cooking, it didn't take long before we became friendly.

Most of the women had time to bring home their purchases from Town Center, our upscale mall, so they could dig into their new duds immediately and not wait for a delivery. Some preferred to squirrel away what they bought only to bring it out two weeks later with the "Oh, I've had this for ages" routine to unsuspecting husbands.

Mark never discouraged me from shopping, particularly when it was for kitchen implements, which he knew would lead to more seductive dinner parties, but he still questioned the contents of every shopping bag I brought home from Saks or Macy's before I discovered the great consignment shops in our area. I guess it was a control thing because he knew I wasn't extravagant, especially compared to our neighbors.

When we first moved into Forest, Mark jumped at the honor of obtaining the club's own credit card. The status symbol carried a special degree of snobbery. Sales people gave us a knowing nod when the shiny chartreuse card was produced, and although at first I thought it was just one more superficial display of the nouveau riche, I pulled it out wherever it was accepted, even at Brendy's, the local yogurt shop.

Once I became so busy with our entertaining schedule, almost all of my supplies except for the basics were ordered on line. I received a quantity discount from many of my routine purveyors, and was also able to save time, which I devoted to developing new recipes.

While shoes and overpriced designer tee shirts from Neiman's were being delivered to my neighbors I was jumping for joy over a Le Creuset five-quart Dutch oven or the latest in Italian espresso makers. Dex, being a weekend cook, couldn't wait to open these delights for me, and usually hung around to see if I was going to test out a new concoction.

Dex was in his late thirties and if you looked up "tall, dark and handsome with eyes the color of the Atlantic Ocean" in Wikipedia, you'd see a picture of him. He mentioned a lady friend a number of times, but never talked about an engagement or wedding date. I came to rely on his compliments as well as his criticism of my food:

1. He pronounced Poulet Seville too salty, so I left out half the capers.

2. Roasted Veal Brisket was bland, in name and taste, so together we created Vitello Oreganata.

Mark's business soared with the help of our dinner parties. Granted, I did have to cancel my weekly manicures and hair appointments as our social pandering increased, but Mark said he loved my new natural look, which amounted to:

1. A brush cut.

2. Fingernails with ground pepper stuck underneath.

Even before his no-show at the hospital, I should have picked up on the clues, but I was so elbow deep in marinades and pickled peppers that I barely noticed the not-so-subtle changes in my husband that began around April, the most startling being his waning interest in selling our dinner guests. Even my most winning desserts (Plum Good Apple Tart, to name one) couldn't get Mark to discuss business with our company. I took advantage of the evening he was almost rude to one of our guests who'd asked for a bit more wine to start up a baby conversation.

As we prepared for bed I pointed out that unless he was going to continue to try to attract new business during our dinner parties that perhaps we might be able to eliminate them altogether or at least cut down to once a week for any existing clients. Mark hadn't complained about money in months, but I still offered to reduce my spending.

I wanted to reclaim my life, our life together. The golf league would welcome me back; my short game was way better than average, and I'd grow my hair out and have it highlighted, and start salvaging my fingernails. Mainly, I'd take a break from entertaining and start cooking the simple meals that my husband and I always enjoyed before getting sucked into our current schedule.

"Let's get off this treadmill," I said, with a whiny tone I knew my husband hated, yet always laughed at. Mark was brushing his teeth but sputtered his agreement. We made love that night after a rather long hiatus and I drifted off to sleep dreaming of babies and happy years ahead.

Chapter 7

The Beginning: New York

My father, Harry Khan, was a living legend on the fashionable east end of Long Island. He and my mother, Stella, owned land from South Hampton all the way out to Amagansett. Dad had a nose for eking out property no one else wanted to touch. Then, sometimes just by cutting down a few trees and clearing the land, he turned his purchases into prime real estate that started bidding wars, resulting in doubling and tripling his original investment.

He bought up land, piece by piece, begin to build a spec home, and before the foundation was poured he'd have a buyer.

My mother had a knack for sketching out elaborate house designs detailing where the de rigueur pool and tennis court would best be situated. She gave these drawings to brokers who were only too happy to share the plans with clients who had trouble visualizing how a weedy lot could morph into an impressive homestead.

They were a good team, my parents, and it was the 80's when everyone had money. Wall Street was on the rise igniting land sales in the most prestigious area of Long Island for vacation and summer residences.

My parents finished only one home in all the years they

were in business; a modest upside-down house that sat in the middle of a potato field in the small town of Sagaponack. The term referred to an upstairs living area and master suite with a view of the ocean, and other rooms assigned to the lower level. Everyone who lived in a cement-bound Manhattan apartment, including my parents, wanted to see water.

Harry and Stella also bought dilapidated homes in good locations and refurbished them to lease out. Even though they had a reliable builder who did renovations, they quit after amassing five rental properties.

During the summer, my folks commuted from our Fifth Avenue co-op every Thursday afternoon and returned Tuesday morning, bringing my older sister, France, and me along when we weren't at camp or in my sister's case, working at a summer job.

I had a privileged upbringing and an easy life, but rather sheltered. When I finished college, my graduation present was a summer in one of our rental homes in East Hampton, right in the village and fifteen minutes away from my parents. Although I had a car, I loved being able to walk almost everywhere in town, and for two months my life was bliss. Friends visited for long weekends, there were parties and dinners out in expensive restaurants, and eventually I met my husband-to-be, Mark Marshall.

My sister, whose given name was Francine, is ten years my senior. Although we're the same height at 5'5" and have the same brunette-colored hair and brown eyes, my sister has all the curves and in all the right places.

When she studied at the Sorbonne during her junior year abroad she transformed herself into a Francophile and legally changed her name to France upon her return. It suited her and no one (with one exception) dared call her

31

Francine or Frannie again – including my parents and me. She was introduced to her husband-to-be, Redmond Baxter, while living in Paris. He was visiting vineyards studying winemaking, and they hooked up during a tour her host family invited her on. My sister and Redmond became engaged before the end of her senior year and married soon after she graduated from college. Although France has her master's in education, her passion has always been art.

They settled in Redmond's hometown of Winston-Salem, North Carolina, where France taught at Wake Forest University for a couple of semesters before becoming pregnant. After their son, Wesley, was born she opened up an art gallery, simply called "France." There wasn't a creative person in the Piedmont triad who hadn't heard of her studio. Many local artists were delighted to leave their works there on consignment, and at a time when business had taken a dive, France and "France" did well. She displayed her own pastels and watercolors, but always staged the big picture windows with works of her guest artists.

Once a month they'd partake in Avenue Stroll Night. Redmond would set up some of his wines, and France would bring in ready-made snacks for the browsers.

They had a nice life and raised their only child who later married a local girl, Priscilla Paine. Redmond's family and the Paines lived within a few miles of my sister, and I often thought how fortunate they were not to have to board an airplane to celebrate a holiday together.

My sister never liked Manhattan and was only too happy not to return to our parents' co-op after college. My mother couldn't understand why any New Yorker would choose North Carolina over Manhattan, or eventually Florida, but somehow my dad saw the wisdom in the move.

"They'll have a good life there, Stella," he said, "and they can live well. France can teach, Redmond has his wine territory and makes plenty of dough. He knows half the town so they'll have built-in friends, and they won't have to wait forever to make us grandparents. I like it."

"I can't believe what I'm hearing," my mother said, "but maybe you're right. Our France was never the cosmopolitan like Dina. So we'll visit."

They did better than visit because instead of staying at their Sagaponack home for the summer season, they sold it and found a condo in Asheville, which was about a two-hour ride into Winston-Salem. My parents still held on to their New York apartment, but when the winters became too severe for them, and before Wall Street tanked, they sold it along with every east end rental property.

Stella and Harry moved to Boynton Beach, Florida, where they became permanent residents, and spent five months a year in North Carolina. The transition was easy because most of their friends had already made the move south to one of the many adult gated communities South Florida had to offer, and a good portion of those friends had also bought condos in and around Asheville.

I graduated college just before my twenty-first birthday and for the first time in my life had no place to live. My mother begged me to relocate with them. Having bought a spacious home in an active adult community, they invited me to stay in their guesthouse where they swore I'd be allowed to lead my own life. I saw that lasting for about five days, and I'm overstating it, and turned them down.

I still had a couple of weeks before I had to vacate the co-op and I'd use that time to:

1. Find my own place.

2. Find a job.

3. Let my parents support me in the meanwhile.

"Mom, I love you and Daddy, but I want to live in New York. I'll visit and I'll think about moving into your guest house. Promise," I said, crossing my fingers behind my back.

Chapter 8

Dating

While I searched for a studio apartment and a job in New York, my sister's former college roommate, Deborah Gibbs, invited me to stay with her. She lived in an enormous two-bedroom terraced apartment in the West Village that had been handed down to her from a wealthy aunt when she died. I took her up on the offer.

"It'll only be till I find something of my own. Wanda was supposed to look for a place with me but she moved in with Linz instead. He's okay in small doses, but at least she doesn't have to pay rent, speaking of which, Deb, I insist on doing that," I said, knowing I'd have to continue accepting money from my folks.

Once I had the apartment thing out of the way, I could concentrate on job hunting. Wanda had already been hired by a major hotel chain to book conferences and elaborate parties for any business doing well enough to afford it. It was a dream job and I hoped to find something equally glamorous. My resume was out at the top headhunters in our field, which was food and hotel management, but nothing exciting materialized. I knew I could always work as a food writer and I'd also been offered a couple of jobs in decent restaurants, but I needed to keep my evenings open for my growing relationship with Mark.

"You don't have to pay anything. Just do the cooking," Deborah said, "and start dating already. Let me fix you up with Stu Downing from my office."

"You know I'm seeing Mark," I said, peeved at her for eschewing my relationship with my boyfriend.

"What I know is that you met this guy in East Hampton who had a share in a beach house – he doesn't own it no matter what he tells you – and he never took you out because he said you out-cooked every chef on the East End. And you fell for that?"

"You're exaggerating," I said, "he had lots of parties at his house too. And we liked being at home even if it was my dad's rental. I know he doesn't own the beach house; he said he was trying to impress me, but came clean on our second date. Who can afford their own place out there these days? You're going to blame him for that?"

"No, I'm just saying that he doesn't seem to be as serious about you as you are about him. I'd hate to see you waste your time."

"Deb, I'm not even twenty-one. I think I can afford to spend a few more months to see if it's going anywhere. I have a feeling we're going to end up together. And if Stu is so great, why aren't you dating him?" The words were out of my mouth before I could control the outburst. Deborah was a recent widow and I blurted out an apology.

"Oh, I'm so sorry – I didn't mean…"

"Forget it. I know you didn't mean anything, but I'm not ready to date. Phil was, if you'll pardon a trite expression, the love of my life. We had it all until he got sick."

"Oh, Deb, he was a wonderful man, but you're only thirty-two; you have your whole life ahead."

"Yes, that's what they tell me. Okay, let's get back to you and Stu."

Since my unintended faux pas, I decided that meeting Stu would make Deb happy and maybe she was right.

1. Was Mark really serious about me?

2. Should I give up other chances just to wait around for him?

Mark, being a year or so older than I was, had just begun his career when we met, and although he worked long hours during the week and over the weekends, his salary barely covered his living expenses in East Hampton and New York. Eating at Palm, or Nick and Tony's was out of the question. I didn't think too much about it, but it sure bothered Deb and Wanda, and they never let up.

"So, you're going to meet Stu. Do you think I'd set you up with a jerk? And how many times have you seen Mark since you left the Hamptons; you're not exclusive with him," Deb said.

"He's come over almost every night," I said, defending my unpopular boyfriend.

"For dinner, right? At your parents' place? Well, I don't mind buying food for the two of us if you'll cook it, but three's company, if you get my drift."

I didn't need a dead cat thrown in my face. The battle was over so I agreed to meet Stu.

Deborah was a highly regarded interior decorator who refused to bill herself as a designer, calling that title trendy bullshit. Stu wasn't a partner in Deb's firm, but he was a top ranking sales person. Deb's showroom was in the famous Decoration and Design or D & D Building on Third Avenue, and was frequented by clients whose homes appeared in the likes of *Architectural Digest* and *House Beautiful.* Customers could browse through her gallery accompanied by one of four designers on staff and place orders, or they could buy accessories off the floor.

Stu apparently had an uncanny knack for knowing just which two thousand dollar candelabra would appeal to his favored clients – society matrons, and clever young men and women who spent hours poring through the latest objects d'art.

"Listen to me, Dina," my roommate said, "Stu is straight, he owns his own home in the Hamptons, not a tenth of a share, and can you even do that anymore? He's recently divorced – so you can go out with him as a friend. Neither one of you will be looking to jump into anything; I'm just asking you to give it a shot. Who knows? You might end up having a lot in common."

"Okay, give him my cell," I said, defeated.

Stu and I met at Japingo's on University Place that Friday evening. We had nothing in common, which was clear within five minutes of meeting, but I was hungry and promised Deborah I'd give it a fair chance. Most of the conversation centered around his divorce.

"That whore of a wife took everything," said Stu.

Everything didn't include the Jaguar he referred to several times during the course of the evening, or the eight-room floor-through on Park Avenue that he called his man-cave. The Hampton place, offered as part of the divorce settlement from his uber-wealthy wife, turned out to be in Hampton Bays, the step-child of its grander relatives.

"Yeah, we were going to cash it in and build out in Water Mill, but Miss Pain-in-the-Ass decided the marriage wasn't working for her anymore," he explained, "but at least 'Bayside' is on the water. I'll make a fortune when I sell."

"That seems pretty generous of your wife, I mean ex-wife," I said, trying to figure out how to end this painful evening.

"Hey! It's the least she could do. So, Dina, what's your situation?"

"Um, I've been seeing someone, and it's pretty serious," I said, trying to discourage him while nursing the minis-cule cup of sake my date had poured for me. "Deb thought you and I should just meet as friends. She wasn't quite sure about your status," I said, knowing it was a lie.

"My status? She knows I'm divorced. Christ, everyone in the place knows it and they're all fixing me up like crazy. Dina, I'll be frank. I have enough friends," he said, finishing the last of the sake he kept to his side of the table for the last hour, "and since we're not going to work, let me give you a piece of advice: don't be a tease."

I thanked Cheap Stu for dinner, which consisted of:

1. Sharing one sushi roll.

2. A quarter ounce of sake.

3. My leaving an eight-dollar tip before catching a cab home.

Chapter 9

Taffie Time

The Thursday after Mark's departure, I skipped my bridge game. How could I be away from my house and still make sure Taffie the Terrible didn't enter the great halls of granite, plus I wanted to stash away a few of Mark's things so he'd have to stop back. I hadn't begun to move on. My husband would return to our home in Forest, and not just for his favorite golf glove that I'd hidden in one of the kitchen canisters.

Mark must have been stockpiling some of his belongings at Taffie's for weeks because I was astonished at how little there was left. We had separate walk-in closets in our 'his and hers' dressing rooms, and if Valentina, my lovely Brazilian housekeeper who was taking English lessons, had studied the chapter on telling the missus that the mister was cheating on her, I'm sure she would have alerted me to the upcoming exodus.

My husband arrived at two. I heard a key in the door, and seconds later the doorbell rang. Score one for courtesy.

I sauntered to the door and scanned the driveway

through the glass side panel to make sure he'd come solo, as promised. My heart dropped a few inches when I caught sight of my good-looking husband, and I gave an audible sigh before opening the door. I forced myself to remain cool and not beg Mark to give up his girlfriend and return home.

"You might as well give me your keys while you're here," I said in my most sang-froid voice. "Keep the gate clicker; you'll need it to get back into the club. They'll be expecting you for the pro-am," I continued on in a cold-front mode while my intestines twisted into a figure eight.

"Dina, didn't we agree to be civil to each other? I've told you over and over on the phone how sorry I am that I hurt you – I thought by doing it quickly it wouldn't be as hard on you, like pulling off a Band-Aid, but that was crappy of me to do it at your birthday dinner. Can you forgive me for that? I'd really like us to stay friends," my husband said, looking like a kid who'd just batted a ball through a neighbor's window.

Although Mark had kept his affair a secret, at least from me, he was never much good at telling a simple basic lie. I knew he felt like a heel.

"You are forgiven for ripping off the Band-Aid," I said, with a flourish of my hand, "but you are not forgiven for eating junk food. Top-Burger? Seriously?"

"Dina, no one is a better cook than you, but sometimes hanging out in those places can be…fun."

"Depends on who you're hanging with," I said, freezing up.

"Okay, if you're going to have an attitude, then let's not do this. I just want to pick up the rest of my things."

Mark's eyes turned toward the kitchen.

"Something smells good," Mark said, knowing he could always get me off a topic he didn't care for by encouraging a food conversation. "New recipe?"

"As a matter of fact, yes," I said. In anticipation of my husband's arrival I knew what I had to do.

My love formula:

1. Mark loved my food.

2. I loved to cook and bake for Mark.

3. I loved Mark.

4. Ergo, Mark would love me.

"Cheddar Flake Biscuits, and I made some pumpkin butter. You hungry?" Boy, was I tough, or what?

"I'm starving; missed lunch. Do you have any coffee made?"

"What, no Burger World today?" I said, unable to restrain myself.

"It's Top-Burger and please, don't."

"Couldn't help it. I can make you a fresh K-Cup, and there's a little country ham left over, want some with the biscuits?"

"If it's not too much trouble, yeah, thanks. That'd be great. Did your sister send you the ham? I've never known you to make that, unless it's another one of your new recipes," Mark said, keeping the food discussion going.

"No, you were right the first time. France sent it to me."

I invited him to sit down for a snack on the condition that he would tell me the tale of Taffie. We'd both dish, but I wanted more than food.

"Dina, you don't need to know the whole story," Mark said, after I insisted for the third time, and after his third biscuit.

"I actually do, Mark. I think after almost fifteen years of a pretty damn good marriage, as you put it, you owe me that."

"Okay, but it's not going to help."

"Why don't you let me decide," I said, forcing him to go on.

"One of the guys knows her family in New York, and when Taffie moved down here she called him for a referral. She wanted to take control of her finances so she asked me to review her portfolio over lunch. Dina, I can't explain it, but I knew I loved her the minute I laid eyes on her. She feels the same. We're going to move out of Boca; I don't want to cause you more pain than I already have. I really meant what I said about being so awful the way I did things."

"You're moving out of Boca? Where? Back to New York?"

As much as I was repelled by the situation, I felt a certain amount of security with Mark living nearby.

"No, not New York, down to Key West. Taffie has a place on the ocean. I'm retiring; this job's killing me anyway. I already gave notice at the firm, and just think, you won't have to cook for my clients anymore."

"You're retiring?"

"Yeah, Taffie wants us to spend as much time together as we can, you know, boating, snorkeling – all that stuff."

"But you hate all that stuff," I said, throwing a swarm of flies into the ointment.

"Well, I don't love it, but I guess I can learn to."

"Well, I guess you can learn," I repeated without cause

or reason. My brain had shut down just hearing that he wouldn't be working anymore. There was no way I could go back to my parents for money at this stage. They were getting older, and although they weren't surprised when I told them about the break-up, I didn't want to stress them further. Now that Taffie was managing her own finances, maybe she wouldn't mind paying me alimony.

Because my parents had done so well with land development and real estate up north, they were able to pay cash for their home at Venetian Gardens in Boynton Beach in addition to gifting us a hefty down payment on our Forest house, but being retired with too much time on his hands, my father made some bad investments. They could support their current lifestyle and have enough for their old age, but I knew there wouldn't be much extra. They loved their surroundings and took part in all the activities with a myriad of friends, but my mother's voice conveyed the worry and fear she had for their future. I couldn't complicate their world with my financial woes.

My sister and Redmond had just celebrated their silver anniversary and money wasn't a problem for them. My hope had been that Mark and I, along with my sister and brother-in-law, would be able to take care of my parents if it became necessary. Mark's folks had moved to Mexico City years ago and lived a luxurious lifestyle.

The Marshalls were cold fish and never bothered to involve themselves in our lives. His mother made sure to send us a trinket on anniversaries and birthdays, and there were always promises of visits or sending tickets to come stay with them, but nothing ever transpired. I'm sure they had no knowledge of our separation and probably wouldn't care if they did.

Mark had no siblings and rarely mentioned his parents whom he'd last seen at our wedding reception in Florida:

1. They flew up for two days.

2. They stayed at the Boca Raton Resort.

3. Made an appearance at the party.

4. Took off, leaving behind our wedding gift - a silver(ish) pitcher.

5. The tag was still on it: Made in China.

My folks had grown fond of Mark over the years, in opposition to their first impression, and were pleased when he agreed to call them Mom and Dad. To him, they represented the warm, loving parents he never had. I couldn't believe we wouldn't be making them grandparents.

Now, while Mark was licking the last of the pumpkin butter off his fingers, I presented a plan.

"Mark, I've done a lot of thinking in the past week (I hadn't, but I'm not bad at improvisation and my plan wasn't exactly the Monroe Doctrine), and this is what should work for both of us. I need an agreement from you. Let me stay in the house for one year with you taking care of the monthly dues and expenses. If this, this thing with Taffie doesn't last, we could always reconcile and you'd just move back in, but if not, we'll sell the house and get a divorce."

Mark sat there nodding his head in agreement.

"Sure, Dina, I can manage that. But, honestly, don't hold out for a reconciliation. This thing, as you call it, with Taffie is real and it's going to last. But a year won't kill us.

Taffie doesn't want to get married for a couple of years anyway until she's twenty-five; that's when her trust fund kicks in. I'll figure out your expenses and send you a monthly check, and I'll call Ted and tell him to hold off on any legal papers until our year is up. But you're going to need to lawyer up, at least for a consultation. Florida law is pretty clear cut about divorce, but you still need an attorney."

Mark acquiesced a little too quickly to my suggestion and I panicked when he mentioned the word divorce. Fifteen years of living together with good sex and great food was falling apart quicker than my Almond Chip Soufflé the time my mother slammed the oven door after taking a peek.

"Thank you. Let's see how it goes. I know I need a lawyer; Wanda gave me the name of someone to contact."

"Who?" said a curious Mark.

"Millie Rise, why? You know her?"

"I was afraid you were going to say that name. I know of her and they say she's a real bitch."

"Why is it that a great female attorney is a bitch, and a great male attorney is just great?" I said, proud of myself for cracking wise.

"Oh never mind, go to whoever pleases you, but do it," Mark said, turning up the hostility in his voice.

Ignoring the building unpleasantness I returned to the pre-lawyer conversation.

"I'll try to get a part-time job to help out, but I haven't worked in so long, and frankly, I don't know who would hire me or for what," I said.

"Don't worry too much about a job. I'll try to cover the expenses for the year. But if you wanted to work, any restaurant would love to hire you. You're really an amazing cook. The best. Taffie doesn't have a clue in the kitchen," he said with a puppy-love sigh, buttering yet another biscuit and adding a few drops of cream to his coffee. "Any more of that ham?" he said, coming out of his reverie.

"Mark, you better gather your things now," I said, having had my fill of Taffie-talk.

"Oh, geez, you're right," said my husband, glancing at his Cartier watch, which must have been a gift from his girlfriend. "Dina, it's not that I don't love you – I guess I always will – it's just different this time."

Different? It was:

1. Easy.

2. Unhealthy.

3. Cheap, just like fast food.

Chapter 10

July

Work

When Mark's first check arrived the last week in June, it was clear that I would have to get a job, and not just part time. My estranged husband had either forgotten how much it cost to live in a country club, or had squandered money in an effort to impress his young lover. He must have been spending on more than burgers because the amount of his check was short by about thirty percent. I had a good idea of what our expenses were, but Mark had always handled the bookkeeping. He discouraged me from checking statements saying everything was being taken care of. I went from my parents taking care of me to my husband doing the same. Now it was time for me to take control. I might be willing to give up my husband for a year, but he had to live up to his obligations.

Everyone at Forest found out about our separation and obviously, I no longer had to cook for Mark's former clients. I should have been relieved, but at least the activity would have filled my empty days. After a few weeks of general speculation and discussion as to why my husband deserted me, it became old news, and a few of the women began to call; no, not to invite me to lunch or to partake in my former card or golf games, but to see if I was still willing to drop off cakes, pies, or even a box dinner.

At first I hedged on the delivery service not wanting to blow my restricted budget on the expensive ingredients my recipes demanded, but it was the one line of communication left open between the residents of Forest and me.

Dex gave me the idea of becoming a semi-professional caterer. My house was last on his route the Friday before July 4th, and he was delivering two Madeleine baking molds that had been back-ordered from before my separation. As much as I loved the delicate French cookies, I'd have to return the pans. Forty-five dollars was now an extravagance.

"How about a cup of coffee for an old friend," he said, leaning against the front door.

"Sure, come on in," I said, leading the way to the kitchen.

This had been our routine for the last few weeks since Mark vacated the premises, and we'd fallen into a late coffee break time.

I laid out the mugs and matching porcelain plates my mother gave Mark and me as an anniversary present one year, and handed Dex a brief explanation of our separation, leaving out the terms. I hesitated telling him the story although it was common knowledge among his clients at Forest, and because I was sure they'd shared the entire account with him, he didn't need to hear it from me.

"It's about time you dumped him," he said. "Hey, Dina, I'm sorry, I know that sounds cruel, but your husband wasn't doing you any favors."

"Did you know about…" I said, hoping that he wouldn't have a clue, but when he closed his eyes and nodded, I knew he did.

"Like I said, sorry. And trust me, it's a flash in the pan. He'll come crawling back, and it won't take long. If you still want him."

I was about to say that we'd had a pretty damn good marriage, but that term no longer seemed true. I should have seen it coming. There were so many signs; his not coming to the hospital, putting a halt to the dinner parties when Mark needed the business more than ever, and the lack of sex during the past few months we lived together. We'd always been so compatible in bed and that was only one of the reasons I was looking forward to the night we were supposed to make a baby; it was my most fertile time of the month, and I'd already envisioned the nursery.

Starting to cry, I couldn't reply. Of course, I wanted my husband back. How was I going to manage without him? It wouldn't just be financially that I'd have to struggle, but the thought of dating was beyond my grasp. Mark had been my first real boyfriend and the only man I'd ever slept with. Living under my parents' wing all those years never gave me the flexibility or freedom to propel any relationships with men into bed, and even my college years and the Hampton summer had been celibate until I met Mark.

"Hey, I didn't mean to make you sad. Sure, he'll come back to you as soon as that Paris Hilton wannabe gets tired of him...and trust me, she will. Uh, someone said something about coffee?" Dex said.

Changing the subject was a specialty of his.

"Oh, yeah, that was you," I said, starting to smile. "I'll get it. I mean, how many more Fridays am I going to have coffee with you? This is the last of the supplies I'll be ordering, and these are going to have to go back." I said, pointing to the cookie trays that he'd already unwrapped for me. "Nothing against PPS, but with shipping rates so high these days if I should need something, which I doubt, I'll just run over to Town Center, or drive down to Coconut Creek to that kitchen store…"

"Sur La Table?" Dex said, completing my sentence. "I'm there all the time. They have great stuff. Hey, you know, I could meet you down there, look over the specials, grab a latte at Starbucks…"

"Well, like I said," interrupting him, "I won't be needing any further supplies right now. I'm not doing much cooking these days, except a few things for the girls – you know – my loaf cakes, stuff like that."

"Yeah, 'Dina's Drop-Off Service,'" he said in a biting manner. "Hey, be honest with me. If things are a little tight with Mark gone, why are you giving stuff away? You should be charging them."

And with that comment, the seeds were planted for my catering business.

Dex and I sat for the next few minutes sipping our coffee and nibbling on my Lemon Coconut Squares. I'd experimented on these old standbys by adding a layer of blueberry jam.

"Are they too sweet?" I asked my coffee buddy. "Is the jam over the top?"

"Not for me," said Dex. "Dina, did you hear me before?"

"I did. You're saying I should charge my friends," I said.

"Friends? Have any of these friends invited you over for dinner, or even called to see how you're doing?"

"Nancy Frank called just last week. I'm not a total outcast," I said, defending my honor.

"And she called you because…" Dex continued.

"She needed someone to fill in for Gabriela Loft, you know, for a bridge game."

"Oh, I see. So she calls you to play for Gabriela, whose real name, by the way, is Gertrude, and did she say anything else?"

"What? Gertrude? You're kidding," I said, starting to laugh.

"Hey, you didn't hear it from me, but it's true. So back to Nancy, what else did she want?"

"Well," I said, feeling my honor deflating, "she did ask if I had any of my Key Lime Pound Cakes in the freezer."

"And did you?"

"No, but…"

"But you whipped one up for her, right?"

"Well, I couldn't come there empty-handed," I said.

"Dina, I've been there when she's had a bridge game going on. All I've ever seen is some store-bought garbage in the kitchen, which is the only place I'm allowed to leave packages unless she's saved up her handyman projects for me. And, she doesn't even go Publix bakery; instead she buys those Little Wendy's Chocolate Pies or whatever they call stuff that tastes like it came out of a chemistry set."

Dex had me on all points. There was no value in continuing on about the afternoon at Nancy's because when I arrived:

1. Gabriela, formerly known as Gertrude, had been able to make it after all.

2. They didn't really need a fifth.

3. Thank you very much for the cake.

No, I didn't have to tell that to Dex because in all likelihood he already knew about it. News, good and bad, travels at warp speed in an open-book community like Forest, and some of the women were only too happy to share stories with a good-looking guy like Dex. They'd never get away with cheating, but they sure as hell could flirt with their hunk of a delivery man. I assumed he decided to take it easy on me because, again, all conversation stopped and the only sound was the loud hum of my refrigerator, which was on the fritz again.

"Dina, just listen to me for a minute. Instead of letting the women take advantage of you – and you know they will as long as you allow it – tell them that you're asking a nominal price to cover your expenses. They don't have to know how much profit you're building in, and they won't care. Oh, I don't mean that you can't drop off a cake or a pie now and then as a gift, that's peanuts, but you could cater dinners and parties at their homes. I can serve and tend bar, even help you cook and clean up, and if you need outside help you can always hire servers and dishwashers from agencies. My evenings and weekends are pretty free these days."

"What about, uh, what's your fiancée's name?"

"Sue-Ellen, but she's not my fiancée. Let's get back to your new business."

I admired the way Dex could cut clean from a conversation about his personal life; I wish I had the same self-control in my feelings toward Mark.

"Dex, come on, you know Forest doesn't allow anyone to run a business from home."

"You're not serious? Everyone's running a business from their homes – oh, not the schmucks who wouldn't know an invoice from a check, but really, many do. And no one seems to care or at least, no one's reported the goings-on. And who the hell gives a damn? Anyway, you don't have to call it a business, officially. Just let people know that you'll cook for them if they'll pay for the food. I have a van – we can't be running around in the PPS truck after five – so I can help you haul everything you need. You'll have to manage the daytime stuff on your own, keep it to luncheons, that kinda thing and you'll be fine."

If there was a flaw in Dex's plan I didn't see it. At first the thought of charging my so-called friends for the meals they'd consumed for free at my house was a little off-putting, but I did need the extra money and with Dex willing to help out, I decided to give it a shot.

Our house had been built with a generous-sized kitchen, which was one of the reasons it appealed to me. Aside from having a brief stint as a food writer back in New York, I'd always had an interest in cooking and baking. Wanda and I signed up for local cooking courses all through our college years, and I continued on with lessons in New York and East Hampton.

When Mark and I first bought our home, a rare foreclosure at the time, my parents thought we were being extravagant by replacing some of the perfectly workable appliances with a convection double oven, an over-sized Sub-Zero refrigerator/freezer, and a six-burner gas range. Everyone had granite counter tops at Forest, but I'm pretty sure I was the only one who needed a marble pastry slab. Mark must have had his entertaining ideas in mind way back then because he was the one who suggested the improvements.

Even with all the present equipment, I realized it might not be sufficient for a full catering business. I couldn't ask Mark for money for renovations because the first area to be demolished would be his paneled home office. Screw resale, I wanted a butler's pantry.

When I mentioned all this to Dex, he suggested that it might be safer not to jump the gun, but to start small with the current gear I already had.

"You've done plenty of dinners here for eight or ten, haven't you?"

"Sure, even twenty at times."

"So begin with a couple of bridge luncheons first, or small dinner parties, and if you get big enough, then you can make some adjustments. In the meanwhile, I'll bring over some stainless carts that you can stick in that office back there; we have a ton of stuff in the warehouse and those'll be handy to have."

"Nothing seems to be a problem for you, Dex, but you're right. I'll start small. I'm going to speak with Wanda, let her know what I'm doing. I don't want to step on her toes. She's the head planner over at Platinum Pantry and does those ginormous parties. This shouldn't interfere with her business. I hope she'll understand."

"Hey, she'll probably be delighted to shift some of the smaller jobs to you. Platinum's one of our steady customers and they have more clients than they can handle."

"Wanda's been such a good friend to me. She was the first person I told about Mark. She said it was about time we got separated."

"Yeah, I sort of agree with that."

Chapter 11

July

Setting the Stage

Before Mark left, which was soon after our dinner parties ceased, his clients took it hard. After being weaned from restaurant food, they wondered where their next gourmet home-cooked meal would come from. I could still fulfill their needs, but now they'd have to pay for it. I managed to create menus with prices that were still far less than what their favorite restaurants were charging, and I'd play up the fact that they'd be entertaining in their lavish homes – a much more pleasant and impressive evening.

I designed colorful postcards on my laptop announcing the opportunity to hold at-home meals without mentioning any form of payment. The first step was to see if there was any interest, plus I had to be careful about not advertising too blatantly.

Walking into the club's dining room at lunch the day after my discussion with Dex, I passed out cards to my former dinner guests with a brief explanation of what they could expect.

"Hi girls, I'm going to leave these cards with you; just give a call or shoot me an email if you're interested. And, keep it on the down-low, please," I said, distributing my postcards.

"Dina! Where have you been?" said Gabriela, née Gertrude, who headed up the brat pack.

I heartened at her exclamation thinking I misjudged the group and that they hadn't forgotten about me. Although the players had just come in from a tennis match, each, with slim legs stemming from short tennis outfits, managed to look flawless. The majority were Caucasian, but Forest being an equal-opportunity snob fest was also home to Asians, Afro-Americans, Eastern Indians, Native Americans and others.

The Forest Look:

1. Hair was straightened and highlighted or left loosely curled.

2. Makeup barely-there.

3. Acrylic nails done in either the fancy and outrageously overpriced pink and white French design (which my sister swore was unheard of in France) or deep cordovan, the signature color for the insanely gorgeous Chan twins, Belle and Bailey.

Not all the women were beautiful, but the overall appearance was one of glamour, style and wealth. I'd never before noticed the glow that emanated from these Boca babes maybe because I'd been in the thick (well, not exactly in the thick, more like the outskirts) of the herd.

Before I started cooking for Mark's clients I followed along and had the tannest legs, the streakiest hair, and the pinkest and whitest nails. I was a babe. At just under five and a half feet, I certainly wasn't model tall or dazzling in any sense of the word; I'd settle for pretty even though my mother thought I was gorgeous. I had large brown eyes fringed with dark lashes eliminating the need for mascara, and my long chestnut-colored hair was naturally wavy until the club's salon got a hold of it. They used the latest process for wringing out any sign of a curl, leaving my locks straight and swingy. Aaron, the colorist from Israel, then highlighted it with a tortoise-shell technique, weaving in different shades of dark blonde and auburn. It was a look and I'd had it.

Because I was aware of all kitchen sanitary standards learned back in my college courses, my long artificial nails had to go and in lieu of wearing a cap or a net, it was just easier to have Aaron cut my hair very short and leave it wavy. I believed my husband when he said he loved the look on me, but thinking back, I know he didn't really care anymore. It was all about keeping his clients happy.

Mark and I never truly fit Forest's standards. We weren't rich. When Mark and I were first married and lived in New York, I wrote a column for the now defunct *Gourmet* magazine. My husband always made a good living, but we were not on the same latitude as most other couples who lived at Forest. We were accepted for two reasons: Mark was a phenomenal golfer, just short of being able to go pro, and I was a fantastic cook. As a couple, we had gifts to offer and were in constant demand.

Our house in Forest wasn't in the estate section; instead we purchased the relatively cheap foreclosure. Aside from replacing the kitchen appliances, we lived modestly and the year that Mark made a killing, paid off the mortgage.

The house was spacious with three bedrooms, one of which we turned into Mark's office, but it wasn't decorated by Darlene's Interiors or Fred's Place, the two top design firms in Boca.

We weren't exactly K-Mart, but spending thousands of dollars on a sofa without room to sit for all the silk pillows just wasn't our taste or in our budget.

I didn't care about those things. We had more than enough to keep up a good lifestyle and I loved my husband. I was content throwing together a meal of spaghetti and salad for us, or grilling the occasional sirloin steak. I sensed Mark wanted more; he wanted what I had growing up: everything. Now Taffie could provide what I couldn't. Or, maybe he really was in love with her despite Dex's opinion.

"You're never at the club anymore and we could use you in the scrambles," said Gabriela, yanking me out of my daydream and then reaffirming my original thought. "Nobody can chip and putt like you."

"Well, Gaby, I've been sort of busy now that I'm single," I said without much conviction. "And, I'm trying out some great new recipes, so stay in touch."

"Poor Dina," I heard Gaby say to the group before I even turned to walk toward the lunch bar-counter, not wanting to sit alone at another oversized table after I hadn't been invited to join them. "How terrible. Her husband leaving her for that young girl, but she should have kept up better. Dina's not exactly the nature girl type, if you know what I mean. That hair! What was she thinking?"

I kept walking, already upping the price of the entrées.

When you hear about mean girls in high school, I'm pretty sure that Gaby and her posse fit the description.

1. They were the ones who lived in upscale towns on the right side of the tracks; the moneyed burgs light years away from their counterparts.

2. They were the ones who didn't need scholarships or even good grades to get into colleges of their choice because they came from families with connections.

3. They were the ones who had a cadre of cashmere sweaters in shades not yet found on a color wheel, and bought expensive lingerie before Victoria had all her secrets.

4. They were the ones who went to concierge summer camps with fancy bunks and decent food in the dining halls.

5. High school graduation gifts were cars and trips to Europe.

6. They were the ones who became engaged the day after graduating from college with diamonds as big as marbles, and although the girls were smart and some even had careers, the pinnacle of their success was to marry and settle down with a rich guy in the suburbs, raise a family, join a fancy country club, and eventually move to an even fancier country club in Boca Raton.

My existence had been strikingly similar to Gaby's and the rest of the women who sat at her table until the day Mark walked out. I was part of the privileged class growing up, and belonged to the right cliques, sororities and clubs. I was everything they were even without a major bank account, but I don't think I was ever mean. At least I hoped I hadn't been. I know now that I'd never trash someone just because she found herself suddenly single.

Chapter 12

July

Wanda's World

I knew I'd have to let Wanda know about my plan to start a small catering service because otherwise there'd be hell to pay if she heard it from someone else. We arranged to meet at Saquella, my favorite Italian café in east Boca, the day after I spoke to the Forest girls.

"I'm glad you could meet me down here because my next client is at that fancy apartment building over on the ocean. They downsized from a seven-bedroom McMansion to a three-bedroom penthouse, poor things, and they're giving an open house for seventy of their closest friends," Wanda said after we placed our order.

"You can't do a sit-down dinner for that many, can you?" I said, needing insider information.

"In some of these apartments I could, but not that one. We'll do a cocktail buffet with tons of pick-up appetizers and maybe a station or two. The living room is tremendous; they knocked down a wall just so they could continue entertaining. I've done stuff for them before when they lived over at Bocaire. Nice people and big tippers. The staff loves working for them, and trust me, no one is leaving Platinum with the salaries they make. Platinum did have to fire one of the chefs, stealing filet mignons right off the truck. I mean how stupid do you have to be?"

I knew I had to stop the upcoming rant and relied on a little sweet talk.

"Well, that's just one bad egg. You've been their top salesperson for the past five years. Good for you."

"Thanks, it's worked out well for Linz and me. You know his office is on the ground floor of our building, which he likes, and I like being out of the apartment. Otherwise, he'd be in my hair between appointments, if you know what I mean."

"Well, it's great that you each have your own career. How's the psychiatry business these days?" I said.

"Oh, Linz does a lot of good work. I mean, he doesn't heal leopards or anything, but his patients love him," Wanda said, using one of her most outrageous misappropriations of the English language. I often wondered how such a smart woman could come up with such wrong phrases, but that was Wanda. "He really cares about them and I love him for that. I wish you and Mark had never moved into Forest with all that competition keeping up with the Johnsons. That's not who you are."

"Maybe you're right, but Mark wanted it and it worked for a long time," I said, again trying to defend my position.

"It worked because Mark played golf with the bigwigs while you cooked for them. How is that even fair to you?"

"Let's not talk about Mark right now. Tell me about Platinum. Are you only booking the big stuff?" I said, cajoling her into the next segment of our conversation.

"Platinum treats me right and I can't believe how that business is growing. You'd think people would be cutting back, but the rich still have money and they like to show it off. Platinum won't even touch the small jobs anymore; not worth the trouble," said my friend, giving me the opening I needed.

"Well, I'm sorta glad to hear that because Dex came up with an idea for me. You know that Mark is paying a lot of my expenses, but I need to get a job."

"Oh no, were you going to ask me to get you an interview at Platinum? I wish I could, but they just hired their last sales person and she's doing great – not really any competition for me because we handle different types of accounts – and she's willing to schlep up to Fort St. Lucie, but if they decide to put someone else on, I'll definitely recommend you."

"No, Wanda, nothing like that, well nothing exactly like that anyway. Dex and I thought I could do some catering at Forest."

"In the dining room? They have more than enough staff plus they wouldn't hire a resident."

"No, not for the club, but privately for the residents. Small stuff, like the stuff you said Platinum doesn't want anymore. There's still a need for brunches, bridge lunches, small dinner parties – things you've gotten away from," I said, almost trembling awaiting my friend's judgment.

"You would cater for the people at Forest? Aren't they your friends? Awkward."

"I played a lot of golf and bridge with the girls, but Mark and I never socialized with couples that much except when they were at our house for dinner. No one's reached out to me since he's left."

"Well, you're not exactly the Keeping-up-with-the-Kevorkians typical country club type so maybe it would work out. And Platinum's parties start at four thousand dollars and that's a cheapie. Bill your parties under two or so and we'll be fine. I can probably throw some business your way, and you can let me know of any big events someone is thinking about."

"Two? Two thousand?" I was thinking more around five to six hundred."

"You can do those too, in the beginning, but if you sell too cheap you won't make a decent profit, and it'll be harder to reach the two mark, which is where you need to be. Start aiming for a thousand and inch it up for bigger gigs."

"Thanks, sweetie," I said, appreciating my friend's knowledge and experience. "I never thought I could help you out, but why not? There are certainly, or hopefully once I get off the ground, going to be parties I can't handle and Dex already told me how busy Platinum is and that you might swing a few little things my way."

"Dex? How many times are you going to bring him up?" Wanda said. "Anything brewing there? I thought he was engaged and you wouldn't take up with anyone who's involved, no value in that."

"No, on all accounts. He says he's not engaged and I didn't ask for any details, and no, I'm not taking up with him. I want to work to make some extra cash so I can keep the house going till my husband gives up his eye candy and comes home," I said quite a bit louder than planned.

"Okay, don't blow a casket, but you could do worse than ending up with someone like Dex. Okay, okay, I'll stop," she said, after I put my hands up in a defensive position. "Give yourself a year and see where you guys are then, I mean you and Mark."

"That's exactly what we're doing. Here's the food, wanna

split?" I said, knowing she would because that's what BFF's did. I decided not to mention that Dex would be helping.

The next evening I received a phone call from Marcy Gold.

"Hello, Marcy," I said, recognizing the name from the caller I.D.

"Dina?" she said.

"Yes, it's me," I said, wondering who she was expecting to answer. "What's up Marcy?"

"Well, I'm looking at your postcard, it's so cute. How did you do that with the pictures and everything?" she said, and not waiting for a reply went on to describe a small luncheon she wanted to host in her niece's honor.

"You remember Brittany, right? Weren't you here when she and Brian got engaged?"

"Um, no, Marcy. I wasn't, but I think you introduced us at the club. Congratulations, by the way. She's a lovely girl."

"Oh, yeah, thanks. She's my only niece and I told my sister – you know Lana, don't you – that I wanted to have a ladies brunchy-luncheon for her, not a bridal shower, but just a chance for Brit to meet all my friends here at Forest. Is that what your postcard meant, that you'd do that kind of thing?"

"Yes, that's correct. And, I did meet Lana at the pool, but don't tell me you're going to invite your sister even though she doesn't live here," I said, hoping to inject a little humor into the conversation while trying not to sound sarcastic.

"What? Oh, right, sure I am. You're funny, Dina. Anyway, she lives at Delaire so she's used to country clubs. Can we talk about a menu?"

"Sure, but I just want to make it clear that I'll be charging so if you tell me how many you'll be, give me the date and time, and a budget, I'll email you a note with all the info."

"Uh, Dina, would you mind dropping it off?" she said.

I'd forgotten that Marcy hadn't yet joined the twenty-first century by using email.

"I'll leave it at your front door in an envelope."

"And of course I expect to pay. I think it's neat that you'd do this for us. The party will have to be on a Sunday sometime in early August."

Scheduling my first event on a Sunday would make it possible for Dex to help out since he didn't work weekends. I had to be careful not to take advantage of his good will, but he seemed so excited about the project that I was sure he'd say yes.

"And Dina, it's not going to break the bank, is it?"

"No, I'll be careful to keep it reasonable, but I do need some idea of what your budget is?"

"Budget? I don't really use a budget, do you? Oh, sorry, I know things must be a little tough going for you now, and I'm really happy you're doing this catering thing. Budget, hmm, I guess around a thousand; no more than fifteen hundred or Burt'll have a canary. We won't be more than twenty-two women, so let's plan on a max of fifteen hundred."

I gasped as I figured out the profit I'd make on this deal. Even if she had thirty guests it would still come to fifty dollars a head, and unless I was serving Beluga caviar I could bring in an appetizing and delicious meal for much less than that and best of all, there'd be no competition with Wanda.

"Marcy, that shouldn't be a problem, and it'll probably be somewhere between those two figures. And, since you're my first client, I'm going to do an over-the-top party for you. Let's take a look at the menu next week, okay? I know we have over a month, but we'll need to discuss table settings, flowers, wine, and all that business as we get closer – unless you want to take care of it on your own."

"Oh Dina, don't leave me with that. You're the expert; it always looked so perfect at your house. And if you need me to buy anything extra, no problem, but I think we have plenty of china and stemware."

"Sounds great. I just want to give you a heads up on one more thing. I'll be hiring Dex Ryder to help out; that's not going to be a problem, is it?"

"Of course not. We all know him, such a nice guy. Cute, too."

There was a slight pause before she continued.

"I'm really sorry about Mark. You didn't deserve that treatment. We all knew he was cheating on you; I guess one of us should have said something. I wanted to, but Burt said to stay out of it," said a contrite Marcy.

"Well, I'm putting that behind me now, but I appreciate your thoughts. It's kind of you to say so," I said. "I know it must have been difficult for you girls not knowing what to do. It's okay, seriously."

Another longer pause this time.

"Marcy, you still there?"

"Dina, thank you, and thanks for all the great dinners we had at your house. Burt is still talking about the apricot cobbler. I just know this brunch is going to be fabulous if you're handling all the details! Oh, wait; there was something I want on the menu: Beluga caviar. Can you do that?"

"Sure, Marcy," I said, seeing my profit shrink by half. "And I'll throw in a cobbler for Burt."

As soon as I hung up with Marcy, the phone rang.

"Yeah, Marcy, what'd you forget?" I said, not even checking the caller I.D.

"Mrs. Marshall? It's Chuck Wilkins."

1. Chuck Wilkins, the club's general manager.

2. Screwed before the first cheese puff was served.

3. Someone squealed.

"Oh, hello, Chuck," I said in the saddest tone I could muster up. Maybe if he took pity on me, he'd let me run my little cooking business without raising a fuss.

"I'm calling for a few reasons. I haven't had a chance to tell you how sorry I was to hear about the…the separation," he said, clearing his throat about ninety times until he got it out.

"Thanks, Chuck, I appreciate that. Mark and I are on good terms despite everything," I said, wondering why I had to tell that to everyone. Although my ex, and that was how I was referring to him now to keep some semblance of pride, had done a lousy thing, I still needed him more as a friend than an enemy.

"That's part of the reason I'm calling."

Part? What was the other part? That the club was giving me forty-eight hours to clear out my pots and pans, and high-tail it back to New York?

"I haven't been able to reach Mark on his cell, and since he's officially a Forest resident I was hoping he'd still be playing in the pro-am golf tourney coming up next month. We were supposed to be partners," he said, apparently saving the worst news for last.

"He may have gone down to the Keys, and you know, the reception can be spotty down there. Did you try texting him?"

"Well, I'm not so good at that," he said. I'd have to introduce him to Marcy; maybe the two of them could take a beginner's course in modern technology. "Would you mind contacting him and tell him to get in touch with me?"

"No problem. I'll send him a text as soon as we hang up. Uh, is there anything else?" I said, still expecting the walls to cave in on me.

"Well, yes, there is. I feel kind of funny asking you, but before everything happened, Mark offered to bring those cupcakes you baked for us last year, you know, the ones with the green frosting and the little flagsticks. They were a big hit," he said.

"Sure, Chuck, glad to do it. How many do you need?" I said, breathing a sigh of relief that could have been heard in Ft. Lauderdale.

"Six dozen ought to do it if that's not a problem. The pastry chef will be baking a few sheet cakes, but everyone kept talking about your cupcakes last year; even Chef André and you know how picky he can be. I keep notes on that stuff, so that'd be great if you don't mind."

The man keeps notes on cupcakes but doesn't know how to text?

"Consider it done. Just let me know when you need them."

"Thanks, Mrs. Marshall. We could get by with just the cake, but I sort of like to show off a bit for the non-members who'll be here. I bet you're the only one who knows how to bake like that."

I bet he was right, but I didn't make the wager.

The conversation had gotten a little surreal for me; here was a fifty-year-old man running a multi-million dollar country club obsessing over cupcakes.

"So, Chuck, is that it then?"

"That's it, Mrs. Marshall."

"Okay then, six dozen cupcakes for the pro-am. And how about some little meringues that look like golf balls; it's a new recipe and I wanted to try it anyway," I said, throwing monetary caution to the wind in exchange for not being discovered. "I'm sure I'll be able to reach Mark for you. Good night," I said, waiting for his reply, but there was a prolonged silence.

"Good night," he said, "and I just wanted to say, good luck with everything."

I hung up the phone not knowing if he was wishing me success with:

1. The cupcakes.

2. The separation.

3. Texting Mark.

Chapter 13

Family Ties

My mother said the same words to me when I told her I was going to marry Mark, and when we were separating.

"Oy gevalt!" said Mom, "You're what?"

That was Stella's cry when I called her years ago to tell her and my father about Mark. My parents were already living in Florida at the time, but had met my intended during the summer I spent out in East Hampton. Although my father said he didn't trust him, my mother was ready to marry off her younger daughter and the thrill of planning a wedding took precedence over any of my dad's opinions.

"He proposed? Wait, let me think a minute." My mother's minute was someone else's nano-second because she'd already formulated a plan.

"Okay, of course you'll marry him. Daddy and I will come to New York City (she never got the hang of just calling it the city even when they lived there) for the entire week. No, wait! I have to come now to find a place for the reception and help pick out your dress. I don't want you walking down the aisle in some schmatta."

My mother, an Italian Catholic, had taken to sprinkling

her conversations with Yiddish phrases ever since moving to Boynton Beach, and had gotten quite good at it.

"Mother, we don't want a big wedding. We're getting married on the beach in East Hampton. Mark has access to a beautiful house overlooking the ocean and we'll have a small reception there. You and Daddy are more than welcome to stay with us, or I'll book you into a hotel."

"On the beach? What kind of shoes can you wear in the sand?"

"Flip-flops."

She detected sarcasm in my voice and handed the phone to my father.

"Harry," I heard her yell, "Come talk some sense into your daughter. She wants to get married on the beach with flippers. Oy vey ist meir!"

Stella got a lot of things wrong, but her expressions were spot on.

"Sweetie? You and that guy getting married?" he said. "You're sure?"

"Yes, Daddy. We're both sure and once you get to know Mark better you'll be sure too. I'm going to be a June bride and we want you and Mom to come up for the wedding."

"What's with the flippers?"

"Nothing's with the flippers. It was a joke. But we're getting married on the beach so you won't need a tuxedo; just something nice and casual."

"Thank God," my father said. "We'll be there; just give Mom the dates. Bye, honey." That was one of the longer conversations I had with my father, a man of few words – leaving most of them to his wife.

"Dina? Does France know?" my mother said once she had the phone back in her hands, "because they'll have to make arrangements to come up with Wesley from that farkakte airport they fly out of."

"Mom, that would be Greensboro, and I'm sure they won't have any problems. I'm sending France an email now; I wanted you and Dad to be the first to know."

"Honey, why don't you and Mark come down here?"

"Because we can't get a lot of time off in June, and because it's probably two hundred degrees then."

"You get used to it, and I meant why don't the two of you move down here."

What should have sounded ridiculous didn't at all. Being a good athlete I liked the idea of having access to outside sports year-round and Mark hated the northern winters. Although we never mentioned it to our parents, we'd actually discussed the move as a possible plan way down the road once we were established.

"You could move to Boca – that's where the young people go – and you can always find deals, even in the country clubs. I'm not saying move to where Daddy and I are because you have to be fifty-five to get in, but being close by wouldn't be so terrible. And then the family would only be in two places, here and North Carolina. Who needs New York?" said my mother, advertising genius for South Florida.

"Mom, there's no way we could afford a place in Boca. And don't those clubs have all kinds of expenses once you're in? Mark's doing well, but he's just starting out," I said, feeling myself weaken. "Plus, I love my job at the magazine."

"Dina dear, even I know they can't be paying you much for your column and what about if you just sent it in? By email, you know?"

"Yeah, Mom, I know, but I think I'd miss the excitement of the city," I said trying to interject reasoning into the conversation that she was taking control of.

"Sweetheart, how much time do you have for excitement? Your husband-to-be works twelve hours a day and must be exhausted by the time he gets home. Tell me, how many nights a week do you even get out for dinner?"

She had me there. Mark and I tried to go to a restaurant on the occasional Saturday night when he wasn't catching up on paperwork, but most of the time I cooked for us, and maybe for the few friends we made in East Hampton. Occasionally, Wanda and Linz, who were now married, would invite us over for dinner, but Mark and Linz were the proverbial oil and water, so we kept our socializing with them to a minimum.

"Darling, listen to me. Living in Florida is like being on vacation 24/7. Even if Mark comes home late you can still go for a swim or a bike ride, you'll love it. And, since it seems you're going to forego the fancy wedding by having it on the beach, what do you need there besides a huppa and some champagne?

Mark's Jewish, right, so you'll have a rabbi. And you can say you're Jewish too because Dad's reformed so it counts. Go find a nice dress on your own, not too expensive, see when Kleinfeld's is having a sale, and your father and I will give you the down payment for a house. We'll even pay the dues for the first year. Your father is standing right here so he knows what's going on and he's shaking his head yes. Honey, we miss you, and with your sister in North Carolina we have no family here."

My mother had it all wrapped up with a bow and a lollipop, and there was little that didn't make sense. With my parents' generous donation, Mark and I could swing a low interest rate mortgage provided the house wasn't out of our price range.

"Mom, do you really think we could find a place that's affordable?"

"I'm sure of it and one of my Maj girls is a top notch broker. I'll mention it to Frosty and she can start looking."

"Frosty? Don't tell me her last name is Winters, because if it is, she's definitely in the wrong business. Hold off for a while," I said, knowing she wouldn't. "I have to ask the magazine if they'll accept my columns from home and just fly me up once in a while if they need me," I said, remembering back to the last staff meeting when we were all told that there would be stringent cutbacks. "Mom, I promise to talk it over with Mark, but I don't know if he'll accept your offer. About the money."

"Pish posh – I won't take no for an answer. Mark's the champion golfer, right? Well, I bet he'd make a better living down here with what he does. Sweetheart, what do you think men talk about for four hours while they're on the golf course? Their feelings? Please! They discuss golf and business."

We chatted on for a while about the scaled-down wedding plans, but my mind had jumped ahead to the Boca move. Bunking with Deborah worked out well, we never got in each other's way, but it would come to an end when Mark and I were married. His studio with a tiny kitchen was not feasible for the two of us, and instead of renting or buying a one-bedroom apartment in Manhattan, we could find, or at least my mother and Frosty could, a house in a country club. Somehow, I'd have to convince Mark that it made sense for us to do it. If he sold his studio and stopped paying rent for his room in the East Hampton place, which was all it'd ever been, we could make it in Boca.

It didn't take much to convince Mark when I brought up the subject that evening over dinner at Deb's. Now that I was engaged and about to be married in a couple of months I stopped the search for my own apartment. Deb was working late, which was fine because she still wasn't crazy about Mark, however, after the flopped date with Stu, she kept her mouth shut. I set aside some tasty leftovers, which would placate her later in the evening in case she felt like making a stinging remark about my intended.

"They'd make the down payment for us and cover the first year's dues?" he said, incredulous that his future in-laws were being so generous. "I didn't even think they were that fond of me, I guess I was wrong."

Not wanting to correct his version, I nodded my approval.

"They're getting older; they want family around them."

"What about your sister and her husband?"

"There's no way they'll make a move to Florida. Redmond's a wine distributor and makes a fortune, and he's not about to give up his territory. Plus, France is entrenched in the whole southern way of life with her gallery and friends; Winston-Salem works for them. It's up to me, I mean us. Do you think your parents would mind very much?"

"Dina, my parents wouldn't mind if we moved to the North Pole," my fiancé said, with a harsh tone. "Are your folks okay with your conversion? It would mean a lot to me. The rabbi is reformed so he'll marry us anyway, but since your Dad is Jewish I didn't think it would be a big transition."

"According to my Italian-Catholic mother, who i.m.'s with God, because my dad's a reformed Jew, his children may be recognized as Jews. I won't need a formal conversion. We celebrated everything growing up, but I always gravitated toward Judaism; France went the other way and we're happy with our choices. And I chose wisely with you," I said, leaning in for a kiss.

"Thanks, Dina. I'm one lucky guy to be marrying you and inheriting such great in-laws as part of the deal," said Mark, his voice bittersweet. "I tried to be a good son, but even as a young kid I remember my mother telling her friends that children were a lot of work and one was enough. I yearned for a sister or a brother when I was growing up, but that was out of the question. They must have known I was lonely because they picked out a parakeet for me as a surprise, but got rid of it the first time I forgot to clean the cage."

I knew Mark didn't get along with his parents, and this wasn't the first time I'd heard about the bird. What kind of people couldn't put up with a bird? With no siblings, he was pretty much alone in this world. A move to Florida would mean family for him, and along with almost year-round sunshine, golf courses and palm trees, his answer was yes. He wanted to relocate to Boca.

"My office has a branch in Boca; I don't think they'll mind putting in a transfer for me. I brought them all that East Hampton business, which kept everyone happy, and I'll continue with those same contacts from Boca. Plenty of them already live there. *Gourmet* will probably be thrilled not to have you as a full-time employee, and you won't need their benefits because I'll cover you with my plan once we're married."

After a marriage ceremony in the rabbi's study of a

nearby synagogue with Wanda and Linz as witnesses, we moved to Boca. Since Mark sold his apartment quickly, we didn't have time to plan the beach affair of my dreams. We told my parents and sister not to bother coming up; but promised my mother she could give us a reception after we moved down.

True to her word, Mom and her broker friend, Frosty, a killer in the business, located a great deal for us at Boca Forest. Wanda and Linz made a move south two months later.

Chapter 14

July

Chez Marcy

The ladies luncheon at Marcy's turned out to be a sensation. Most of her guests were women I knew from the club, and along with Brittany, her mother and a few cousins, there were twenty-two hungry women. My price came in just under the middle of Marcy's budget even with the Beluga. Her husband, Burt, had a wine closet filled with champagne and white wine, which Dex uncorked and poured for the women.

Even though the luncheon was a relatively small party, I was happy to have Dex on hand for support. Marcy had opted to use her dining room table as a display area for the gifts the women would bring, so I needed to rent three large round tables with appropriate sized cloths and twenty-two white ballroom chairs. I used Acorn Rentals, courtesy of Wanda's referral, and they delivered everything the Saturday before the luncheon and set up seating in the center hall rotunda of Marcy's home.

The day before the party I unstuck price tags from Marcy's exquisite linen napkins that went nicely with the Acorn cloths.

"Oh Dina," she said in her Legally Blonde voice as I

was folding the napkins. "I can't wait to tell Burt we're finally using all this stuff."

"Sure, it's so beautiful, why not? You want everything to be elegant and perfect, don't you? Let's take a look at the china; you said you had enough for everyone, right? You know, we could have rented it, but you said you had it covered."

"Can I tell you a secret? I only invited twenty-two because that's all I had enough for. I used to have two more place settings, but they broke when we had them shipped down from New York. I didn't realize you could rent dishes."

"Well, keep it in mind for the future, but I'm getting ahead of myself. Let's concentrate on tomorrow."

My helper, Dex, arrived the next morning just before eleven and after loading up, we arrived at Marcy's in plenty of time to finish our preparations. We dressed the three tables including champagne flutes, wine and water glasses. I've never been a fan of huge floral arrangements and the few bouquets of white roses I brought along were all that we needed to fill low crystal bowls. Marcy wrote out place cards for each guest, using her calligraphy skills.

Once we arranged the tables, Dex and I plated the main courses in Marcy's spacious kitchen. I poached salmon filets at home and we placed them on a bed of romaine, frisée, and radicchio. Cubed yellow and red roasted beets gave the greens a pop of color, and I topped it off with dried cranberries and sugared pecans. My own secret-recipe salad dressing would be trickled on at the last minute.

Dex peeled two dozen tiny clementines and fanned them out at one side of the plate, leaving room for a dollop of papaya salsa on the other. He plucked fresh dill from the washed and dried bunch I brought along and snipped it over the salmon. Finishing the plate with paper-thin lemon slices he stepped back to inspect his masterpiece.

"And?" he said.

"Perfect."

We laughed at the verbal shorthand just as Marcy entered the kitchen wearing a green silk kimono that accented her Prell-green eyes."

"Oh, my god!" she said. "How did just the two of you do all that? And the tables look beautiful. You were right, Dina, it's about time I started using my dining room, well, the foyer anyway. The salad is so colorful; isn't that what Dr. Oz says we should do?"

"Yes, Marcy," said Dex, picking up on the reference. "This is one of the healthiest meals you could have chosen, plus it's going to be delicious."

"Oh, Dex, Dina was the one who suggested…"

"I can see you have exquisite taste, Marcy," said Dex, interrupting her on purpose, "in food and in your home."

I thought he was pouring it on a little thick, but she lapped it up.

"Well, I can't take all the credit for the food idea," said the hostess, almost blushing.

"Oh, don't be modest," I said, getting my game on. "You're the one who made the final selections."

"Well, I guess I did. Thank you, both," said Marcy with a touch of humility confirming that she was a genuinely nice person.

"Our pleasure, Marce," said Dex, shortening her name that neither of them flinched at. "Now, even though that robe is a knock-out, you don't want to get salad dressing on it."

"Well, if you don't need me, I'll finish getting ready.

You know, no one here, I mean at Forest, has ever done anything like this; usually they have bridal showers and lunches at the club or out in a restaurant somewhere. No wonder you used to like entertaining at home. They are going to be so jealous," she said, practically clapping her hands as she skedaddled out of the room.

Did the residents believe that I did all that cooking for them because I liked it so much? Didn't they realize it was a business ploy of Mark's that he drummed up during the golf games?

"Marcy's a little ditzy, Dina, you have to take anything she says with a saltlick of salt," said Dex, reading my change in mood.

I didn't have time to feel sorry for myself or my own empty dining room, which once held guests more often than not. Today, Dex and I had twenty-two people to serve and keep happy; being morose would bring everyone down.

Dex and I continued working side by side piling an assortment of rolls into three baskets, and carving butter swirls to be placed on individual bread plates. I fashioned a low-fat vichyssoise for the first course, which we ladled into small black bowls that Marcy dug up from one of her guest room closets. Dex sprinkled chopped chives on top of the cold soup and set the bowls out on rosewood chargers.

"Ready for dessert?" I asked.

"Let's do it," Dex said.

Again we worked as partners placing apple slices onto six-inch rounds of cookie crust dough that would be transformed into individual open-face tarts. With just a bit of cinnamon, crystallized ginger and crunchy raw sugar, the pastry would be placed in the oven in stages right before the main course was served, and the aroma would certainly be better than the heavily scented candles I talked Marcy out of using.

Since Marcy requested decaf, setting up the coffee urn was a breeze. I felt entitled to a smug smile. Dex caught me at that exact moment and seemed to know what I was thinking.

"See," my assistant said, "I knew you could do it."

"And you're sure you don't mind giving up a Sunday? Isn't there a football game you wanted to watch?" I said, a bit more coyly than intended.

"Golf, and I Tivoed it. I'm having fun, Dina. First time I've ever done anything so fancy."

"You're a natural and if I haven't said thank you in the last ten seconds, I really mean it. I couldn't have done this without you."

"I'm glad," he said.

We had our moment and then it was my cue to inspect the tables. I stepped back from the dining tableau now adorned with linens, flowers, the first course, and sighed. Everything was in place. It would work.

The day went by quickly and smoothly. Every detail had been attended to including the outfits Dex and I decided to wear: khaki's and a white shirt, with white aprons. We looked casual, but professional. Almost everyone knew Dex and me, and treated us with friendly courtesy. We served food, poured wine and cleared like we'd been doing it forever.

Not a drop of champagne was spilled, and the crowd was awed by a dramatic caviar presentation during the social half hour before they were called to their places. Because I'd instructed Marcy to turn the air conditioning to its lowest setting, the chilled soup remained at just the right temperature.

"No," I heard Marcy say to one of the Chan twins, maybe it was Belle, but very well could have been her identical sister, Bailey. "It's not a cream soup; Dina promised me that lunch wouldn't be fattening."

I was refilling the bread basket when I heard the exchange and with a relaxed return to the dining area, placed the basket on one of the tables in full earshot of the conversation.

"Dina, isn't that so? The soup doesn't have any cream, right?" asked Marcy, this time not so sure of herself.

"Not one drop. It's all skim milk and pureed potatoes with leeks and a little seasoning. Is everyone enjoying it?"

"It's divine," said the twins in unison.

"Thank you, Belle, Bailey," I said, using both names because I could.

"I must say, Dina, you're really making the best out of a bad situation. Lucky for us," said Gaby, with her usual inappropriate aplomb, "and what a great idea hiring Dex to help. I'm sure he can use the extra bucks."

I was grateful that Marcy told everyone in advance about Dex's role in today's luncheon. Aside from Gaby's statement, no one else had anything to add. I thought perhaps they were embarrassed by her remarks, but I realized they were too busy eating to make any further comments.

The salmon salads were devoured in much the same way the soups were, and Dex had an easy job loading the dishwasher. The desserts were just out of the oven, their heavenly fragrance wafting throughout and they'd still be slightly warm when served. Dex whipped heavy cream, which he plopped on top of the tarts right before we brought them out. The coffee was ready and the urn sat on the dining room sideboard where the guests had already begun to help themselves.

After dessert and coffee, the unexpected happened. Dex and I were back in the kitchen straightening up when we heard the ping of a spoon being tapped against a glass.

"Attention, everyone," said Marcy. "Dina, Dex, come on in here please."

Dex and I were trying to remain as unobtrusive as possible, but we couldn't ignore the host's summons. As we walked into the dining area everyone was sitting quietly with a raised flute of champagne. Gaby looked a little discomforted, but she held up her glass as well although not quite as high as the others.

"I want to make a toast to the chef, I mean chefs, today. Dina and Dex, thank you for a magnificent lunch," said Marcy.

Brittany who hadn't said much the entire afternoon piped up with "awesome, you guys."

With that, everyone lifted their glasses and sipped while I stood there in somewhat of a stupor. Dex nudged me to come up with some sort of a response. He realized the day was mine even though I never could have done it without his help.

"I'm so pleased you enjoyed everything. Brittany, all the best to you and Brian. Marcy and Lana, thanks for being so gracious," I said, about to go on when I felt another nudge from Dex, silently telling me to shut it down.

Then, they actually clapped. I hoped Marcy was intuitive with her prediction of forthcoming jealous friends who would turn into a line of clients.

1. How long would that line be?

2. How long would it last?

3. Could I keep the price under a couple of thousand so I wouldn't be treading on Wanda's territory?

4. Would I stay small enough to dodge the club rules about a home business?

It took Dex and me less than an hour to clean and pack up our supplies. The rolling carts did most of the work for us and as we loaded the van, we burst into laughter.

"They toasted you!" said Dex.

"You, too! And they were flirting with you the entire time, as if you didn't notice."

"I was just being friendly. Everyone was in such a good mood; great food does that to people, and Marcy was pretty cool."

"Definitely; I agree on all points. I'm glad my…our first job was for her."

"Well, don't be giving Marcy too many accolades because I heard her tell her own sister that you only did parties at Forest," Dex said.

A feeling of satisfaction overtook my exhaustion thinking that I'd be exclusive to Forest. Hopefully, I'd get enough business to make ends meet easier than they presently were. Dex and I spent a total of about five or six hours in preparation, serving and cleaning up with Marcy's event, and I'd figure out my profit in the morning, but it had to be close to eight hundred even with the Beluga.

There were plenty of leftovers in Marcy's refrigerator,

but I kept out a small portion of salmon for dinner. I invited Dex to stay for a light supper, and over a glass of Chardonnay we dissected every facet of the party trying to find areas that could have been improved.

1. There were none.

"You really did it, Dina. But, if you want my advice, try to make sure the girls keep it within the club. Even if they invite outsiders, like today, ask them not to give out your cards. Management here is bound to find out and it may not cause you any trouble, but people are jealous; if they can burn you they will. Just be careful."

"I'm pretty sure Chuck already knows, he probably got a hold of one of my postcards; not much gets by him, but he's probably also aware of my situation and as long as no one complains or gets hurt he'll leave it alone. He's a decent guy. But I know you're right and that's why I didn't put any mention of money on the cards, plus I think the girls are getting off on having me all to themselves. Okay, let's eat. I'm starving and I'm not exactly Wolfgang Puck yet. I just hope today wasn't the beginning and end of my career."

"Trust me, your phone'll be ringing off the hook by the end of the week. Belle and Bailey were jabbering away in Cantonese, and I think I heard 'I wonder if she can make fried rice' in the conversation."

"Oh, stop. Those two are more westernized than anyone else here. And they get their fried rice from Judy at Wok Out, like the rest of us. I'll be lucky if another job comes in, but in the meanwhile I made a very nice profit today thanks to you. I couldn't have done it by myself. Dex, I feel

I need to offer you part of the money…"

"Now you stop. It's fine for you to say that you hired me, that makes sense, but I told you I wanted to help you get on your feet. I had a blast today. I love to cook and this is a great outlet for me. My company's doing well and I just don't need the extra cash. If I do, you'll be the first to know. Now, is there any more of that salmon?"

After Dex left the phone rang. It was Belle Chan.

"Hi Dina," she said after I greeted her. "I must hand it to you; that was a great party you catered."

I was about to thank her and pay a false compliment on the hideous platformed shoes that only she or her sister could make look stylish when she continued.

"Can you do Chinese? And I don't mean Asian," she asked in that clipped tone picked up at the various British boarding schools she and her twin probably attended.

"Sure, Belle. What did you have in mind?" I said, grabbing a notepad and pen.

"It's Bailey's and my birthday December 3rd and our husbands want to throw us a party. The parents, in-laws and our Uncle Tai will be there so we want to honor them and have a special type of dinner, part Cantonese and part American. Would you do a Saturday night? I know that's the busy season, but I wanted to get to you before anyone else did to book it."

"Um, Belle, that could work…let me check my calendar…it's around here some place. Did you have a budget in mind? That's how I worked it with Marcy," I said while pretending to search for my non-existent date book.

"It's just going to be family, nine altogether. They're not big drinkers so probably some of that Tsingtao beer and white wine will do it. Can you bring it in for around a hundred a piece? That's what Marcy said she paid."

I silently thanked Marcy for upping the fee for me, and accepted the job.

"Belle, I found my calendar. December 3rd is free. It's right after Thanksgiving so people haven't been booking December yet. I'll pencil you in and work up a menu."

"Pen me in," she said, "and email me the menu tomorrow. My addy is in the directory."

"Will do, Belle. Thank you, I've already got a few things in mind. I'll send it all to you tomorrow. I don't think we'll need any rentals for a small group. You can fit nine around your dining room table, right?"

"Dina, we live in the Willow section. Marcy's entire house could fit in my dining room. Don't rent anything. I want to keep the cost down. Got it?"

"Got it," I said, suppressing a laugh.

"And can you wear all black instead of that yuppie get-up? Tell Dex the same if he helps out. Actually go ahead and hire him. The two of you made a good team today. I know you're paying him, but I'll put a little on top if you can keep it to a hundred per person."

"Sure, Belle," I said, happy that Dex would pick up a little cash from the Chans, if not from me.

"Oh, one more thing," she said.

I prayed it wouldn't be Beluga.

"My uncle was a chef at the Peninsula Hotel in Hong Kong for years when the British were there. He knows authentic Chinese food so no fried rice!"

"Wouldn't think of it," I said, although I already had.

Belle hung up with a ciao, which seemed a little affected, but for a nine hundred dollar gig she could have said sayonara.

I sent Dex a quick text and he confirmed back that he'd be on board at the Chan's.

Belle and Bailey were married to brothers, hence the same last name. As if the girls weren't rich enough – their parents owned a chain of luxury hotels all over Europe – Jim and Sonny Chan, the husbands who'd been chosen for them, hailed from one of the wealthiest families in Taiwan. The twins, astute businesswomen in their own right, ran an online dating service for Asians, and the brothers Chan, who unfortunately hadn't inherited their parents' savvy, were content to play golf and bridge. They were short, plain-looking men who blessed the day they were set up with the two glamour girls. The couples were always together and even with different physicalities, their parents had chosen wisely for them.

It was nice to know that as westernized as Belle and Bailey were, they still respected the old traditions, and honored their family's wishes by accepting the grooms selected by both sets of parents.

Maybe I should have listened to Harry and Stella.

Chapter 15

September

Holiday Dinners

The Jewish holidays were coming up and I was in demand. I booked the first night of Rosh Hashanah with Mollie and Julio Rasco, Cuban Jews, and the second night at the Weitzenbaum compound in the Oaks section of Forest. The Oaks only had fifteen residences and each was at least 10,000 square feet. Roz and Charlie Weitzenbaum invited their immediate family for the second night of the holiday and because it was a small group, we agreed to set it up in their screened-in patio.

My Italian mother, who wasn't a bad cook, was never much good at making brisket, but it was nonetheless one of my specialties. By this time, I'd confessed to my parents that I was making extra money by cooking for my neighbors.

"Is that such a good idea?" Mom said when I met her for coffee one day at her club's café.

"It's working out okay so far. I did a great luncheon in August, and now I have two holiday dinners plus a dinner party coming up in December. I have an assistant and nothing's too unwieldy for me to handle and I'm going to keep it that way. I can make enough to help out with the expenses. Please don't tell France; I'll do that at the right time."

Stella zeroed in on only one part of the conversation. "I thought you said Mark was paying your way for the year? What happened to that?" she asked, ready to initiate a full scale attack on my husband.

"He is, Mom, but things have gone up at the club; it's a stretch, which is why I'm doing this. I love to cook so it's a win-win," I said, signaling our waitress, whose name-tag identified her as Maizie, to refill our coffee cups, and hoping to sidestep the interrogation.

"Here you go ladies, and how about a nice piece of Russian babka? Made fresh today; not here, but somewhere!" our peppy server said.

"Come on, Mom, let's splurge. Two pieces, please," I said to Maizie who was already en route to the kitchen. "So, Mom, what's new here at Valencia Point? And I thought you said Dad was going to meet us."

"It's Venetian Gardens as you well know, and plenty is going on – wait till you hear," said Stella, unable to disassociate herself from local gossip.

The holiday dinners went off without any snags. I prepared four briskets, which would be enough for both nights, tweaking an old standby recipe from one of the first issues of *Bon Appetit, Gourmet's* main competitor, and the magazine which eventually won out. It was easy and probably a lot of people used a version of it. My trick was to brown the meat first, even though the recipe didn't call for it, but it was worth the effort because aside from creating a nice crust on the meat, it sealed in the juices. I was never a fan of electric slow cookers, and instead, used old-fashioned enameled roasters.

Holiday List (although not in order):

93

1. Lay a few pieces of Publix corn-rye bread in the bottom of the pan to thicken the gravy without adding flour.

2. Add meat, cut up onions and carrots, and cooking liquid, which consists of beer, broth and chili sauce.

3. Skip the recommended but too salty dried onion soup mix. Use my own seasoning pack.

4. While the meat braises in the oven, make chicken soup, honey cake and fruit compote.

5. Roast fresh asparagus in hot oven for ten minutes before serving.

6. Heat up noodle kugel.

7. Order round challahs from Publix.

8. Cheat on gefilte fish. Buy at local kosher store and doctor it up. Serve with freshly grated horseradish, sprigs of parsley and a few sliced carrots.

Almost everything could be done ahead of time, and cooking for two meals was as easy as doing it for one.

Dex wasn't able to help with the first night's prep because I had to leave for the Rascos around four to serve their meal on the early side as requested. Since Mark had the Hummer, which I could have used, I made two trips to transfer all the food. I missed Dex as I set the table, and when I plated the first course. The soup was simmering in the Rasco's kitchen, and the desserts were on standby for the end of the meal. I knew Dex would be late that evening as he had to fill in for one of the drivers who was Jewish, and I wasn't sure he'd be able to show up at all.

Julio came into the kitchen with a check for the agreed upon amount right before they left for temple and asked me to lock up.

"Just leave the key in the planter. The security is so tight around here I don't know why we even use these," he said, holding up the key. "Thanks, Dina, dinner was delicious, and it was nice having Mollie being able to sit down through it.

I'm not sure if you're aware of this, but Mollie's been going through radiation. She's almost at the end of it and is doing well, but I've taken over most of our meals when she's not up to going out."

"Yes, Julio, I heard about it and it can't be easy, but she's looking fine. I'm leaving you with plenty of leftovers to get you through the next few days."

"Thank you, I'm sure she'll appreciate it. I'd ask for that brisket recipe, but I'll never make it. My mother taught me the basics in Cuba so we won't starve. Anyway, I'll stick to the easy stuff in the kitchen; this is probably way too complicated," he said, clueless about my go-to recipe.

"Thank you, Julio," I said pocketing the check. I was going to add that the recipe was indeed immensely complex but couldn't bring myself to fib about it. He'd been so gracious I thought about dropping off another brisket, gratis, but Dex's words rang in my head: "charge 'em!"

"Uh, Dina, I know this is awfully short notice, but if you could, Mollie and I want to invite a few couples from temple to break the fast next week. Do you think you could fit us in? We were going to go over to TooJays, but I'd rather have it at home, maybe eight or ten of us?"

Without thinking or checking my sparse schedule for the moment, I said I would.

"Can I fax you a menu tomorrow?"

"Oh, don't bother; just the usual fare will be fine. Lox, bagels, whitefish – you know the drill," Julio said. As he'd seen Mark and me at services he knew we were Jewish and assumed I'd have no trouble planning a meal to break the fast.

"Wait a minute. If you're going to fast, you won't be able to do the meal or even work on Yom Kipper. I'm sorry, didn't mean to insult you, we'll stick to the original plan. TooJays will be fine; I'll give them a call in the morning."

"Really, it won't be a problem. I'll get all the fixings done the day before and everything will be served chilled or at room temperature if that's okay with you. And I'll heat up a dessert kugel at the last minute."

"If you're sure, it'd be terrific. Everyone enjoyed the meal tonight, which reminds me, I better get the family going so we can find decent seats for the service. Thanks again, Dina, and if I can offer you some advice," he said, not sure if he should actually do that.

"Of course," I said, willing to listen to anyone who came to this country with nothing and became a multi-millionaire making caps.

"I don't think people would mind if you charged a little extra for doing holiday events, especially the religious ones. Most here, or at least the ones hiring you, can afford it and it's only fair. You're giving up time with your family to wait on ours; it just seems like the right thing to do," said Julio, my new best friend at Forest. He took a hundred dollar bill out of his wallet and stuck it in my apron pocket.

"I couldn't, really, it's not necessary," I said knowing I'd already made a huge profit on tonight's meal.

"It makes me feel good, and I think maybe you could use a little extra. Okay, I've got to run; I already feel guilty leaving you with this mess, but I think I heard Dex come in. Good night, Dina and thank you," said my client as he went to gather up his guests to leave. He'd been so gracious, just like Marcy.

Maybe I'd been hanging out with the wrong crowd at Forest and ignoring the nice residents.

"Hey, Dina," Dex said, entering my workspace. "I wanted to get here earlier, but we were swamped. Let me give you a hand," he said. "Was it tough going alone tonight?"

"Hey, you. Nope, no problem at all, but you can help me pack up the leftovers. Leave most of the brisket here."

Dex gave me a quizzical look but by the expression on my face he didn't question me. I'm sure he knew about Mollie and must have realized why I was going against protocol. Wanda told me that large catering companies always left a good amount of leftovers so the clients would feel they got more than their money's worth, even though it was factored into the original cost.

Because my events were small, she advised not to be overly generous, but to leave the hosts enough for one extra meal and take home the rest for myself. I packed up the brisket in three small containers and left a note that they might want to stick one in the freezer for a future dinner. The rest of the clean-up went quickly and before long we were headed back to my house.

By the time I returned home, with Dex following me, we were both starving and I fixed two he-man sized brisket sandwiches on the rest of the rye bread. Dex opened a couple of cold beers and wished me a happy new year.

"Did you want to be at services tonight?" he asked.

"I haven't really had time to think about it," I said. "Mark and I used to go to the temple over on Yamato for the high holidays, but it was mainly for him. Now, I need the money more than the sermon. What about you? Is religion a big part of your life?"

"It used to be when my folks were alive. They were killed in a car crash – drunk driver – ten years ago, and I sort of lost faith."

"I'm so sorry, I didn't know," I said, tears welling up in my eyes. My parents were such a big part of my life that I couldn't imagine my world without them.

"Well, I try not to talk about it. I did go to grief counseling for a few months; that's where I met Sue-Ellen, but in the end I had to find my own solace and it wasn't in the group or in church. Sue-Ellen was important to me then and for years afterwards. She's a good person and a good friend. She wanted more out of the relationship, but I was never in love with her and tried not to lead her on. She pushed for a while until I felt I had to back off spending time with her," he said, finishing his beer. "Got another one of these?" he continued, clearly ending the conversation about his personal life.

"If you think you can drive afterwards," I said, joking around, but instantly regretted my remark. "Oh, I'm so stupid, I didn't mean anything."

"I know you didn't, and with this pot roast and bread sticking to my ribs? Are you kidding? I'll be fine," Dex said, ignoring the reference to drinking. "Really, Dina, I'm a big guy; I can handle a couple of beers especially on top of all this food. Got any dessert left over?"

"Sure," I said, handing him a second brew, "and I'll make a pot of coffee. If you're available, I promised Julio I'd do a breakfast for them next week; that's an easy job and I can prepare most of it the day before."

"Sure, be glad to help. Will you be fasting?"

"Mark and I used to; this will be the first year that I'm doing it without his being here." There were a lot of firsts since he'd been gone, but I kept those to myself.

"Now, since we just polished off the last of the brisket, let's get to that honey cake sitting on the counter. I'll make the coffee; then we'll clear up," he said, more like a husband than a helper. "And Dina, nice of you to leave that much brisket for the Rascos."

His smile was compassionate so I knew he understood the circumstances.

Chapter 16

September

In Demand

During the rest of September, in addition to the holiday events, I booked several more small parties. Marcy and Burt scheduled a cocktail supper for his golf-mates and their wives, but because they wanted a wide variety of hors d'oeuvres I knew it would be a lot of preparation. I decided to stop by Marcy's and discuss the cost even before working up the finalized menu.

"Come on in, Dina," Marcy said, opening the door to an ultra clean house. Since Mark left, I had to let our housekeeper go; there just wasn't enough money to keep her on. I felt bad because Valentina had worked for us almost the entire time Mark and I lived at Forest, but my slowly growing finances still couldn't cover a weekly maid. I offered her a spot once a month for heavy cleaning, which she was nice enough to accept, and had no trouble filling in with other jobs.

Keeping the kitchen and Mark's study-cum-pantry tidy was an impossible task. I swept and vacuumed almost every day, yet there was always a film of dust on every surface. Trying to cook, bake, book parties and clean was a task for more than one, and even with Dex helping, I was so stretched that I decided to see what the market would bear as far as pricing.

"Hi Marcy, your place looks beautiful. How do you do it?"

"I don't. I probably shouldn't tell you, but your ex-housekeeper is working here now. Valentina comes in three times a week and what a gem. I can't believe you let her go. Her English is great and she knows what she's doing."

Now she learned English?

"Well, with living in the house alone and my doing so much cooking I just clean up as I go along and it works out better that way. I can't have anyone mopping up in the kitchen while I'm prepping, but I'm really glad you were able to hire her. She's wonderful," I said, envious that my house would never again be this clean.

"So, what did you want to discuss? You can do the party, right? Burt's all over it because they usually do their once-a-year golf dinner at the club, but it's a bore for the wives. At least here we can walk around and not have to listen to their trumped up scores all night. Will Dex be coming with you? Can he make martinis?"

"Yes and yes. Now, let's see, you'll be eight and you want an assortment of finger foods, but if you're serving hard liquor, then we really should do a dinner buffet. I don't mean a heavy sit-down deal, but maybe one hot entrée like sliced steak or a chicken and rice dish alongside all the hors d'oeuvres, and I'd feel better if we served some bread or rolls. I like to be careful about people drinking a lot if they're driving, even a short distance."

"Two of the couples can walk over, and Mack and Florence aren't big drinkers, so we're safe, but I like the idea of the steak. You know, since the lunch you did here, all Burt's been talking about is having another party at home. I've never seen him this pumped up about entertaining, maybe because we've always gone to the club, like everyone else, or to your house," Marcy said.

"Well, you already know how much I love to entertain, and if I can't do it at my house, this is the next best thing," I said, hating myself for being so phony. "We do have to discuss pricing. Can we sit in the kitchen?"

"Sure, sorry, come on in. I have some coffee if you'd like," Marcy said.

We sat at her granite and wrought-iron breakfast table, almost identical to the one in my house, and I brought out my notebook.

"I've done some preliminary figuring and before we go further, I need to discuss the cost. I know you want a big variety, but that bumps up the price because I have to buy so many different provisions and it's a more time-consuming job. The steak isn't that expensive; I'll do a marinated London Broil, not a filet, but the other stuff is what brings up the price."

I laid it on the line and left it up to my client to decide.

1. I didn't want to give up the gig.

2. I couldn't give it away either.

3. Who was I kidding? Even with all the work, my profit was enormous.

4. Was I getting greedy and taking advantage of my clients?

5. No one was complaining so it was all good.

"Dina, Burt told me to pull out all the stops for this party. He said he didn't care how much we spent as long as we did it at home. You see, each year, one of the guys treats the rest of the foursome, and this is Burt's year. I probably shouldn't tell you all that, but I know you'll be fair. Dina, I'm sure things have been tough without Mark. You may like entertaining, but now you're doing this for a living and I respect that. So does Burt," she said.

I decided not to go crazy with the estimate and we settled on a figure of no more than eight hundred. Burt would use his own liquor, but Marcy insisted on rentals.

"For eight people?" I said, incredulous. I'd make a small profit, but not enough to have her spend needlessly.

"I know, I have all that china but Burt wants everything to have a golf motif. He bought martini glasses with all these silly golf sayings, but he asked if that Acorn place had plates, and whatever else. I told him you'd know."

"I'm sure Acorn has what you want. Shouldn't come to a whole lot and it'll be very festive," I said, "I'll ask Sammy about it."

As if reading my mind, Marcy said, "He was the one who brought the rentals for the luncheon, right? Maybe you could have Sammy stop by with samples. Do you think he'd mind? "

"Good idea, that way you can select the pattern you like; I'm sure he has more than one design to choose from."

"We'll use the dining room this time – I won't need tables and chairs like we did for the lunch, so I guess that's it then," said my client, signaling an end to our meeting.

I made almost fifteen hundred dollars for the month of September plus Marcy's initial luncheon, and began to feel more relaxed about my financial position. If I continued on supplementing Mark's checks I wouldn't have to ask him or my parents for more money. I'd still have to be careful, and shopping for anything other than food or supplies was out of the question. My only extra expense might be asking Valentina to come twice a month.

I needed to prove to Mark that I was willing to do everything possible to make our marriage work again, and running my own business would surely impress him. Competing with a Taffie-type person was impossible, particularly in the physical and age categories, but Mark and I had history together. He had no real family other than mine and they'd be sure to forgive him once he got through this pre-mid-life crisis and returned.

Although Mark said he was retiring I doubted that would happen, even with Taffie supporting them. He'd grow weary of not manipulating the purse strings as he'd done throughout our marriage, and maybe Taffie would start demanding that he kick in for some of their expenses. My husband would be proud of me and I could continue on with my business if we stayed at Forest.

Or:

1. We could downsize and avoid expensive club fees.

2. I'd find a job in my field.

3. Our marriage would continue on and my husband and I would be closer than ever.

Because my status was now "caterer," I was canceled out of my one remaining bridge game and although I played in the weekly golf scrambles, I could tell my presence was only accepted because they knew I could knock a few strokes off the total score. After a couple of games when I wasn't invited to join the foursome for lunch, I opted out.

The residents didn't want to socialize with the help.

Chapter 17

October

Priscilla and Wesley

In my spare time, aside from meeting Wanda once a week, I had lunch or coffee with my parents, and decided to invite Wesley and his girlfriend, Priscilla, to visit for a long weekend. I'd make a family dinner so my folks and I could get to know Priscilla, and although Dex might enjoy the interaction, I didn't want to be grilled by my mother about him.

Just as I was leaving for the airport, the house phone rang. Craning my neck I was able to see that the caller was Mark. I grabbed the phone like it was my lifeline.

"Mark! Hello," I said, sounding chipper and upbeat although I knew I'd be late if I stayed on the phone for more than five minutes.

"Hi Dina, how's it going? You sound a little rushed, got a few minutes?"

"Sure, go ahead," I said, frustrated that I wouldn't be able to extend the conversation. I couldn't come across as needy, but wanted to play every card to get him to come home.

"Just wanted to let you know that the check's going to be late this month. I'll try to get it in the mail next week. Can you manage till then?"

"I'll have to," I said, knowing I could get by anyway,

but maybe sounding a little distressed would tug at my husband's heartstrings. I'd pulled that move more than once when we were together, and now because he couldn't see my on-demand puppy dog look, he ignored the intonation. "Why, is there a problem?"

"Yes, there's a problem. When Ted drew up the financial agreement I didn't realize it was going to be such a burden now that I'm not working. I'm pulling the money out of an account I had before we were married because neither of us can touch the joint account until everything is finalized, and I'm having a tough time of it."

There was no way I was going to mention the money that the catering business was bringing in because being tied to Mark financially could only work in my favor. Once he was back everything else would fall into place and he'd be done with his Key West fantasy.

"I thought Taffie was paying all the expenses," I said, hitting him where it would hurt.

"Look, I'm living in her house rent free, but I'm not a gigolo. When we go out for dinner, which is almost every night and almost always includes a few of her friends, I'm expected to pick up the tab for everyone. And whoever said the Keys were cheap must have been drunk on cheap beer because that's about the only damn thing that's cheap around here."

"What about going back to work?"

"Yeah, I thought about that, but Taffie likes me around especially when we go diving and snorkeling," said my land-lubber mate.

"How's that working for you?" I said, not bothering to hold back a laugh.

"Shitty!" Mark answered, clearly upset. "And I got a

damned ear infection to end all friggin' infections the first time we went deep sea diving so I'm off the hook for that, but I still have to be on the boat when she goes."

"Boat? Don't you get seasick?" I said, remembering the time we went out to Montauk to watch the whales. What I tried not to watch was Mark puking over the side of the boat every ten minutes till we got back to shore.

"I use a patch and those wrist bands so I'm usually okay, and Taffie keeps some crackers and ginger ale on board. I tell you, working was easier than this."

Now was the time for me to make my pitch. My husband sounded depressed, not only about money, but also his daily routine was not as idyllic as planned.

"Listen Mark, I have to run, but why don't you come up one day so we can really talk. I'll make lunch for us," I said, thinking food-love-food-love.

"That's not such a good idea, and what's your rush now?"

"I'm picking up Wes and his girlfriend at West Palm. They're staying for the weekend," I said, trying to hide the disappointment in my voice.

"Oh, really? I'd like to see them; maybe I could drive up on Saturday."

Now he could drive up? No way.

"Ya know, Mark, that's not such a good idea," I said, repeating his turn of a phrase. I didn't need him to think I was a total sap. "Please get the check to me as soon as possible. I'm running low. Gotta go, bye," I said and hung up the phone.

Tough love? Was I going for that? Absence makes the heart grow fonder came to mind along with every other cliché, but Mark was already living a Nora Ephrom novel:

1. Man in late thirties leaves wife for hot young blonde.

2. Wife hunts for a way to reconnect with husband.

3. I don't know about Nora, but in my book they reunite after Taffie gets eaten by a shark or spells her name with a Y.

My nephew and Priscilla arrived on schedule that afternoon and I was glad to save them the expense of a car rental. Wesley had recently been hired by a local television station and aside from leasing a small studio apartment in Winston-Salem, or Winston as they called it, he was socking away every penny. He and Priscilla were twenty-three and France thought they'd be getting engaged soon. Although they were both young, France said she knew they were soul mates.

Just like Taffie and Mark.

My nephew and his girlfriend carried their luggage on board so we were able to zip right out of the airport on to I-95 and were home by five.

As my guests, they had every service and activity open to them at the club, and I offered them my car should they feel like doing a little sightseeing. My parents were at the house by the time we arrived, and Mom had set the table and warmed up the dishes I prepared that morning.

"Well, kids, Grandpa and I are going to take off," my mother said after helping me with dessert.

"Your grandmother is taking us on a nature walk at eight in the morning so I want to make sure we're rested. I hope we'll see you kids over the weekend," said my father.

"Sure, Grandpa," Wesley said, "so awesome to see you both. Priscilla and I'll take a ride up to see where you live and all."

"It's not as fancy as this place, but we like it," Harry was fond of saying even though their club's lobby looked like a replica of the Metropolitan Opera House.

Wesley walked them out to the car and Priscilla helped me clear up.

"That's a beautiful name you have," I said, not exactly sure of how to open up a conversation with the girl who was probably going to be my niece. She was polite enough during the ride back from the airport and throughout dinner, but like my dad, hadn't said much.

"Everyone thinks it's from Priscilla Presley, but it's not."

"I thought perhaps it was from the pilgrim days," I said, glad I hadn't revealed my love for everything Elvis.

"That's exactly right. Our ancestors go way back in this country and my mom wanted to honor them. My brother's name is John Alden Paine. Kinda weird, don't you think, I mean with John and Priscilla being married and all, but he doesn't use his middle name very often."

"Well, your mom did good; the name suits you," I said.

"Aunt Dina," said Wesley as he came back in the house, "I don't mean to be nosy, but what's with you and Uncle Mark? You guys were a great couple."

"We're trying to work it out, Wes," I said, not adding that Mark would have driven up to see his nephew if I encouraged it.

110

"Where's he living? Mom said some place down in the Keys?"

"Key West, he's staying with a friend," I said, not wanting to reveal anything else.

"Uh, Aunt Dina, we know about Taffie. Sounds like a cat," Wesley said, cranking out a laugh from me. "But Key West. I've always wanted to go there. Does he do all the water stuff?"

"He had a little trouble with that, but his friend is a diver so he's on the boat a lot," I said before pulling a Dex and abruptly changing the subject.

"So, Priscilla, where do you work?"

"She's the new buyer for the best linen store downtown, not one of those big box places," said Wesley, jumping in to speak for Priscilla who was still a bit shy.

"Oh Wes, I just started there so let's not jump the gun. They've had three buyers in the last six months," Priscilla said, "but I hope they keep me, I just love it there. I've met the nicest people and some have even asked me to come to their houses so I can suggest color schemes for them. Mrs. Blum said no one's ever done that before. She's thrilled because I dressed the store windows in a slightly different style than they're used to and the customers compliment her on it all day long. She's so nice, gives me all the credit and I guess that's why I'm developing my own clients. Oh, I'm sorry for monopolizing the conversation, didn't mean to," said the girl who hadn't spoken more than a paragraph in the last three hours.

"Hey, don't be so modest. That's quite a talent, and speaking of linens, let me show you where you'll be staying," I said, hoping Priscilla would approve of the sheets I bought on sale at Target. "Oh, leave that door closed, please," I said catching them just before they walked into Mark's office. "Mark has his stuff all over the place – it's a mess."

I hadn't yet told France about my catering business and didn't need her fretting about me from a thousand miles away, and I certainly didn't want Redmond supplementing my income.

"Okay, Aunt Dina, thanks for dinner, it was great. I wish Mom could cook like that. Priscilla and I are both pretty good in the kitchen, and once we're married and have our own place, she's going to plant a vegetable garden for us. Oops, the cat's out of the bag, I guess."

"You two make a lovely couple; I had a feeling an engagement would be coming up," I said.

"Yeah, we're going to save it for Thanksgiving when Grandma and Grandpa are up; wish you could be there too," Wesley said.

"Not this year; too much going on," I said, not explaining any further, "but I'm so happy for both of you."

"Thank you, Dina," said Priscilla. "We've known each other forever even though I moved to Atlanta for a few years."

"Worst years of my life," said Wesley. "So, come on, honey, let's unpack and maybe take a walk outside. Hey, who are those guys cruising around in golf carts – the ones wearing all black?"

"We call them ninjas, they're part of the security system here. They ride around, make sure garage doors are closed, check the perimeters, stuff like that."

"I thought I saw them carrying guns. Do they really need that?"

"It's just a precaution; things are pretty secure. There've only been a couple of robberies since I've lived here, and they called those inside jobs, but like I said, the residents feel safer with the added protection."

"Well, there's certainly a ton of money in this club; every other car is a Jag or a BMW."

"Yeah, Forest attracts a lot of wealthy people, and then there are couples like Mark and me who got a fantastic deal on a house and manage to pay the dues."

Priscilla had gone into the guest room to do the unpacking leaving my nephew and me to talk further.

"Are you happy here, Dina?" he said, leaving out the aunt as he was prone to do at times. "I mean especially now that Mark's gone?"

"I'm okay by myself. It's mainly a couples society, but I do my share of socializing," I said, not wanting to add that most of it was done in other people's dining rooms and that it wasn't exactly socializing. "And Mark's probably going to come to his senses even before our trial separation is up; then we can decide if we want to stay here or not."

"Good enough," said my nephew, "but you know, if things don't work out, why don't you consider a move to Winston, you know, be near Mom and Dad. Pris and I plan to stay there also. Now that Grandma and Grandpa have a place up in Asheville, we'd all be together for at least part of the year."

"Oh, honey, I don't see that happening. My life is here. What would I do in Winston besides hanging out with you guys?"

"There's plenty happening and I'll be honest, from what Dad told me, he thinks that Mark is probably going through with the divorce. Wouldn't you want a new life then? New surroundings, get out of this fish bowl kind of place with Police Academy cops riding around in golf carts?"

Although Wesley used the same fish bowl reference I did when I talked about downsizing to Mark, I was annoyed that Redmond and now Wesley and probably the entire state of North Carolina knew more about my circumstances than I did.

"Oh, oh," my nephew said, lightening the moment. "There's that frowny look that Mom gives me. I won't butt in anymore. Let me go see if Pris is ready – it's a beautiful night – just hope we don't get stopped by the ninjas."

Chapter 18

October

Sammy

The kids went out for an hour giving me just enough time to go over the menu for the Chans. Belle and Bailey were pleased with my initial suggestions and felt sure their Uncle Tai would enjoy the meal in his honor even though it was technically a birthday celebration for the girls. Hacked Chicken was a big favorite of mine and it was a simple dish to prepare. The mahogany-glazed birds would present well on my teak carving board, and Dex was the appointed hacker. At the last minute I'd sprinkle the pieces with chopped scallions. Belle had a rice cooker and insisted upon making the rice. I'd have to be sure to tell Uncle Tai that his niece had a hand in this special dinner.

The Chans didn't want any appetizers, but the food on the table had to be plentiful. Along with the chicken and rice, I was going to steam a whole sea bass in ginger, garlic and vegetable broth, fry up a flat noodle dish, and have two or three green vegetables as sides. Belle also liked my idea of stuffed mushrooms as a garnish, and she talked me into candied carrots, which were Bailey's favorite. Although the meal would be partially Chinese, the twins requested an ice cream sundae cart with all the fixings; seemed like Uncle Tai had taken a shine to the American dessert tradition.

I sent off a final fax to Belle asking her to confirm the menu, and to send me a deposit check at least two weeks before the party. I hadn't asked for any payments in advance from the few parties I'd previously done, but Wanda advised that covering the cost of food was usually a third, and tacked on to that could be rentals and servers so I asked for fifty percent. If for some reason the client refused to pay the balance I wouldn't be out the full amount. Belle sent a return fax saying she'd have her husband drop off a check to me in the morning.

Wanda was truly a wonderful friend, malaprops notwithstanding; conversely, they endeared me to her. Did her clients notice her special way of mixing up words and sayings? Since she managed to close on almost every pitch she made since joining Platinum Pantry maybe they thought it was cute.

"What's your secret?" I asked the last time we met for lunch.

"Easy, I hire one server for every ten guests. Even if the food is halfway decent the event will be successful. No one will have to wait, hors d'oeuvres and drinks will be at their fingertips during the entire cocktail hour and if there's more than about thirty, I hire two bartenders. There's never anything out of kilter at my parties because I plan ahead.

Dina, these are very wealthy people I deal with. I don't take advantage of them, but I have to give them what they expect, and taco chips and salsa just doesn't cut it. Why do you think Platinum is so successful? It's because nothing fails. And the food is never halfway decent – it's one hundred percent delicious and perfectly prepared for every party."

"Hey, you don't have to sell me. I've been to one or two of your parties. That New York training paid off; Platinum's lucky to have you," I said, awestruck by my friend's expertise.

"New York was nothing compared to the clientele in Boca. Up there it was a lot of business events; down here it's like the Spanish Imposition going out on calls. The things people ask you. And the best is that most wouldn't know a Hollandaise sauce from the Holland Tunnel, but I have to listen and in the end I book most of the calls I go out on."

"Who turned you down?" I said.

"Well, actually it only happened once. A couple over at Boca West – something just didn't sit right with me about them. Found out later the house was in foreclosure and they never would have paid the balance. I turned them down and gave some excuse and didn't even refer them to anyone. You know the old saying," Wanda started to say as I shuddered.

"Lie down with dogs and get up with flies."

That wasn't too far wrong so I let it slide.

Although an unwritten law evolved not to reveal information about Forest's newest home caterer, everyone at the club, including Chuck Wilkins, knew it was me, and no one raised a red flag.

There was a Halloween bash for the Signorellis, who had four children living at home, and a Thanksgiving Day dinner for Marla and Andrew Burke. Although the Halloween party was for thirty-five kids and adults, it was informal or I wouldn't have been able to accept the job. The party was in the afternoon so it was all about apples, juice, cupcakes decorated with ghouls and witches, and individual bags of candy for everyone. There was pumpkin ice cream, and Dex made a hard cider punch that he served over ice cubes embedded with fake spiders.

Our routine was simple. Dex would come over two hours before the start of a party, which was usually right around his quitting time, help me finish up whatever was necessary, then load up the van with provisions and equipment.

Wanda made the initial introduction between me and Mr. Max Friebling, the owner of Acorn Rentals. Platinum Pantry was their biggest client and Max agreed to accommodate any small orders I might place. He understood that my events would be nowhere near what Wanda booked, but on the occasion when I needed some round tables or extra chairs, he'd give me the same price as for his regular clients.

The Signorellis' Halloween party would be the third time I needed rentals, Marcy's ladies luncheon and golf dinner being the other two. The routine was to have everything delivered to the client the day before and picked up the day after the party. Max gave my account to his son, Sammy, who, up till that point, worked in the stock room.

If there were a Jewish Mafia, Sammy Freibling would surely be the capo di tutto cappi. But underneath his bravado and gangster-like get-ups, Sammy was a decent guy in his thirties who wanted to make something of himself and prove to his dad that he was capable of more than loading boxes.

Sammy put on a suit and tie, albeit a black and white pinstripe deal, when he met me at the Signorelli home where Acorn would deliver extra tables and chairs. Although he had a tough-guy appearance, Mary Lou Signorelli listened attentively and a bit flirtatiously as he made his recommendations in accordance with my party plan. Along with the extra seating, he showed her samples of specialty dessert plates, which she agreed would put the finishing touch on the party.

"I'll write up the order back at Mrs. M's and we'll be sure to get everything just right for you," Sammy said, with what looked to be like a giant wink. "Everything will be perfect, just like you, Mrs. Signorelli."

"Oh, call me Mary Lou," said the now very playful lady of the house. "And, thank you so much for all your suggestions."

"Well, we really should be going," I said, breaking up the one-on-one going full force.

"Oh, Dina," she said, just seeming to notice me, "thanks for stopping by with Sammy, but you really didn't have to. Sammy, if you need to come back, just give me a call," said Mary Lou.

"You got it. Be seeing you soon," Sammy said.

I gripped his arm and led him out of the house before they decided to kiss goodbye.

"Sammy, do you think it's a good idea to get so familiar with the clients?"

"Hey, it doesn't mean anything. These babes are usually starved for a little affection, I'm not gonna follow through on anything. It just makes 'em feel good, know what I mean?" said Sammy the Lothario.

"I guess so," I said, easing up because he really was very engaging.

We wrote out the order for the Signorellis in my kitchen over some peach iced tea and plain old sugar cookies.

"So, Mrs. M., when you gonna start bumping up these gigs? I wanna show Pop I can sell as good as him. Wanda just placed an order with us for six thousand bucks. She's doing a frickin' clambake or something at one of those oceanfront homes. Ya know, I don't understand people some time. What's wrong with good old paper plates and a case of cold beer?"

"Well, Sammy, nothing's wrong with that, but I guess these folks want something fancier. Wanda told me they ordered Cristal Champagne to go with the lobsters and she's putting up tents and a dance floor."

"Yeah, we got all that stuff except I had to order a few more grills. That's one party I'd like to crash. Hey, Mrs. M. how about it? You and me going together? There's going to be so many people hanging out they won't notice two extra."

"Uh, I don't think that's such a good idea, but maybe Wanda can put you on as one of the servers; there's bound to be an extra lobster or two. And please, just call me Dina."

"Yeah, I know, but I think Mrs. M sounds classier. Nah, Wanda won't put me on to serve, but she said I should stop by for the set up, learn more about the business. Wanda's cool. She said I have a lot of potential. She's the one who told Pop to let me take care of you."

"Right, she mentioned that to me, but I'm afraid I won't be much of a customer for you because mostly the stuff I do can be handled by what the client already has," I said.

"Yeah, you may think that, but did you see how Mary Lou went for that orange and black china, and the dessert napkins? Always, and even if you're serving tea and crumpets to six year olds, always tell the client they need dessert napkins. Not much more in money, but it all adds up."

"Sammy, you have a pretty good business head and

you're right. My first party was a ladies luncheon, and I noticed by the time dessert was served that the linens looked a bit, well, not exactly dirty, but tired. Dessert napkins, hmm, good point," I said, making a mental note.

"Even though I don't book the parties, I see every order that comes in; that's how come I know this stuff. You oughta ask Wanda about the extra crap she orders, you would not believe it, but no one's ever complained."

"She's very successful and I don't think she's milking anyone, she just makes sure that everything runs smoothly. Wanda's given me some great advice and I don't know what I'd do without her," I said, choking up.

"Yeah, she's good people, not like your ex. I heard about him and that hot little number he's screwing on the side. Some guys just don't know what they have at home. Why go out for hamburger when you got steak at home? I think Paul Newman said that," Sammy the philosopher said.

I laughed in spite of myself.

"Ya know, Sammy, I think he did. Anyway, let's add up the order. I've got to get over to the Burkes' to finalize their Thanksgiving menu."

"Way to go, Mrs. M."

I'd have to remember to put in a good word with Mr. Freibling about his son because Sammy had done a remarkable job listing everything that the Signorellis would need: tables, chairs, orange and black plates and barware, and a couple of large punch bowls with cups.

As if reading my mind, Sammy said, "You're my only account, Mrs. M., so if everything's okay, maybe you could mention it to my pop. I'd like to get out of the frickin' stock room and build up my clientele. Work the country club set."

I was about to tell him he'd have to give up the frickin' this and frickin' that along with the George Raft suits, but I realized he was probably a walk on the wild side for the women here. Mary Lou Signorelli had already sent me a text saying how cute Sammy was.

"Sure, Sam, be happy to do that. Hey, do you have holiday china with you, I mean for Thanksgiving?"

"Ya mean plates with the turkeys and shooters?"

"Pilgrims, yes, those are the ones."

"Yep, I got a few samples in the truck. Just let me know how many you need and I'll put some aside. We do a big business for turkey day, so give me a heads up. Oh, and Mrs. M., think about that clambake – I mean going with me – I wouldn't mind having a good-looking babe like you on my arm. I like your style, not all phony tits and ass."

"Uh, Sammy, I don't know what you've heard, but my husband and I are only separated right now so I'm not dating."

"Well, don't wait too long. You're a classy babe, like I said, and you oughta sign up on one of those dating sites. I can understand your not wanting to go out with me, business and all, but why not give some other dude a shot? Your husband must be nuts walking out on you. You'd rock the singles scene."

"Thanks for the vote of confidence, but I think I'll put my energies into the catering right now. I'm only doing small parties and only at Forest, just enough to make some extra money. I love what I do so it's better than trying to find a job somewhere else," I said, opening up to Sammy who was now straddling a barstool. "Well, I better get over to the Burkes'. Sam, if you're not busy, how 'bout meeting me there so you can show her the china?"

"That's using the old noodle. Sure, I got time. I know they'll like the turkey china, but I bet I can talk her into our new tablecloths – orange and gold with green leaves – she won't have anything like it. I got that in the truck also. I got a lotta tricks up this sleeve."

"I have a feeling she'll agree to whatever you suggest; just don't push too hard."

"Nah, that ain't my way. I'm smooth. So, Mrs. M. let's go get 'em!"

Marla Burke, besotted with Sammy, decided to order everything needed for Thanksgiving Day dinner and not use any of her own china or linens. We walked out with an order totaling nearly five hundred dollars.

Chapter 19

October

More Money Blues

Even with the business that was coming in I was just covering household expenses because Mark had been slow in getting the promised checks to me. My last phone call hadn't gone well when I told him he was behind in his payments.

"I don't know why you need so much money," he said.

"You're the one who made up the schedule, I'm just asking you to stick to it. I don't want to get behind. This house still costs a lot to run even with you paying the dues. I've got to get the refrigerator repaired, again, and there's probably going to be another assessment because the roads are beginning to show wear and tear so you better plan on kicking in for that."

"Hey, Dina, you're the one who came up with the idea of staying in the house for a year hoping I'd come back. I never should have agreed because it's not going to happen the way you want. And for damn sure, I'm not paying any more assessments. You want to stay at Forest, you find a way to pay them. Otherwise, put the house on the market and we'll split whatever you can get for it. It's gotta be worth a lot more than we paid, even with the recession.

I'll say one thing – you were right about the home office because that's going to appeal plenty to a buyer these days; the built-ins alone are worth thirty grand."

I was about to lower the boom of tearing apart the home office if my business increased, but decided not to add fuel to the fire. I needed money.

"Let's wait for the economy to pick up a little, and then I promise I'll think about selling the house even before the year is up. It's just been a few months and I'm only asking for what we agreed on."

"Okay, I'll get it to you. Actually, Taffie and I will be in town for a wedding in a couple of weeks so I can drop off the check then."

"Mail it!" I blurted out. There was no way I could let Mark see the condition of our house as it stood now, particularly his office, which was home to several stainless steel carts covered with recipes, trays, and sacks of flour and sugar.

"Geez, Dina, chill. Okay. I'll put it in the mail. What's the big deal?"

"Uh oh, our connection is getting bad…breaking up. Thanks for sending the check," I said, while making a rattling noise in the background.

"What's that sound? Taffie just got me a new iPhone; it must be on your end."

"What?" I said, holding the phone away from me before disconnecting in the middle of my next sentence. People don't usually hang up when they're the ones doing the talking, so I was pretty sure he bought it.

The Halloween party at the Signorellis' went off like clockwork. Sammy delivered the rentals as planned and set them up himself. I got his call when he was just about finished.

"Hey, Mrs. M., we're all done here. Looks great, and Mary Lou sure is happy. I threw in a bunch of plastic jack-o-lanterns, no charge, and we're gonna fill 'em up with candy for the kids. Wait, hold a minute," he said.

I heard Mary Lou's voice in the background asking if he wouldn't like a nice cup of coffee and some cake because she just defrosted a Key Lime Loaf (mine) by mistake so he'd be helping her out by having a piece.

Oh brother, was Sammy going to fall for that?

"Mrs. M., I gotta go, we're gonna have coffee and cake, and don't worry, nothing else. She's just a nice lady who likes more attention than her hubby is giving her. Foolish man. Let's hope he's not screwing around like your jerk is," Sammy added before saying goodbye.

I hoped he wasn't either because it sure as hell didn't feel good.

Chapter 20

November

Parties

Before Thanksgiving dinner at the Burkes' I did three more parties in November. Belle and Bailey were so nervous about the December 3rd family dinner coming up that they insisted upon a trial run.

This time it was Bailey who called to make arrangements.

"Dina, hi, it's Bailey. I wanted to ask you a favor. You know the birthday party you're doing for us and the relatives in a few weeks? Well, Belle thinks it'd be wise to have a tasting dinner beforehand in case there are any changes or if she doesn't like something," said Bailey, the twin with the milder disposition.

"I can do it, but unfortunately, I have to charge you close to the full price for the food because I still need to poach an entire fish and it's basically the same amount of work. Are you sure you need this? You've both been here for dinner more than once; was there a problem with any of the food?"

"Are you kidding? It was the only time we had a decent home-cooked meal, but really, this tasting thing is Belle's idea. She's never gotten along well with our mother and if anything goes wrong, she'll go postal. So, you're thinking about a hundred a person for the tasting?" Bailey said, coming in way above my target price.

"No, that's too much. Let's call it two fifty including dessert. Just give me the date and I'll make dinner for the four of you, okay? At your house, or Belle's?"

"It has to be at Belle's so she can see how everything flows."

"Bailey, you know Dex works with me, and if it were a different menu I wouldn't need him for this, but he has to hack the chicken at the last minute while I'm getting everything else to the table," I explained.

"Right. Belle said she wants him to come, and because this is kind of last minute she asked if a hundred would be appropriate for him," Bailey said.

I realized she meant one hundred dollars.

"That's quite sufficient and I'm sure he'll appreciate it. I better send him a text so he can hold the evening; what date did you want?"

"Dina, I know this is crazy, but can you do it this Friday night?"

"That only gives me one day to shop, prep…"

"I know and I'm sorry. Even Belle was too embarrassed to call you so she said if you can do it that she'd put twenty percent on above the cost of the real party," the lovely twin said.

I hesitated a moment letting Bailey think I was considering it when actually I was doing a happy dance around the kitchen. Twenty percent was an enormous overage. Granted, it would be extra work for me to get this tasting together so quickly, but I didn't have anything else going on so agreed to the terms.

"Oh, and one more thing, Belle said to remind you and

Dex to wear black. I guess you know about that already," Bailey said.

"No problem," I said, responding for both of us even though I had no clue about Dex's regular wardrobe. Either he was in his work uniform, or the catering khaki/white outfits we'd stuck to. I'd send him a detailed email including the dress code along with a mention of the enormous tip coming his way. That should be enough to cover a pair of black pants and shirt.

The tasting was even better than I expected as I hadn't made Hacked Chicken in a couple of years and forgot how delectable it was. I roasted one sizable chicken and there wasn't a scrap left over. The bass weighed close to three pounds and the four of them would have enough for lunch the next day. The twins and their husbands couldn't have been happier, and tipped Dex and me a hundred dollars each even though I told them it wasn't necessary.

Belle, who'd always been a bit cool and officious, hugged me after Dex and I cleaned up and were ready to leave.

"Dina, I can't tell you how much I admire you for what you're doing. Bailey and I started our business after we were married off, not because we had to, but because we wanted to have our independence. Our parents are really old fashioned and were horrified that their daughters insisted upon working, but Sonny and Jim were thrilled that their wives were executives.

I don't know how much longer we'll continue in the business because Bailey and I both want to have children, and become full-time moms. We're almost thirty and she and I want to become pregnant at the same time. Our husbands are so wonderful they'll agree to anything that makes us happy.

We're even hoping to have twins; runs in our family."

"Your husbands seem very proud of you and Bailey. You've been so generous to me tonight, and Dex. Thank you and I guarantee your party will be a success," I said, trying to end the conversation because not only did I have to load up the van with Dex, but I also felt tears beginning to surface thinking about the baby I had hoped for just a few short months ago. I was six years older than the Chan twins with no hope of starting a family unless my husband returned and that chance was lessening each day.

"Dina, you'll do alright with or without Mark. If he comes back it has to be for the right reasons, and not just because he wants to live at Forest and play golf and do business here. He has to want to come back for you, and frankly, you are such a fine person he'd be crazy to stay away.

You know, when our parents first introduced us to the brothers we were shocked that they expected us to marry their choices and not pick our own husbands. We really shouldn't have been surprised because our family is steeped in tradition and the old ways. You saw a little of that tonight because even though we're twins, Bailey looks to me as her older sister because I came out a minute before she did. Bailey and I knew we didn't have to marry Sonny and Jim, but it would have devastated our parents had we not. In the end, after almost seven years together, Bailey and I both know how lucky we are and how wise our parents were. The old ways aren't so bad after all."

Belle was on a roll now, and because this was the closest we'd ever come to forming a friendship I let her continue.

"Sometimes, Dina, happiness is right within your grasp, you don't have to hunt it down in Key West. Now, I'm sure that's enough Chinese philosophy, Boca-style, for one night, and you must be tired. The dinner was wonderful. I know it will please my parents and Uncle Tai when they're here in December. Here's the check for the balance. I'm going to let you pack up now, Bailey's about to leave," she said, and walked her beautiful self out to the patio to say goodnight to her sister and Sonny.

For a moment I thought she would ask if I'd like to have lunch with her one day, or even coffee, but realized:

1. I was getting ahead of myself.

2. Better I should stick to business.

3. Boy, did I sound like my mother and her mentor, Frosty.

"You ready to go?" said Dex, meeting me in the hallway. "I've got a big day tomorrow."

"Thanks so much for helping, or I should say hacking, tonight. Even with only four, it's a lot easier with you around. Unfortunately, there aren't any leftovers for us. You hungry?"

"Starved," he said, "how 'bout running up to Sefa in Pineapple Grove, they'll be open. Great Turkish food."

"I thought you wanted to get home," I said.

"Gotta eat, right?"

Because there were no perishables to stick back in my fridge, I agreed and hoped we wouldn't bump into any Forest people.

"Don't worry, it's not a date, and trust me," he said, glancing at his watch, "the Boca crowd doesn't eat at nine o'clock. I'll even treat, pretty nice tip tonight."

Running through my mind:

1. How did he know I was a little worried?

2. What if some people did eat at nine?

3. He was going to treat me.

4. Was it a date?

Tucking a strand of hair behind my ear in what I thought was an appealing move, I said, "Bailey told me they'd take care of you because it was so last minute, but they gave me the same and insisted I take it. Then Bailey said Belle was going to add on twenty percent to the cost of the family party just as a thank you for helping them out with so little notice for tonight. How nice is that? Maybe I never took the time to get to know some of the people here. If only Gaby weren't the ringleader."

"Well, she's not giving up her post. You'd think as tough as Belle seems to be, at least on the outside, that she'd stand up to her, but none of them ever do. Okay, ready? Let's go and since you got tipped also, we'll go Dutch if that makes you feel better," said my almost date, "just let me get that scallion out of your hair."

Chapter 21

November

A New Client

By the time Dex dropped me off at home there was a voice mail from Portia Goodlove saying that the Chans highly recommended me and could we have coffee and discuss a few things coming up. I didn't want to call after eleven, so emailed her instead. The phone rang two seconds later. It was Portia.

Portia Goodlove hailed from St. Thomas and had a beautiful lilting accent that made everything she said sound aristocratic. She was tall, slim and good-looking, with skin the color of my Mocha Whip Parfait. Portia never married and at close to forty, she'd established herself as a player in the clothing boutique game, owning over thirty shops throughout the country in the most prestigious cities. Boca Raton, Naples and Palm Beach in Florida, Hilton Head in South Carolina, several up and down the coast of California plus those in other resort areas like East Hampton and Newport.

"Shells" carried items such as luxurious beachwear and bags, and also a line of expensive body lotions and perfumes that were nothing like you could find anywhere else. Portia began her career by modeling swimwear and casual clothing in several large hotels in the Bahamas when she started sketching her own designs. She sent them off to one of the manufacturers she modeled for and they immediately set up production for her own line. It was an instant success and with that income, plus a loan from a local bank, she came to the States and opened her first boutique in Boca; and then, when Shells expanded, Portia was able to buy a home at Forest.

"Dina, Belle called the minute you left. Said I had to book you for something before everyone else does," Portia said. Her singsong voice went on to describe the two meetings she held in her home twice a month, and was there a way I could serve a breakfast and dinner for about ten to twelve.

"You see, Dina dear, we do volunteer work for Gilda's Club – you know, the support group for cancer patients and their families – and we meet on the first Tuesday of every month at seven in the morning and that goes till about eight thirty. Then, on the second Monday we have a dinner meeting."

"And it's always at your house?" I said, wondering why the others didn't offer.

"We tried a round robin, but frankly, most of the women work or have young children, and it was too much of an inconvenience even to throw together a breakfast by seven, or make dinner by six. It's easier for me to do it, and I don't mind, plus the girls like coming to Forest."

"So, when will this be starting?" I asked, looking at my datebook, which I now kept next to the phone.

"Starting? It's been going on for over a year."

"And you've been serving them…?"

"I order breakfast from the deli, and dinner is usually

takeout of some sort, but these women work so hard and for such a worthwhile cause, I want to treat them to something special," Portia said, whose stock just went up in my book. "You know, I don't hang out at the club a lot because my business needs me and I do almost everything online, but I used to see you there with the golfers or at lunch. Belle told me about your circumstances; I don't know Mark, but sorry this happened to you if you didn't want it to."

Wanting to get the business end over with, plus being dog tired, I dived right in.

"It'll all work out for the best. So, you'd like me to bid on breakfast and dinner, once a month for about a dozen women. I can probably bring in the morning meal for about twenty a person, that's with regular and decaf, and a variety of teas, but dinner will cost more. I'm assuming you want to work while you eat, so maybe a buffet would be best rather than having me serve you," I said, not revealing that I'd grown so dependent on Dex that I was nervous about handling even a simple breakfast without him. There'd be no way he'd be able to do the early prep with me.

"Yes, exactly, that's what I do now. I lay it all out on the bar and the girls help themselves. We like it that way. So, you'll be able to do it?"

"I'd love to. It's a worthy cause and I'll give you a ten percent discount. If you don't mind, I just got in and really need to get some rest. How about if I drop off several menus, and you make your choice for each month once we get going. Oh, two things: just let me know if there are any vegetarians in the group, or if anyone has any allergies. I keep it healthy, but everyone likes a slab of roast beef now and then."

"No problem with any of that. These women eat anything, and Dina, they eat a lot, so don't skimp. I don't care about the cost, and no discounting. You can make a contribution to Gilda's Club instead."

"Done. And I promise, no one will go hungry and you'll have leftovers. Oh, I almost forgot, do you have enough china and linens for your group?"

"I hate to admit this, but I use paper and plastic. I know that's awful but I didn't want to have to do dishes after everyone leaves. I have my regular business to attend to and my housekeeper refuses to help. Can you imagine that? You don't know of anyone without an attitude, do you?"

"Give Marcy a call; she hired my former housekeeper, but Valentina may have the early morning and dinner hour free," I said. "She speaks perfect English."

I was a little fixated on Valentina's new language skills.

"Thanks, I'll speak to Marcy about that. Any chance you could start a week from this coming Tuesday?"

"Yes, I'm free," I said, taking a quick look at my calendar for that week, "I can hold those dates and times for you, but I do prefer regular plates and silverware. I take a lot of pride in my cooking, and well, it's just not the same on paper. You can always buy some big buffet plates and stainless for twelve at Pottery Barn or Crate and Barrel, and then you'll always have it."

When I didn't hear a response forthcoming I dropped the Sammy bomb.

"Or, if you like, we can rent everything and you can choose from different patterns. I can set up a meeting with Sammy from Acorn rentals. He keeps loads of samples in his truck," I said.

"Now, that idea I like. I heard that you do the most

magnificent table settings so sure, let's make a date with Acorn. And Dina, I've met Sammy; tell him to save the charm, I'm gay."

I thanked her for the business and we hung up. I threw my cat burglar's black get-up into the laundry room, washed my face and fell into bed.

My last thought before sinking into a deep sleep was the variety of clients I had amassed:

1. Gay

2. Straight

3. Cuban

4. Asian

5. Italian

6. Caribbean

All I needed was an Afro-American or an Indian (eastern or Native American) and I'd have a Benetton commercial.

Chapter 22

November

Thanksgiving

I was glad to have the job at the Burkes' for Thanksgiving because it gave me somewhere to be. Usually, my folks came over for dinner, but this year they made reservations way in advance to visit France and Redmond. My nephew, Wesley, would be there with Priscilla and that's all Stella had to hear before calling the airlines and booking flights. My mother was now in competition with others in her community who were up to their necks in grand and great-grandchildren, and she was not about to be left out of that club.

France extracted a promise that neither one of our parents would make any mention of marriage or babies. I could just hear my mother saying, "Who me? Who would do such a thing?" She would, and we all knew it, but there was no stopping her from going to North Carolina for Thanksgiving.

"Are you sure you won't come with us?" she asked after having lunch with me one day. The weather was cool and she was wearing her usual winter attire – a velour tracksuit and sneakers. "We're going to be seeing Wesley's girlfriend again. Priscilla Paine, that's some name. I bet her mishpokhe

138

came over on the Mayflower; oy, they'll plotz when they find out what a patchwork quilt our family is. Jews, Catholics, Uncle Will's a Baptist – everything they'll look down their Protestant noses at."

"Mother, that's the most racist thing I've ever heard you say! It's certainly not how you and Daddy brought us up. We had Hanukkah and Christmas, and France and I became what we wanted."

"Oh, I didn't mean anything. What else do you know about her?"

"Did Wes tell you they went to grade school together? Then her family moved to Atlanta, and they didn't see each other until they reconnected at Duke University," I said.

"You'd think Wes would have told us he was so serious with her when they came down here to visit. Did you know anything?" my mother said.

"I figured they'd be getting engaged sooner or later. You know, Mom, maybe they'll do it at the Thanksgiving table."

Stella continued on. "They're awfully young to be getting engaged, if they're thinking that way."

"Mom, France got married right out of college and it's worked for them. Wes is a smart guy and Priscilla's a lovely girl; I hope they do get engaged," I said, keeping all conversation away from my situation. I didn't need my mother to remind me that it wasn't working so well for Mark and me.

"Who knows with these kids today? I just hope they don't get married on top of some meshuggah mountain and we all have to schlep up there like a herd of goats.

And what's with the mess all over the counters? I know you're doing a lot of cooking, but it looks like you're packing or something. Are you moving? I thought you and Mark were going to wait out the year before making any decisions. What do you hear from him anyway? He still with blondie?"

"Mom, I don't want to talk about Mark right now. I'm just doing a little spring cleaning and rearranging in case I have to sell the house. You know, if Mark doesn't decide to come home."

"Home? You'd take that putz back? He doesn't deserve you after what he's done."

"Mom, don't start. Mark and I have had our differences and we're going through a rough time, but he's been a good husband and a good son-in-law. I don't want you to say anything about him that you might regret later on."

"A good son-in-law is Redmond who wouldn't run off with a shiksa to Key West and leave you here to take care of things!"

"Mom, I'm half a shiksa and so is France. You're all shiksa."

"Watch your tone with me, and I still don't understand why you can't come to your sister's for Thanksgiving. I told you we'd pay for the ticket."

"I know, Mom, Daddy told me. I appreciate it, but I want to stay here."

"What are you going to do all alone in Boca on Thanksgiving? Go to Wanda's and that schmendrick of a husband of hers?"

"No, they go to his family down in Miami, and Linz's not that bad, just annoying at times, but he means well. I'm catering dinner for my neighbors."

"Well, if you put it that way, it's not such a bad idea if you're going to stay in this fancy-shmancy country club," my mother said.

"Mom, you and Frosty are the ones who found this

house for us. Remember?"

"Of course! That Frosty is one balabusta. Still selling real estate like she was giving away fifty-cent dreidels. I tell you, Dina, once you find something you're good at, stick with it and you'll make a fortune. You making anything cooking for people here?" she said. "Because Daddy and I can help you out if you need money."

"I'm actually doing pretty well, but thanks for the offer."

"You used to have such a passion for cooking, and writing about it too. Your columns were fantastic; I saved every one. Believe you me, I sat shiva when *Gourmet* went kaput."

"Well, I need to work, but my lawyer told me to hold off on getting a job until I reach a formal settlement with Mark, so I'm doing the catering in the meanwhile."

"A lawyer? This is the first I hear of a lawyer."

Stella was about to go off on her next outburst, but I brought out her favorite dessert and pushed the Keurig to brew coffee for us.

"Pineapple Upside-Down Cake? You made that just for me, didn't you," she said.

"Yep, Mom, I did and you can take home whatever's left. I know Dad loves it too. Let me get some vanilla ice cream," I said, and all talk of lawyers, jobs and Thanksgiving was preempted.

Chapter 23

November

Party On

Any fears I had about my business not being able to help support my lifestyle were allayed by the amount of emails and phone calls that came my way each week.

"It's about time we started eating at home" became the new mantra. Although what they considered eating at home was a far cry from the meals I used to prepare for Mark and me during most of our marriage, they'd gained new status by having a semi-professional caterer in their kitchens.

True to my promise to Wanda, I kept my fees under three thousand dollars, up a thousand from her original two thousand mark. Business had expanded for Platinum Pantry where they now wouldn't book anything under five thousand, still leaving a two thousand dollar bridge between our services.

I also did more business with Acorn, and Max gave Sammy two more accounts. Sammy called with the good news and I was genuinely happy for him. He was a sweet guy who was developing into the partner Max always wanted, and becoming better at his trade with each event he handled.

I made up new postcards at Dex's suggestion, finally

giving a name to what I did: "Dina's Dinners." Although more than half my business was still in brunches, pool and cocktail parties, now that my limit was raised I wanted to try my hand at larger events and buffet dinners for more than the Gilda's Club women. As long as I kept the price in accordance with Wanda's parameters I could manage and still make a great profit.

Mark's checks were spotty but I didn't bother reminding him. I was doing well enough to cover the expenses that came in and I was determined to keep peace between us. I didn't want to nag him; hopefully, Taffie was taking care of that. He got into the routine of calling me a couple of times a week, usually on the pretense of telling me he'd be mailing out my check soon, or asking if he left a putter in the garage. Well into our sixth month of separation, I thought perhaps he was laying the groundwork for a reconciliation.

I already had a preliminary meeting with Millie Rise who advised that it might be wise to set myself up as a small business. She wasn't thrilled that I was running it out of the house although I explained it was par for the course at Forest.

"Yes, Dina, I realize that, but those people are probably paying taxes. Yours is a cash business. Please speak with an accountant if you continue and certainly after your trial separation is up. You can get away with this for just so long; all it takes is one unhappy customer. Take my advice; if you must do it, keep it small."

"I'm only working within Forest and no one's saying anything. Can't I say that they're paying for the food and I'm just setting it up?"

"You can say whatever you like; just be careful."

Thanksgiving dinner was a raving success. Marla Burke's

house looked like the third floor of Bloomingdale's china department with every conceivable size patterned plate stacked on her buffet. Sammy had done his job well, even talking her into five sets of ceramic pumpkin salt and pepper shakers that we set out on her dining table, which was covered with the autumn leaves motif table cloth that Sammy also suggested.

My twenty-pound turkey was beautiful enough to be photographed, and once again, I mourned the demise of *Gourmet* magazine. Dex made the stuffing using chopped apples, apricots, toasted pecans and roasted chestnuts sautéed with celery and onion, which was then stirred into crumbled-up homemade cornbread. He moistened the mixture with a cup of apple brandy and some juice from the roasting turkey; then baked the dressing until a crust formed on top, which had us panting to take a bite.

"I'm way ahead of you," said my sous-chef as he pulled out a small ramekin that had baked alongside the large casserole.

We didn't let it cool down before digging two forks into the heavenly ambrosia. I'd never again add sausage or chicken livers when such a tasty dish could be prepared sans meat.

Once again Dex played bartender, waiter and all-around helper at the Burkes'. Like a highly trained surgeon, he carved the turkey before putting it back on the frame. Serving fifteen guests was just a matter of lining up food on the sideboard and having people help themselves. Once they dug into the meal, Dex and I came around with platters for those who wanted seconds. They all took another helping of every dish we prepared and Dex gave me that knowing look of "well, partner, we did it again."

Being that no PPS deliveries were made on Thanksgiving

Day, Dex arrived at my house early that morning to assist with the entire meal. Lately, he was showing up way before I really needed him, but insisted that it'd be easier for two of us to do the prep work, and he wanted to learn more of my techniques. It was only when I had a weekday event that he'd appear just after five to load up his van with food trays and supplies before heading out to that evening's party. Dex still refused a portion of the profits.

"Dina, my food bills are way down because you give me so many leftovers and my trucking guys are busier than ever – so don't worry about me. And no one likes to be one-upped around here, so all your clients are tipping me, which, if you can stand one of my metaphors, is gravy. Let's just get you through this year."

It was clear that I was twisting the club's documents by running a business out of my home, but who was going to rat me out?

1. Surely the members wouldn't sacrifice their Roasted Duck Breast stuffed with chopped Granny Smith Apples, Walnuts and Gorgonzola, laced with a Cabernet sauce, or their beloved Pina Colada Layer Cake, to turn me into the Grievance Committee, the chairman of which was Jim Chan.

2. It was only for a year, I rationalized, until either Mark returned to our marriage or, well, I didn't have an 'or' yet.

I now had no time for any golf or card games, which the girls had slowly and cautiously invited me back into, but realized I didn't much miss the typical club life. My clients invited me to lunch occasionally, mainly to keep tabs on me so I wouldn't get any ideas about catering at other clubs.

"Let the Polo Club and Boca West hire the big caterers in town and pay twice the price of Dina's. Have you seen what Platinum charges?" they gossiped amongst themselves.

The day I met Portia for a cocktail at Bar None to go over the menus for her Gilda's Club group, the leader of the pack approached us.

"Dina," said Gabriela. "I've been hearing good things about you; so nice to know that we don't have to go elsewhere anymore. You and I will have to talk soon. I'm sure you've come a long way since Marcy's little luncheon for Brittany."

I felt the sting of her use of the word little, but was so flattered by her otherwise decent compliment that I practically flubbed my reply. "Sure, Gaby, anytime," I said, a little puffed up now that the head honcho was interested in me. "Just give me a call."

"I'll be doing that. Oh, my husband's here, we're going to Winners Circle for dinner. I didn't feel like cooking so it's just the two of us," said Gaby.

"Oh, so normally you cook?" said Portia, well aware of Gaby's status in the community.

Gaby gave a half puh, half snort sound before saying, "not in this lifetime, but I order in from the same places you do, Portia. Goodnight, ladies."

"Oh lordy, save me from that girl," said Portia. "I don't know what kind of a hold she has over the others, or why they drag along after her. When I first met her I thought she was beautiful, all that long streaky hair and big blue eyes but then as I got to know her, I thought just the opposite. Everything attractive about her is on the surface. And she sure as hell shouldn't be wearing Missoni with those wide-load hips. I don't even know any lesbians who'd like her. She certainly doesn't deserve to have a chic name like Gabriela."

Portia, honest and down to earth, was correct in her assessment, but I was happy that:

1. I'd protected my previous nemesis.

2. I didn't give up Gaby's real name.

"Well, don't be too hard on her. She did like the luncheon at Marcy's and she said she's been hearing good things about me," I said, slightly star struck from our brief interaction.

"Be careful with that one," said Portia, "she'll be just the person to destroy you."

"Portia, you're not going to put a voodoo curse on her, are you?"

"I'm not from Haiti, you twit," she said. She joined me in a laugh and since we weren't driving, another cocktail.

147

Chapter 24

December

More Mark

At the beginning of my catering career, I was thrilled to handle the jobs that were too small for Platinum Pantry, the premier caterer in Boca. Wanda was only too happy to pass along the women's charity breakfasts, small birthday luncheons and Sunday family brunches to my kitchen. I filled a niche that was missing in a town, or at least in Forest, where most parties were being billed at two and three times what I charged.

My breakfasts were priced for as little as two hundred dollars, and I still made a profit. My luncheons and teas blossomed into dinners, and cocktail parties, and eventually a small engagement party for the Haywood family. Even with Wanda's permission, it was rare that I had to charge three thousand dollars, and rental fees were paid directly to Acorn, who in turn paid me a small commission in cash.

My reputation spread throughout the club and I attained a level of success that was quickly bringing my private stash up to a decent figure. In addition to Mark's checks, which continued to be late, I could just squeak by living solo in Forest if my husband didn't come back, and if the dues didn't go up. Even if there was no time to partake in any of the club's amenities I'd still live in beautiful surroundings with a nice little business going. Realistically, I knew it would be tough, but just the thought of managing on my own kept me going.

The Chans' birthday party for the family was uneventful as the food had already been deemed acceptable at the tasting dinner, and all nine of the Chan dynasty came into the kitchen to thank Dex and me.

"Miss Dina," said Uncle Tai, "you could have worked in the Peninsula dining room with me. Where did you learn to cook like this?" he asked, more as a musing than a question because he was out of the kitchen before I could answer him.

"Let's hope Uncle doesn't want us to take cooking lessons now," said Bailey. "That's not going to happen, but really, Dina, the meal was terrific."

Both sets of parents were equally appreciative and when Belle handed me a check for the balance, she hugged me. Dex was at the sink trying not to listen as she spoke.

"Dina, let's have lunch one day, you, me and Bailey. We don't have to go to the club, that gets boring, but my sister and I would like to get to know you better, and it's our way of saying thank you for all you've done," said Belle.

"I'd like that. You've been so generous with me, but it'd be nice to socialize once in a while," I said, hoping she would follow through.

"I'll call you. Thanks, Dex. I don't know what we'd do without you two," she said taking off to go back to her guests.

Was it my imagination or did she stress you two?

Our separation was into its seventh month and it still

wasn't clear if Mark would return. He was calling me several times a week and during one conversation dumped all the latest on me.

"Taffie decided she needs a career so now she's selling real estate in the Keys. Forget the quiet existence. Before I only had to pay for us and a few friends when we went out to dinner, God forbid she should cook or even bring in food, but now I have to lug buyers around by day because she doesn't want to be in a car alone with them. Then when she decides they need a little more goosing we have to entertain them at night. It costs a fortune down here; that's why I'm calling; no way I can get a check to you this month. Can you manage?" Mark said.

I was annoyed, but amused at the same time.

1. Mark's little Taffie had obviously become disenchanted with his beach-boy status, and was turning him into her whipping boy.

2. I almost felt sorry for him.

3. He wasn't asking to come back home, yet, but he sure didn't sound happy.

4. This time I'd be more aware of the signs.

"Gee, Mark, your check was so late last month and the month before that I'm learning to live on less, but it's not easy. I'm barely keeping my head above water; maybe I'll ask Mom and Dad for a loan," I said, knowing he'd go ballistic.

He did.

"Please Dina, don't do that. Your parents wouldn't spit on me now and if they knew I couldn't support you, I don't know what I'd do. You've been my only family, even though we're not together, and I still want to make it up with your parents one day. They've given us so much; I really felt awful hurting them," he said.

I knew that was true; he probably felt worse about leaving them than me.

There were so many things I missed about my husband, but I also knew that there were just as many that would have to change if we reunited.

"Mark, I think I can stretch the money for another month, but then you'll have to start sending those checks regularly. What about going back to work? Now that Taffie is working why would she object to your doing the same?"

"I would, but it's not the same down here. Either it's starving artists and writers, or people with money who've had their own advisers for years. I have no 'teeth' here. And between walking the dogs, going out with Taffie and her clients I hardly have a chance to read the paper anymore," Mark said, even more downcast.

Dogs? Did he say Dogs?

"Dogs? She has dogs? But you're allergic," I said.

"Yeah, I know, but I take pills and get shots so that controls it," he said.

"Mark, it's the other line, I have to go," I said, lying to my husband, "it's France. Send the check as soon as you can."

I hung up with such a horrible feeling of doom that I had to steady myself against the kitchen island. Placing my head down on the marble pastry board I sobbed. My husband wasn't coming back to me. Taffie may be putting him through the wringer, but if he was downing pills and taking shots to tolerate her dogs then he had it right.

They were soul mates.

When Mark and I first started to date I mentioned my love of animals and how I planned to adopt a kitten as soon as I rented my own apartment.

"Deal breaker," he said, not unkindly, but stern enough for me to know he was serious. "I am totally allergic to dogs and cats; all breeds – even those hairless monstrosities, or whatever else a vet tells you won't be reactive. Please Dina, promise me, no pets and that includes birds."

So for the fifteen years we were married there was no more talk of animals; only of one day having a baby and even that didn't materialize.

My husband was gone:

1. Physically.

2. Emotionally.

3. Financially.

We'd sell the house, and I'd receive half the proceeds along with anything left in our joint account, plus the catering money I'd put aside. There'd be enough to buy a small condo in downtown Delray; the idea I presented to Mark in an attempt to save our marriage.

When Wanda took her maternity leave, perhaps she'd ask Platinum to interview me for a temporary job. Maybe if I did well, they'd keep me on.

I was projecting into the future, but after giving up all hope of Mark's return to our marriage, I was ready to face reality. Like the lady at Tara said, I'd think about it tomorrow.

For tonight I'd take the easy way out:

1. Fill the bathtub.

2. Pour a tumbler of vodka with a dash of tonic.

3. If I were lucky, drown.

Falling into bed that night I thought about how much I used to enjoy folding myself into Mark's arms and listening to him talk about his day. It didn't matter what the subject was; the physical contact we had during those times kept us connected. Having my own career would have added spice and vigor to our marriage. I wouldn't just be a country club wife anymore. I was an entrepreneur and once he found out about Dina's Dinners, he'd have a new respect for my professionalism.

I had proven myself and it would have been the jump-start we needed, but:

1. My husband had found a new life and a new partner.

2. With dogs.

3. He didn't need me anymore.

Feeling sorry for myself, and with the help of the king-sized drink and bed, I fell asleep.

Chapter 25

December

Gaby's Deal

Dex was indispensible to me. I doubted I'd be able to exist without his help, particularly for weekend functions, which had grown in size but were still manageable for the two of us. When Portia asked if there was a budding romance between Dex and me I looked at her like she was crazy. Where did she get that idea? Dex had never so much as held my hand or kissed me good night. I did catch him staring at me one Saturday afternoon while we were prepping for a small dinner party.

"What's up? Something wrong?" I said.

"No, just admiring the way you bone and poach a giant sea bass without a fuss. Most women around here can't open a can of tuna and look how you've taken that sucker apart," he said. "No wonder the Chans are 'enchanted' with you, pun intended."

I guess it was a compliment of sorts. Did I want more than that? It was a confusing time for me. Dex filled a gap in my life, but only for male friendship and companionship. There was nothing romantic between us. Although my mind accepted Mark's departure, my heart hadn't caught up.

He was still my husband and maybe I'd have a chance to get him back:

1. Maybe if the dogs and the boat made him sick enough.

2. Maybe if he got tired of chauffeuring around Taffie's clients.

3. Maybe if he needed to work again to feel useful.

4. Maybe Mark would come to his senses.

5. That was a lot of maybes.

Not really expecting Gaby to contact me I was surprised and flattered when she called a few days after we chatted at Bar None.

I saw the caller I.D., but decided saying "Hi Gaby" would be too informal. She and I were never good friends, or even friends. She tolerated me in golf games to up her chances of winning, but the few times I sat at her lunch table, she rarely directed the conversation to me.

"Hello," I said, in my most dignified voice.

"We need to talk," said the ill-mannered Gaby on the other end of the phone. "I want a party and I want you to do it. Meet me for lunch at the club and we'll discuss. Make it noon, I'm playing Maj with the girls afterwards."

"I guess I can manage that, but I can't stay more than an hour. I have some things to prepare for Portia's dinner tonight."

"Huh, Portia and her gang. What's the dinner for? She never invites me. Probably some lesbo thing," Gaby said.

"No, it's for women who are working for Gilda's Club.

It's a charity that helps cancer victims and their families and it's a wonderful cause. I don't think you have to be a lesbian to join," I said, my sarcasm lost on Gaby.

"Whatever, in the meanwhile, bring a notebook so you can jot down a few things. See you later. Don't be late," she said and hung up without a farewell greeting.

It was already after eleven, and since most of the meal had been prepped for Portia's dinner I put the rest of the ingredients back in the fridge. There wasn't enough time to bake my Triple-Rich Chocolate Cookies, and I hadn't even showered yet.

I arrived at the Grille just before the appointed time, and grabbed a booth before the morning golfers came in. Gaby was fifteen minutes late and I was on my second iced tea when she stormed through the dining room and sat down across from me.

1. Why did I accept this interview with such an obnoxious woman?

2. Did I really need her acceptance? (Probably)

3. My business with other residents would increase once they saw me catering for the toughest person to please at Forest.

4. And on the face of the earth.

We ordered lunch and I slapped my notebook on the table.

"Well, Gaby, let's start because you don't want to be late for Maj," I said.

156

"Oh, it's no problem – we're five anyway and they'll begin without me. That's how we do it for bridge also."

Again, I was taken aback at her lack of tact knowing that I'd been dismissed from that bridge game at Nancy's after arriving with a Key Lime Loaf and thinking I was invited to stay as Gaby's replacement.

1. Who was I kidding?

2. Even if she did remember, she wouldn't have cared.

3. I was no longer a total outsider, but I sure wasn't part of her inner circle.

"So, what did you have in mind?" I said, politely but semi-firmly (I was still in awe of Gaby), but needed to get down to business and back home to bake.

"I want to give a farewell party for the snowbirds. Dinner. Buffet."

"But that's not till April or May; it's only December."

"You may need more planning time; my list is almost a hundred people," said Gaby.

I gave a laugh similar to a demented hyena's before answering.

"Oh, Gaby, I really appreciate your thinking of me, but there's no way I can handle a party that size. Let me give you the name of the best rep over at Platinum Pantry, she's a good friend of mine and will take excellent care of you," I said, gulping down part of my sandwich in an attempt to end the meeting. I still had to finish baking for Portia's group.

"Wanda, right? She already gave me a bid of twelve thousand. Marty says fine because he says fine to everything, but

I know it's way too high. I told him that you'd be able to do it for far less."

Not wanting to divulge my price point set by Wanda, who'd recently upped me another thousand, I repeated that such a large event wasn't within my realm of capabilities.

"Gaby, I don't think you understand, there's no way I could cater a dinner buffet for more than about thirty or forty, and even that's a stretch. Mostly what I do is luncheons, small dinner parties, you know, stuff that people used to have at the club before they discovered their own dining rooms. I'm honored (Honored? Where was I getting this stuff from?) you asked, but Wanda would do the best job for you. Everyone loves her parties, have you ever been to one?" I said, trying to get Gaby to open up and stop scowling.

"Dina, Marty and I are on the A list. We're invited to all the good parties, and of course, I know Platinum's work; it's great, but I don't feel like spending twelve hundred, much less twelve thousand to say goodbye to the fucking snowbirds."

"May I ask why you're doing it?"

"Because if we don't, somebody else will. No one's ever thought of a farewell party like this before, and I've got to get out those 'save the date' evites. Oh, the date will be Sunday, May 29th. Write it down."

Without checking I knew that was Memorial Day weekend and even Wanda would have a hard time hiring extra help without paying time and a half, if not double. No wonder she quoted so high. It was also the last month before the end of my year apart from Mark, and I would have to know for sure where I was headed by then.

1. How could I possibly have a house full of

party ingredients a couple of weeks before vacating if Mark didn't come back?

2. I'd need that time to pack up and find another place to live if he stayed in Key West.

3. If only my husband would return; then I'd have a breather and not be so rushed to make a decision.

4. Why was I bothering with another head-list when I realized after my last conversation with Mark that we were done?

Not wanting to explain the finite details of my separation, I again stressed how impossible it would be for me to cater her party.

"Dina, let me remind you that we've been to your house for dinner once or twice, and we've been to a few of the parties you've done here so I know you can cook, and I know your boyfriend helps you."

"Dex is not my boyfriend. We are friends and yes, he does help," I said, ready to blow my stack at this insensitive, repulsive woman, streaky hair and enviable blue eyes notwithstanding.

"Whatever, I don't give a shit who you're fucking; you're going to do my party. Now, let's talk about the menu. Eventually I do have to get into the card room. Waiter! Where's my coffee?" she screeched across the room. Leo, the experienced maître d', who rarely left his post at the entrance, raced over with the pot.

Even awestruck people can summon up their courage

159

in times of great need, and summon I did.

"Gaby, I'm leaving," I said in my who-the-hell-are-you-anyway voice. (I had nothing to lose at this point and decided to go for it.) "You're being rude and there's no reason for me to sit here and take it. I will do you one favor; I won't tell Wanda (I couldn't wait to tell Wanda) what an insufferable prig you are. Believe me, whatever she's charging isn't enough to deal with you," I said, standing up ready to make my grand exit.

"Sit down," she said.

Her tone, which had only been repugnant up till this point, was now commanding.

"I said, sit down. I think you're going to want to hear why you'll be catering my party," she said.

"Gaby, I'll give you exactly two minutes," I said, following orders. "What is it?"

"The way I figure it is that you've made quite a nice pile of money since June. You know the club doesn't allow anyone to run a business from their home, especially such an obvious one. Now, of course, Chuck knows what you're doing and although he's letting you get away with murder, it's still a clear violation of our club's documents," Gaby said.

"Well, you have a point there, but there are many other residents who work out of the house, it's just a fact of life today, the new normal is what they call it," I said, breathing a sigh of relief. Chuck already knew what I was doing so her blackmail was garbage. Her next statement wasn't.

"I don't care what anyone calls it; the fact is that Chuck could get fired for letting you carry on the way you do. Moving those carts in and out of Dex's van, probably not paying any kind of taxes and who knows how clean your kitchen is?"

"Stop right there, Gaby. My kitchen is spotless (lie) and I'll work out the details with my accountant (lie) and you wouldn't dare have Chuck fired (would she?); everyone loves him. He's the best general manager in Boca."

"I agree with you there and he gets a hefty salary for the work he does. Trust me, if I don't want him here, he's gone and no one else will hire him. He'll be held accountable for letting your business go on, and stop me if you're getting bored, but you won't be able to call a halt once it's in progress," said Gaby. "Oh, I know you're calling your deal Dina's Dinners – very original by the way, but have you actually opened a business account? Incorporated?"

"I told you I was working on it," I said.

"Dina, you're screwed on all charges. I'm simply giving you a way out," she said, opening her massive Hermès bag to yank out a notebook. "Did you know that you probably need certified ovens for what you're doing, not to mention a sanitation rating from the health department? Oh, you could probably get around all that, but you'll have no control over what happens to Chuck.

Do this party for me and nothing will ever be said, but if I pull the plug, you'll get Chuck fired, and I'll make sure you get sued up the yin-yang for something, and they might even throw you in jail where I'm sure you could work in the kitchen. Now, let's talk about the menu, and if you see the waiter, get him over here," Gaby said, "Leo only poured half a cup."

I felt the blood leave my face as I reached for the glass of lukewarm tea still in front of me. Even if I straightened out all the business aspects as Millie Rise advised, I knew Gaby and her husband had a lot of pull, and she'd make good her word about Chuck's future. In addition to being an ace in running a club such as Forest, our manager was such an honorable person; I couldn't take a chance of his being fired.

1. If I did Gaby's bidding there was no way I could keep the cost for a hundred guests under my committed maximum amount.

2. Since Gaby turned down Wanda's proposal, hopefully, my best friend would assume that the client hired another caterer.

3. She'd never suspect it was me.

4. I could call Wanda and spill my guts, but she was having an uncomfortable time with her pregnancy and even though her idea was to work up until the ninth month, I didn't feel right about worrying her.

5. Platinum wasn't going to get the job anyway, so what would it matter if I accepted it?

"Dina! Wake up and stop daydreaming!" Gaby snapped at me. "You are the most exasperating person I've ever met."

Gaby, meet Gaby.

"I don't think you're making a well-thought out decision, but you have me over a barrel," I said. "I'll take care of filing all the proper papers for the business so there's no point in threatening to sue me (please don't sue me because I couldn't take jail unless Frosty found a good cell for me) but I won't put Chuck's career in jeopardy."

"You have enough problems without that. I'm not going to say anything for the moment and I suggest you keep our conversation confidential."

"You have a game to get to so let me suggest what would work for that many people. I'm thinking a lovely cocktail buffet," I said, wanting to keep the cost and work to a minimum. "Perhaps a nice pasta station, and people are just crazy about those little make-your-own tacos, or Asian chicken-lettuce roll-ups…"

"Dina, this isn't a soup kitchen dinner. I want Beef Wellington, stuffed lobster tails, that roast duck we had at your house and tons of hot and cold hors d'oeuvres, and no dips. I want baby lamp chops being passed around also. That's what people are crazy about. Not Taco Bell. Here's the proposal from Platinum; just copy everything as is."

No wonder Wanda had given an estimate of twelve thousand dollars. Not only was the food portion a fortune, but it also required cooking equipment I'd either have to buy or rent, and according to Wanda I'd need ten servers, three bartenders and a dishwasher. Dex couldn't do it all. Even though he'd be working on prep with me, I'd need at least one extra chef, and would I be able to find all this help for a Memorial Day weekend party?

"Gaby, no one really eats Beef Wellington anymore," I said trying to steer her away from the extravagant menu. "It's a very heavy dish and the end of May can be quite warm. Also, lobster tails get messy. People need plates and cutlery for it, and a place to sit."

"Dina, we live in the Oaks section, near where you did the holiday dinner for the Weitzenbaums. Their house is ten thousand square feet; ours is fifteen. I think we can seat a hundred, a sit-down if we wanted, without too much trouble. And people will be milling around on the patio so make sure you have plenty of waiters passing those hors d'oeuvres. Not everyone is going to eat the beef, but it'll be a spectacular presentation."

163

Beef Wellington, a dish involving a rib roast, pate and pastry crust was to my knowledge never served as a buffet item. Once it got cold, the fat would congeal, and the pastry would get mushy. Stuffed lobster tails? Really?

"Gaby, you're not giving me a choice but to do your party, and you have some very expensive items on this list. I need a chance to cost it out, but with servers and rentals it's not going to be much less than Wanda's proposal."

"I'll pay you eight thousand and that's monumental for you. Platinum is probably working on a huge markup; you don't have their overhead. Eight is fair and I'm sure you'll make up for it with other parties because once people find out that you're working for Marty and me, you'll be flooded with requests for more than the kindergarten stuff you've been doing. You should consider this a big opportunity. Platinum has gotten too big for its britches, and Wanda will probably leave soon anyway to take care of the baby. Listen to me, Dina, your friend will be relieved that she doesn't have to supervise this party," said Gaby, actually believing that she was now my guardian angel.

I was relieved that she was offering me enough to cover most of my costs although I couldn't be sure until I totaled everything up. The mystery was how to cook and serve all the items she was insisting upon. I'd have to get her to modify the menu, but right now I just needed her to leave.

"Gaby, I'd appreciate it if you wouldn't mention the price to any of the girls, and please don't tell Wanda. If you do, it'll be the end of my career and a friendship," I said, laying it on the line and trying to appeal to her sense of decency, which she kept well hidden.

"Don't worry about Wanda. I mentioned that I was going to get a quote from Taste so I'm sure she'll figure that

I went with them. And no one else here has to know what I'm paying. I've got to get to my Maj game; I'll have coffee there. Here, let me pick up lunch today," said my benefactor. "Trust me, Dina, once you do this party for me, your whole world will change.

You won't need that cheating prick of a husband, and you and Dex can get married – and don't tell me there's nothing going on – I think you can agree that I'm not stupid when it comes to picking up on things. Here's my check for half in advance, that's how you work it, right? I'll sign it and you fill in the rest. See, I trust you. Ta ta," she said, and waltzed out of the dining room.

Seeing me in distress, Leo approached the table.

"Mrs. Marshall, everything okay?" he said.

"Oh, yes, thank you, Leo. I wouldn't mind a little more tea if you could ask one of the servers to stop by," I said, unable to stand up.

Chapter 26

December

Marcy's Take

By the time Leo returned Marcy walked over and parked herself across from me.

"Hey Dina, what's going on? I saw you and Gaby having lunch. Are you guys friendly now?" said Marcy.

"Uh, well, we were never enemies. We were discussing a party she wants to throw – don't say anything, she'll be telling everyone soon enough."

"Oh, the snowbird thing? She already mentioned it, said it's going to be a quite an event. Gee, that's got to be good for you, right? You've been doing great so far, but no one's taken a chance on you for a big shindig. They always use Platinum or what's that other one?"

"You mean Taste? They're out of Ft. Lauderdale, but they do a lot of business up here."

"Yes, that's the one. The Millers used them once for a New Year's Eve party and it was fantastic. Your prices are really the best, the girls have confidence in you, and there's no reason you couldn't handle some big parties here. You and Dex are so organized," said the ever-bubbly Marcy. "And Dina, if you and Dex have something going, no one would care – we'd all be happy for you."

There it was again. Why did people think that Dex

and I were a couple? Couldn't a man and a woman work together, or be friends, without being romantically involved?

"Marcy, there's nothing going on with Dex and me. He helps with the catering, and we've become close friends. Can we speak frankly about something else? I've enjoyed getting to know you, Portia, the Chan girls and a few others – before it was just golf or bridge and the occasional lunch – but since I've been on my own and catering, the girls are so much friendlier and it's been a great experience," I said, leading up to the Gaby issue. "How do you account for the change in attitude toward me?"

"Honestly, we always felt you were a little standoffish. I mean, we were invited to dinner at your house, but that was mostly for Mark's business and trust me, that was no secret, but you never actually put yourself into the conversation. You were always jumping up and down, making coffee and dessert at the last minute, stuff like that, so it seemed like our being there was an imposition.

You used to play golf with us at least once a week and then you stopped. When you started to cancel bridge, we needed a replacement to keep the games going. I know some of the women are hard to keep up with around here; believe me, Burt and I are on the low end of the ladder money-wise, but we still take part in most of the activities. Mark used you for his own benefit and then left. Now, you're getting back into your own skin again, know what I mean?"

I was taken aback by Marcy's comments. It had been easier to blame residents for snubbing me than to try to form friendships. I fed them and now discovered why they felt it was a burden.

My rationale for entertaining Mark's clients?

1. Couples try to please each other.

2. Mark's future was also mine.

3. Until Taffie.

"Thanks for being honest with me. I know I put Mark's needs ahead of mine; it seemed like the right thing to do at the time, but I missed out on a lot." I sighed before continuing. "Do you mind if I ask you something about Gaby, just between us, okay?" I said, gearing up.

"That bitch? Ask away," said Marcy, and we both smiled.

"Well, since you put it that way – what's her hold on everyone here?"

"It's not really a hold, it's just that she and Marty owned the original property and helped develop it. It was a good time to buy and they made zillions. But it wasn't just money. They built the first estate home in the Oaks and Gaby went out of her way to meet new residents; you know, so she wouldn't be left out of anything. Because they're so rich, people tended to follow along with whatever she said or did.

She was actually nice in the beginning, always arranging golf games, theatre parties, cards, lunch, and I didn't know anyone so I was happy when she included me. I guess it was that way with most of the new people who moved in, especially those with a lot of money.

She and I were never close, and even Burt was surprised when I invited her to Brittany's luncheon, but if you leave her out she'll get back at you one way or the other. She'll take her revenge, even if it means resorting to rumors or lies. If you're going to do that party for her, it better be perfect," Marcy said. "You know how they say someone doesn't have a mean bone in their body? Well, Gaby's are all mean.

But I have to tell you, the other day after tennis, she started to say something about you, oh, nothing terrible, just her usual bullshit, and one of the Chans, I can't tell them apart, told her to shut it. We were shocked, but it worked. Gaby changed the subject and when I looked at the twins, they gave me that funny look of theirs."

Marcy signaled for coffee so we were silent for a moment.

"Thanks, Leo," she said, "we don't often see you pouring coffee. How've you been? How's your little boy?"

"Oh, just fine, Mrs. Gold, can I get you ladies anything else? We're a little short staffed today so I'm pitching in."

The appetite I'd lost talking to Gaby returned. The busboy had whisked away the rest of my sandwich so I asked for a piece of coffee cake.

"Make that two, Leo." said Marcy.

"Be right back," he said, and disappeared into the kitchen.

"It won't be as good as yours, but he doesn't have to know that," Marcy said.

"Seriously, Marcy, you missed the day they were handing out mean bones. I didn't even know Leo had a family. But back to Gaby, I told her I'd do the party even though it's bigger than what I'm used to. I just hope it'll go well."

"Of course it will, and then you'll have it made. I bet you'll even get more offers as soon as people find out you're doing the snowbird thing. You're probably not charging any of us enough so be sure you make it up with her," said

Marcy, unaware that Gaby would be getting the cheapest deal in Boca-town.

"Dina, none of us thought Mark was a bad guy; I mean leaving you was plain old stupid, but before that, all the men liked him. He didn't have to push so hard; the business people who were in his foursomes would have gone with him anyway. He knows his stuff – that's what Burt always told me.

I can't believe in this day and age that some of the women here, including me, still don't know what's going on with our finances. That's going to change. I signed up for a course at FAU. Burt thinks it's great. The Chans talked me into it. I got a couple of the girls to do it with me."

"That's admirable; if I had time I'd do the same. One day."

After we finished our cake, which was almost as good as mine, we got up to leave.

"I better be getting back; have to bake cookies for Portia's dinner tonight," I said. "How about if I drop off a dozen for you and Burt. My little way of saying thank you, for everything."

"Well, you don't have to, but if there's any kind of chocolate in them, I won't say no," she said, handing the valet her ticket.

"Three kinds. See you later," I said and started the short walk back home.

Chapter 27

December/January

Discovering Dex

December was a busy month for me. After the Chan's dinner, I booked a New Year's Day brunch for Tess and Mick Morgan. Tess wanted to keep it casual, with food that could be left out except for some kind of a hot dish. I suggested my tried and true blintz casserole that was prepared the night before and could be popped into her oven a half hour before serving.

Since I needed a warming tray for the casserole, I decided to buy one instead of renting. It'd come in handy for the next few months because after Gaby's evites went out I was inundated with requests as Marcy predicted.

About two weeks before Christmas I called Dex late one Saturday morning to see if he wanted to look at trays with me.

"Hey, Dina," he said, picking up the phone on the first ring. "What's going on up there at Forest?"

"Uh, nothing much," I said, wondering if he was aware of my bargain with the devil. I hadn't yet discussed Gaby's party with Dex and figured today would be the right time to bring it up. "Thought I'd take a ride down to Coconut Creek to buy a warming tray. Feel like meeting me there?"

"Sure, but why don't you let me pick you up. Promise it won't be in a PPS truck or a van," he said, full of good humor. "And, it's a perfect sitting-outside-day for a latte or something. Maybe even lunch?"

"I just had a big breakfast, but I'll take you up on coffee. I'll be ready whenever you get here," I said.

"Great, just have to take care of a little business and I'll leave," he said and we hung up.

Dex arrived at noon. Not that I was hiding our association, but I decided waiting in the garage would be the least likely place anyone would see me. He pulled into the driveway seated in a white Saab convertible.

"Hope you don't mind the top down. Come on, let's go," he said.

"I've got the right haircut for a convertible," I said, running my fingers through my cropped do to demonstrate.

"It suits you, I'm tired of all those Boca blondes," he said, with a laugh.

"Right, I'm sure."

"Let's just take Lyons; beautiful day for a ride," he said as we drove away.

We passed a few joggers on the way out of the club; they waved and we did the same. Although I could have made this little trip by myself, I felt so miserable since realizing Mark wouldn't be coming back, and combined with Gaby's threats ringing in my ears, I just didn't want to be alone. Aside from Wanda, Dex was the person I felt most comfortable with.

Twenty minutes later we pulled into The Promenade at Coconut Creek and found a parking spot right outside of Sur La Table.

"Do you mind if we do the coffee thing first?" said Dex.

"I had sort of a busy morning and didn't have a chance for breakfast. Starbucks okay?"

"Sounds good. I'm always up for coffee."

The weather was beautiful – cool, sunny and dry, a South Florida winter day to lift my spirits. Dex ordered coffees for us and picked out a sandwich from the refrigerator case.

"Let's sit outside; go grab a table and I'll be right out," he said, while the barrister was filling our orders.

"What were you so busy with earlier?" I said when he joined me. "Getting ready for the week?"

"No, not exactly," he said and then continued after taking bite out of his sandwich. "Dina, I'm thinking about selling my business."

"You're going to retire?" I asked, not believing my ears. Mark's not working was one thing, but Dex? Did he have a rich young hottie stashed away also? "What would you do? Oh, sorry, that's really none of my business."

"No, I don't want to retire. I didn't want to tell you until I was pretty sure of the deal. The three guys who work for me made an offer. They're all in their twenties and think they can run the business as well as I can, even expand it, and I know they can."

"But it's been so successful, the clubs must be thrilled; I know Chuck is always bragging about our special PPS."

"Yeah, it's been good to me, and to the guys. But, well, doing all this cooking and stuff with you has had a major effect on me. I'd like to start up a food business and there's someone in Greensboro who's interested in partnering with me. We'd be supplying universities in the area, and then move on to other venues."

"Greensboro? North Carolina?" I said.

"Yeah, I think I need a change of climate in more ways

than one. Your sister lives there, right? And didn't you say your folks have a place in the mountains?" he said.

"Yes, on both counts. France is in Winston-Salem, about twenty minutes from Greensboro, and my folks bought a condo in Asheville. It's beautiful because the seasons are so defined," I said, not realizing where the conversation was headed.

"Dina, we've never discussed this, but what's going on with Mark? Is he coming back or is it a done deal?"

"It's over. Not officially, because we won't file for divorce until May or June, but it looks like he and Taffie are the real thing. I wouldn't have believed it, but after our last phone conversation I realized how deep his feelings are for her."

As difficult as it had been for me to accept my fate, recounting it to Dex seemed natural and effortless. Normally, I'd be crying my eyes out and whining to Wanda, but for the time being she was out of commission. Her doctor ordered bed rest for the next month at which time he'd reevaluate her condition. She developed high blood pressure with her pregnancy and was advised to eliminate as much stress as possible. Calling on clients qualified as stress so she took a leave of absence from Platinum. Bidding on Gaby's party must have been her last assignment and probably the reason her blood pressure went berserk.

"Dina, you want a cookie or something? I'm still hungry," said Dex, looking nervous.

"A biscotti would be great. Want me to get it?" I said.

"No, you wait here; I'll be right back and then we need to talk," Dex said before heading back into the coffee shop.

While he was gone I made up a new list about my life that was breaking into pieces:

1. No husband.

2. No legalized business.

3. Threats from Gaby.

4. My best guy friend might be leaving Boca.

5. If Dex left before I sold the house there'd be no way I could handle any catering jobs without him.

"Here you go, one almond biscotti and a glazed donut for me, and I got us two fresh coffees," said Dex as he sat down. The brief intermission in Starbucks seemed to have revitalized him and he was full of confidence as he continued the conversation.

"Dina, I'm in love with you…sshh…let me finish. I never would have said a word if you and Mark were going to reconcile, but you just said it's over and I am so thankful for that even though it must be painful for you.

I want you to consider moving to North Carolina with me. Your family is there, and this country club life isn't for you. Yeah, there are plenty of nice people, but it's an expensive lifestyle, and who knows what'll happen in the divorce, but it probably doesn't make much sense for you to stay on at Forest unless that's what you really want. I might be all wrong about this, but you are in love with me, right? Oh Jesus, please say yes; otherwise I'll feel like a total asshole."

I was in shock and couldn't say a word…I even had trouble forming a good list.

1. Moving close to my sister had great appeal.

2. While I wasn't tired of working, it was exhausting to do it just to make ends meet.

3. Was I in love with Dex?

4. Of course I was. I switched #4 with #1 before speaking.

"Dex, I bid on a party for Gaby and if I don't pull it off I may be going to jail," I said.

"You'd go to jail rather than North Carolina with me?" he said, his eyes teasing me.

"It's no joke. Let me explain about the conversation I had with her before talking about us," I said, and then proceeded to show him the menu and repeated how Gaby had bullied and threatened me. After I spilled my guts and tears, Dex laughed.

"Oh, I'm sorry, I don't mean to make light of this, but it's ridiculous. Yeah, you should start a small business, but maybe wait till your divorce is final – less complications. I don't know about the situation with Chuck, but regardless, do the party for her. Even if it's the last gig at Forest, you want to leave with your head held high."

"I have to do it," I said, "but it's going to be tough."

"Yeah, certainly more people than we're used to, and you'll have to get her to ditch that crazy menu, but we'll figure it out. Does Wanda know?"

"No, she's on bed rest and I don't want to upset her. She gave a high bid to Gaby because of the food costs, and right after that the doctor insisted she take a leave. She and I had an agreement that my parties wouldn't run over four thousand. If she knows that I'm getting eight, it'll be a disaster," I said.

"Eight? Thousand? Listen, put it on hold for a minute. I said I love you and want to spend the rest of our lives together. Did that register?" he said.

"My life is so screwed up right now it wouldn't be fair to involve you," I said, weakening.

Then I told him I loved him. I had to work on my priorities.

"How about if we face the worse now, and then just have the better after that. You know, for better or worse?"

I did that half-cry, half-laugh thing before kissing him.

We picked out a cordless warming tray and drove back to my house not saying a word. Stopping at the center of my circular driveway I no longer cared who saw us. Many residents already thought we were having a thing, so why not give them a little extra? The convertible top was still down when I reached over to kiss Dex knowing full well that two of my neighbors were walking by.

Once inside the house, we left the tray on the kitchen counter and walked into my bedroom. The few kisses left me needing more of him and I was past the point of wanting my husband back; it was time to move on.

"Are you sure, Dina?" he said, "I don't want to ruin anything between us by bringing sex into our relationship too soon."

"Remember when we did that rehearsal dinner for the Chans? Think of it that way – if it's good now, it'll be great later," I said, shocked at my boldness, yet happy I was able to express myself.

Dex was different in so many ways from Mark that

there was no need to compare the two men sexually. Mark had been my first and only lover, but that was over and I was ready in every way for Dex.

Except for the few moments in between our lovemaking sessions we never left each other's arms. He kissed every inch of my body and explored me with his hands and tongue before entering me. I don't know who came first, second or last, but the love-fest lasted for hours before we took a break. We looked at each other and both said the same thing: "Hungry?"

We'd worked off every calorie consumed during the day and were ready for dinner.

"Come on, don't bother making anything; let's go to that new burger place up on Atlantic, right across from the ocean," Dex said.

"Not Top-Burger, is it?" I said, the one place I vowed never to visit.

"It's called Burger Fi, great burgers and the best fries ever. We'll drive up the Intracoastal and just be another couple going out on a date. For real. My treat."

It had to be for real because the weight on my shoulders that I'd been carrying around for months was lifted. I was in love with a good man; I'd hire a business manager who'd put my catering career on the books, and make some kind of a fair agreement with Mark. In one day everything had turned around and I was heading toward a good place.

Dex and I walked into Burger Fi, placed our orders and walked hand in hand back outside to a planked table with a view of the ocean.

"Dina, let's get a couple of things out of the way. First,

we should absolutely do Gaby's bash. You've already accepted the terms and taken a deposit, even though she forced you into it, but it'll give you the experience you need if you want to continue on catering. Even if Gaby refuses, I bet you can get letters of reference from all the others you've done work for, and believe me, Gaby won't want to incur the wrath of the entire club by dissing you. So, the second part is, will you come to North Carolina with me?"

"Gaby'll find a way to make trouble for me if I don't do the party," I said, skirting the other issue.

"And?" said Dex, not to be ignored.

"Well, I have to be divorced; I'll set that in motion with my lawyer, then Mark and I will put the house on the market, and I guess after that I'm a free agent. I could move in with France and Redmond for a while. I was so undecided before today, but now everything seems so right: you, the divorce, North Carolina.

"I'm glad you put me first. And listen, I won't push you, but I'm asking you to marry me over the burgers and fries that are ready because this obnoxious buzzer just went off. I'll book one of those extended-stay hotels until you and I decide where we want to settle. Greensboro is close to Winston, right? It'll work out, I promise. Now, for another important question: you want catsup with the fries?"

"Yes, to everything," I said, feeling as lighthearted as I'd ever been.

Chapter 28

January

Going Forward

Dex and I spent a quiet but passionate New Year's Eve at home, and I managed to put together the blintz casserole that had to sit overnight in the fridge.

The New Year's Day brunch was so successful that I decided to make up a special menu for similar occasions. The casserole was easy to assemble and the warming tray kept it at just the right temperature. Bowls of sour cream and cherries accompanied the hot dish, and along with a variety of bagels, smoked salmon, cream cheese, sliced tomatoes and onions, there was more than enough to eat while the four couples enjoyed the day together. The big screen was tuned into one of the six bowl games, and I served coffee and strawberry cheesecake in the great room while they relaxed on deep cushy sofas.

The hosts invited Dex and me to join them for dessert, something we hadn't done before, but in the end decided to have our little treat at home, in bed.

It was now common knowledge that Dex and I were seeing one another, and although there were plenty of knowing glances, no one said an unkind word. Except Gaby.

The following week Portia invited me to lunch at the

club to discuss a few new menus and to get my take on a fundraiser luncheon her group was planning for the fall. As I stopped at Gaby's table to say hello, the girls all greeted me. While I was still standing there, Gaby said, "The cook and the delivery boy, sounds like a porno flick."

Belle and Bailey were all over her and the others chimed in as well.

"Stuff it, Gaby. Dina's separated and they're getting divorced so what's it any business of yours if she's seeing Dex?" said Bailey, feeling her oats.

"Oh, she knows I don't mean it. Right, Dina? We've become quite close and Dex is a doll. I'm really very happy for them," Gaby said in her oily way when she thought she was putting something over on everyone.

"Then act like it," said sweet little Marcy.

I scooted into Portia's booth and we each ordered the spaghetti Bolognese. Forest's head chef, André, was notably very temperamental but Chuck put up with him because he was an extraordinary cook with some first-rate recipes.

Portia looked over my printout of next month's menus, which she approved, and we chatted amiably for the next hour.

"I've got to be going, Wanda's in her seventh month and going crazy being in bed all the time. She's due March 15th and itching to get back to work as soon as the doctor lets her. I've been so busy that we haven't caught up in a while, and I really have to bring her up to date," I said, not revealing how nervous I was about Gaby's party.

"Say hello, I wish we could have used Platinum for the charity luncheon in September, but one of our members belongs to Woodfield, and she's underwriting the food cost, but only if it's held there – so we couldn't turn that down," said Portia.

"That's a super deal and Woodfield's a beautiful club. If I'm in town, I'd love to come," I said.

"Why wouldn't you be here?"

I knew I could confide in Portia.

"Mark and I will be getting divorced and no way can I afford this place on my own. I may be moving to North Carolina, near where my sister lives," I said.

"What about Dex?" she said.

"Portia, I promise, as soon as I know everything I'll be happy to tell you, but a lot is up in the air right now."

"Understood. I won't say a word," said Portia. "Oh, tell Wanda I can recommend a great nanny if she needs one. Okay, thanks for the menu tips, let's get the check."

Driving over to Wanda's I rehearsed my speech about how my business had grown and how Forest residents only wanted to use me because it was so convenient, and every other detail I could think of to excuse the way I was going to flout my agreement with her.

When I arrived Linz let me in and led me to the sitting room off their master bedroom, which had views of the Intracoastal.

"She likes to be in here during the day; staying in bed gets pretty boring," said Linz. He seemed so concerned about his wife that he forgot to ask me the usual forty questions about my life. "She's doing much better, pressure is normal, and the doctor may ease up on the restrictions in a couple of weeks."

"That's great news," I said, breathing a sigh of relief on all counts.

"Hi Dina," said a very pregnant Wanda. "I have to stay

on the chaise, but Linz brought in this chair from the den so my favorite visitor would have a comfy place to sit and keep me company. Did you hear the good news?"

"Hi sweetie," I said, bending over to give her a hug, "yep, your hubby just filled me in."

"I'll leave you girls; I have some work to do, but how about some tea? Herbal, of course," said Linz.

"I just had several glasses of tea at the club, so I'll pass," I said.

"Me too, I'm only allowed to get up to pee, which is every thirty seconds without the tea, so nothing right now, but thanks, honey," Wanda said as her husband departed.

"He's been awesome, waiting on me hand and foot. I told him we could hire one of the servers I know to help out, but he wouldn't hear of it. And you know, he's not a bad cook. So, tell me, what's going on with you and Dex. I know you wanted to keep your marriage together, but it takes two to tango."

She got the dance right. Was pregnancy self-correcting?

"My marriage is over. Dex and I are in love and it's great. I'm really happy. The only bad part is that we're probably going to leave Florida and you."

"Yeah, North Carolina you said. With your folks spending half a year there it sounds like a smart move although I'll miss you like crazy, but you can come back and babysit anytime."

"Well, I still have several months left; then we have to sell the house. All that takes a while. I'll definitely be here for the baby's arrival."

"So, how are your parties going?" said Wanda, unaware of what I was about to reveal. Being confined and with Linz screening her calls, I assumed no one had gotten through to her about Gaby's party. Country clubs are not only fish bowls; they're the fastest source of communication known to man. Someone in Boca West has an affair with the tennis pro at Boca Point, and it's all over Polo and Bocaire that evening. Easing into the conversation, I decided to lay a little blame on Dex.

"Well, Dex has been helping me a lot, and Acorn has been super when I need them, so I started to do bigger stuff. Dex has been so encouraging and supportive that I decided I could take a jump up."

"Oh, I figured you wouldn't stay under a few thousand. People want more and more. You're entitled to make a living as long as you keep control." said Wanda. "The main thing is not to go above about fifty guests, otherwise you'll be dealing with a whole different animal, and even though you're doing well – and I am so proud of you – you just don't have the experience to coordinate anything larger."

"The first thing I have to do is to make my business official, even if I move in a year because I don't want to get in trouble," I said, leading up to Gaby's event.

"Good idea. So, what have you done lately? No one tells me anything. Linz won't let anyone through on the phone except you because he wants me to stay calm, and even when I'm on with you, he pops in every two minutes pointing to his watch. I'm so fucking bored! I need a little gossip."

"Well, he's looking after you and he's excited about the baby. You're lucky," I said, nervous about the upcoming blow.

"Yes, I am. I know he can be a pain, but Linz does mean well and he can't wait to be a father."

"Hey, you never told me what you're having and you must know by now," I said, extending the baby talk.

"Well, I wanted to find out, but Linz didn't. He says

he wants to hear the doctor say, 'it's a boy or girl' just like in the movies. Isn't that too cute? So I never found out either. It'll be a surprise for all of us," said the mother-to-be. "Now, let's talk shop."

"I've done Marcy's luncheon, I told you about that one, then a beautiful dinner party for the Chan family and some small cocktail parties and a New Year's Day brunch, and tons for the Gilda's Club girls."

"That's great! Congratulations. What's the biggest one you've booked?"

"Actually, it's one that you bid on. For Gaby."

Silence.

"Gaby's snowbird party? For a hundred? With that ridiculous menu?"

More silence.

"Yes," I said.

"Dina, I don't care how much money you make off that bitch, you're going to kill yourself and your business. And Memorial Day weekend? How do you think you're going to find help? All the good agencies are already booked, and some of them even call the caterers to remind them to put in reserves now, so you'll be paying double for the dregs. Oh, Acorn will deliver if you give them enough notice, but how can you even think about making all that food in your kitchen?"

"Wanda, please don't get upset. I'm sorry I even brought it up today, but I couldn't have you hearing it from someone else. I'm going to try to talk her out of the Beef Wellington and the lobster, and if I simplify the menu, I'm sure I can handle it. I have to do this party because she's threatened me with all kinds of crap including getting rid of our general manager. I don't have a choice."

"I'm not upset, just totally freaking out because it's so

senseless. Why in God's name would you do her party if you don't have to? You think Chuck or the IRS are interested in the food you bring over to your neighbors? They'll give you a slap on the wrist, a fine and be done with you. What I'm worried about is you two idiots, and I mean you and Dex, not you and Gaby because she knows exactly what she's doing, will never pull it off. That's a big job; I don't care that she turned me down, but she said she was going to get a second bid from Taste, what happened with that?"

"She never went to Taste. She knew she could offer me less and that I'd have to agree," I said. Then in my defense, added, "I need to learn how to do big parties anyway because I want to try to continue on as a caterer after I leave Forest. I'll call some agencies to find extra help. Please stay calm," I said, as I heard Linz's approaching footsteps.

"Girls," he said standing in the doorway, "everything okay in here? I heard some loud voices and Dina, I don't have to tell you how important it is for Wanda to stay calm."

"We're fine, honey," Wanda said, "just a difference of opinion."

"Well," said Dr. Freud, tapping his watch, "I think visiting hours are just about over."

"Linz, just give me two more minutes," I said, knowing I couldn't leave yet.

"Two minutes," he said, and went back to analyzing something or someone else.

I improvised the following lie:

Me: "Wanda, I don't know what's wrong with me. You're a hundred percent right – there's no way I can do this party. Let her do and say what she wants. I doubt she'll have Chuck fired; that's an empty threat. I'll stick to what I know I can do."

Wanda: "Thank God, because you would have bombed. You'd need an enormous amount of food, and remember, you're not Jesus, so your cloves and fishes (no self-correcting going on) aren't going to multiply by themselves. And I wouldn't worry about losing other clients; they'll understand."

Me: "I'm so glad we talked about this, although I could have used the eight thousand bucks, that's what she offered."

Wanda: "Even with a different menu you'd probably cover your costs, but since you've decided not to go ahead, it's a mute point."

Me: "I get it. Now listen up, sweetie, because I'm going to tell you something epic, but first I must swear you to secrecy."

Wanda: "Go."

Me: "Gaby's real name is Gertrude."

Wanda: Nothing, because with all the laughing, she finally had to get up to pee.

Chapter 29

January/February/March

January

hen Dex stopped by later that afternoon I shared the news about Wanda's reaction and my grand prevarication. "I won't spill the beans, but I don't understand why she didn't go along with it. We have plenty of planning and prep time, and you already have the name of a new agency for extra help. Wanda'll make up for not getting the booking once she gets back to work. I can understand if she thought we were going with Gaby's original menu, but you'll talk her into this new one, which looks sensational," he said, holding up my notebook. "This is nothing for a couple of old pros like us."

"Wanda was getting upset, and her husband was giving me the evil eye so I had to tell her I was going to back down from the party. Wanda called us idiots to have accepted it in the first place. Are we?"

"Probably, but not about this. Listen, you won't have to tell her you accepted the job until after the baby is born. We're going to do this party, and it's gonna be incredible. Old Gertrude'll be riding high on the hog when we're done with her. Now, what do we have going on for the weekend?" said my biggest fan.

Chuck half pretended he knew nothing of my catering services, but he couldn't have known that Gaby's threat still hung over my head. I was sure she'd make good on it if I canceled her party.

February
Since Forest held a beautiful Valentine's Day dinner dance, I only had one booking that night for a recently married couple who wanted a romantic catered evening for two.

Residents traditionally had a lot of company during President's Day week and this year was no exception. Business was slow for me because visitors wanted to sightsee and eat out, or sit by the club's Olympic-sized pool and help themselves to the barbeque available all day long. No one wanted to stay home.

Portia's breakfasts and dinners were my bread and butter money for February, and I managed to scrape by to pay a portion of the new assessment just handed down to residents. Mark's check arrived on time, which helped, but aside from that we had no communication.

I gave a baby shower for Wanda, which was held in her living room. Linz set her up on the sofa and I prepared a beautiful luncheon for twenty of her friends, most of whom I knew. The weather was cool and the girls welcomed the butternut squash soup I served as a first course. I topped it with some Greek yogurt and chopped chives, and followed it with Wanda's favorite dish: lobster ravioli in a simple tomato sauce finished with a dollop of sweet butter and fresh basil. There was plenty of green salad and fruit along with popovers that I baked at the last minute.

As my dearest friend opened her gifts, Linz wheeled in a sheet cake decorated with pink and blue ribbons, with the words: "Welcome Baby" squiggled on with yellow icing. He'd ordered the cake from Publix, and it couldn't have been a better finish to the day.

March

Wanda and Linz had their baby girl on March 15th, the exact day the doctor predicted, and a week later she was finally up and around tending to little Hailey Dina Blake. She hadn't told me they planned to use Dina as the baby's middle name and I felt even guiltier about withholding the truth about Gaby's party.

I was swamped with requests during March, the height of the season, when almost all snowbirds were in South Florida. It was before Passover and Easter, and a good time to get away from colder climates. Even those who only came down for a few weekends, or snowflakes as they were called, wanted some sort of catered party.

Word continued to spread like crazy ever since people received Gaby's "save the date" evites; I was in demand. Being hired so far in advance by Gaby was the acid test; I was not only back in the loop, I was in the hot, molten center.

When time permitted I played a round of golf with the girls. The pro at the shop knew I had a better than average handicap and matched me up with like players. We'd tee off at eight, and come in for lunch around noon – just like the old days – or actually, better than the old days. I still couldn't let my hair grow because of all the cooking, but Aaron painted on a few highlights and Marcy talked me into getting pink and white acrylic nails. I'd have to be careful not to let food get caught underneath them, but they did look beautiful. I was trying to live on Mark's monthly stipend and only dipped into my catering funds when necessary, except for the little luxuries I felt entitled to.

Chapter 30

April

Getting Closer

March came in like a hungry lion and continued on with a raging appetite into April. Although Winners Circle served a Passover Seder for over two hundred residents each of the two nights, I was able to book drop-offs for several holiday meals. I handled most of the cooking by myself as the first two nights of Passover were during the week and Dex was shorthanded at work with no time off to help. After the last drop-off, I prepared a mini-Seder, or Passover-lite as my mother called it, for Dex and me as we were both done for the day. Because Dex had split from the church he thought it'd be a good idea to learn more about Judaism.

"It's usually best if the parents are of the same religion, right? So, I'm going to look into classes and conversion once we're up in North Carolina," he said, while breaking up matzo.

"There's probably one or two temples in Winston, and Greensboro has a bigger Jewish population so we'll find you something," I said, glad that my intended was so concerned with our future. "But, it's really not necessary. I'm not all that religious."

"I know, but it's something else we'll have in common.

You know, we've only discussed marriage, what about kids? Were you and Mark going to have any?"

I couldn't bring myself to tell Dex about the negated plan to conceive the night Mark left. It was still painful.

"We were going to start to try, but then put it off," I said, knowing he wouldn't delve into the reasons.

"I'd love to have a baby with you," Dex said, looking so deeply into my eyes that I dropped the potato pancakes back down on the platter and grabbed him around his waist. "Hey, my latkes!"

"They can wait, I can't."

Dex, the mind-reader, led me to the bedroom.

I dropped off food for five Easter brunches and aside from maneuvering a few hams in and out of the oven, it went smoothly. These were family affairs and didn't require service. I set up food on counters or buffets, and told my clients I'd be back in the evening to clean up and collect any platters and dishes that weren't theirs. The day went so well that they all asked to be scheduled for the following year. Not wanting to reveal my pretty-sure plans of moving, I agreed and took the bookings for 2012.

When I walked through the clubhouse I was hailed with affectionate greetings and no one cared that I was running a full-blown business out of my house. Although I'd done a vast quantity of events during the last few months, none were larger than thirty or forty people, with a top-billing price of five thousand dollars. I kept track of all my expenses and fees in case I had to establish a business in a hurry.

I'd be giving a much more elaborate party for Gaby's hundred guests and there was no way I could let any of my loyal clients find out what she was paying. Even though

Gaby was cordial, we were still on shaky ground. As far as she knew, Forest was my home and her soirée would serve to put me over the top.

I was in love with Dex, but Mark and I had a fifteen-year history that made its way into my mind at times. Since he had no plans to return to our marriage I gave my attorney a retainer to start working on the divorce papers. Mark and I were over. I wanted a new life with Dex, a man who'd never leave me for another woman.

I finally discussed my catering business with France during one of our conversations, but only mentioned a slight possibility of a move north. Today's talk was much like every other one we've had in the past six months.

"Dina, there's no reason for you to stay in an expensive country club anymore because even though it was a great place for you and Mark and Mark's business, he's gone and he's not coming back, unless you're still holding out for that, which you shouldn't be, so you need to think about moving," said France.

If Wanda was the queen of malaprops, my sister was the empress of run-on sentences.

"I know he spoke to Redmond a while back, and there's zero chance that either one of us wants to reconcile; it's just easier for me to stay here till the end of June. Then we'll see," I said.

Even with the difference of a decade between France and me, we've always been close, and spoke or Skyped several times a week. She was pleased that I was making my own money and encouraged me to think about it as a long-term career.

"You know, sweetie, with Redmond's wine business

193

and my gallery, we could give you bunches of recommendations, and the people are so wonderful in this town,
and I bet Priscilla could find plenty of help if you need
it; she's doing so well over at Blums, so doll, think about
moving up here because we'd love to have you near us, and
Mom and Dad are usually here almost half a year so we'd
be together a lot and they'd for sure fly up for Thanksgiving and Christmas if you were here," she said, all in one
breath.

"I promise I'll consider it. Even if Mark came back,
which I wanted at one point, we wouldn't be able to stay at
Forest any longer. The club just issued another assessment,
and being house poor isn't a great feeling. Mark's always
done all the money stuff, but believe me, I'm learning,"
I said.

"Good to know," said France. "So, what did you say
you had in the oven? Should I send you any more of those
country hams?" she said, hopping onto my favorite subject.

"I have a freezer full right now, so hold off. I have a ton
of shopping to do for one big party in May, and after that
I don't want to load up on things that I don't absolutely
need," I said.

"Got it, sis. Okay, I'm late because I told Pris I'd meet
her downtown for lunch. They haven't set a wedding
date yet, but let me tell you, Redmond and I lucked out
with her as a daughter-in-law and her family is wonderful
too, even if they did come over on the Mayflower and did
I tell you they love Harry and Stella? They're going to visit
them up in Asheville during the summer. Who woulda
thunk it."

I laughed at the thought of my mother sprinkling her

194

Yiddish like holy water over the Christian couple, but Stella was not without her charm.

"Mom has her ways, but I agree with you about Priscilla. I liked her a lot when they were here. She and Wes make a great couple, like you and Redmond," I said, choking up as I usually did when thinking about how I wanted that for Mark and me; growing old together and being one of those loving couples who held hands walking into the sunset.

"You okay? Are you getting weepy or just making up a list?" France said.

"I miss what Mark and I had," I said.

"Is it more that you miss being a couple, or that you miss Mark?" said my ever-sage older sister.

"Go meet Pris. I have some custard that's not going to caramelize itself. Don't worry; I'll be fine. Say hi for me," I said, putting an end to the discussion.

Wanda resumed her position with Platinum after the baby was born although none of her events were scheduled at Forest so she was still unaware that I had booked Gaby's party. The nanny Portia recommended was in love with the baby and even Linz was satisfied.

My regular clients knew they were getting bargain-rate prices compared to Platinum and Taste even though I still made substantial profits. No one dared ask Gaby what she was paying, and true to her word, she kept it between us. Still being the ringleader, Gaby made it clear that she preferred no big parties take place before hers.

I continued on with small luncheons and a few cocktail parties, but Gaby's snowbird party would certainly be the highlight of the season and a grand farewell to the departing winter residents. I was beginning to look forward to upping my repertoire and my status. It was important for me to go out with a bang and so far, everything was falling into place; I was proud of my upcoming accomplishment.

I was only able to secure two bartenders and eight waiters from a new local service, but no dishwashers. Even with Dex and me doing most of the cooking, I still needed one more chef. My biggest coup was getting André to agree to lend out a sous-chef from the club's kitchen.

It was important to speak with Chuck about it as well, to show respect for his position.

"As long as the sous-chef isn't working at the club that night, and if Chef André can spare someone, it's okay with me. Who'd you take?" said a very genial Chuck. Every couple of weeks I stopped by his office to drop off a cherry strudel or his favorite caramel cake, but the day I presented him with two jars of fresh fig preserves, I knew I had him in my pocket.

"Maximilian," I said.

"Oh, yeah, the guy with one name. They seem to be pleased with him, he's new, you know, but André checks out anyone coming to work in his kitchen. Uh, you couldn't get Keisha? She's been here since we opened," said Chuck.

"Chef André checked his schedule and said I was lucky to get anyone for Memorial Day weekend."

Another important triumph was convincing Gaby to accept a simpler menu.

I called her on the pretense of going over a few details, but had my coup in place. We arranged to meet at Bar None explaining that I couldn't spare time during the day.

We met at five and ordered two glasses of Italian Prosecco.

"Thanks for meeting me at this hour, are you hungry? I could get us a plate of the appetizers," I said, pointing to the little ribs, wings and everything that could possibly be deep-fried that the residents were filling up on.

"Are you kidding? I don't eat that crap and I can't believe you do either. I mean, you have a figure like a boy but at least you're slim, and you didn't get that way by eating junk," she said. "If you're hungry, just order something."

"Oh, not really, I'm fine with the nuts," I said, popping one into my mouth to prove the point.

"Now, why are we meeting? Marty and I have dinner plans at seven and I've got to get home to change, so what's up?"

"Well, I thought maybe you'd like to review an alternate menu. I'm just afraid if you serve all that fattening, unhealthy food like the garbage over there that your guests won't be too happy about it. I mean it's okay to have one special item like a nice sliced steak, (Was I pushing those sliced steaks or what?) but to have three heavy, caloric entrées – I just don't see it, particularly when I can do other things that'll hold up better at room temperature.

People watch their weight around here; that's why the gym is packed all the time. I know I'm flat-chested (come on, I was a full A-cup), but I still have to run a couple of miles whenever I have the time or my stomach would be out to here," I said, holding my hands out to exaggerate an imaginary gut.

"And, I can still do those baby lamp chops you wanted, that's only one bite and all the fat will be trimmed." I knew there were at least a dozen racks in my freezer that I'd gotten on sale because they were always a hit, and along with some less expensive hors d'oeuvres, there'd be plenty of food being passed before the guests hit the more substantial items. "Would you like to review a different menu? I made some notes," I said, pulling out a sheaf of papers.

"Well, I want people to think that I care about health and nutrition, like at Marcy's party, and I don't want them stuffed to the gills even though they are snowbirds," she said, laughing at her own joke. "Let me hear what you can do."

"I'll be honest. The Beef Wellington has to go because I've never even made it, but I know it won't stand up well. What's always popular is a nicely carved whole filet mignon or boneless sirloin. I'll make a couple of sauces to go with it – horseradish and maybe something with whole grain mustard. Then you really need a fish dish so I was thinking about sides of salmon poached or roasted with dill, and some herb-grilled free-range chicken tenders with my special mango-lime chutney."

"What else," said Gaby, not unkindly.

"I make a really delicious low-fat vegetable lasagna, and a seafood paella. Those are all wonderful buffet items and there won't be any experimentation. This is a special party for both of us and it has to be perfect," I said, laying it on as heavily as possible.

"What about salad?" she said, "Wanda was giving me a Caesar."

"A Caesar? Are people still doing that? (Tsk, tsk, I almost added.) What about a nice chopped salad that's easier to manage, and then some grilled balsamic vegetables and an assortment of rolls and focaccia," I said, knowing I'd have to cheat on the bread items because all that dough preparation would eat up too much time. I'd order it all from Publix and no one would be the wiser. There was no reason to reveal the slight deception because I was going great guns now.

Leaning in for the kill, I said, "and your guests will be treated to a fantastic feast and you'll be hailed as Forest's supreme hostess."

"Cut the shit, Dina, what about dessert?" she said, not buying my award-winning performance.

"Gaby, you'll have to trust me here, but that's the time people can go a little crazy. There'll be cut up fruit in a watermelon basket, but I'll also do something chocolate, and a few other goodies. I'm a master baker and no one's ever turned down my desserts."

"Since you're really not a professional, I didn't think you could make the first menu so this is fine. But it's also cheaper and don't forget, you're not supplying liquor or wine, Marty and I have plenty of booze on hand, so I'm cutting your fee to six thousand. You already have four and I'll give you a check for the balance after the party. We done here?" said Gaby.

"Yes," I said, discouraged at the thought of losing two thousand dollars, but she had a point; the new menu was a little cheaper, but more importantly, far less time consuming and totally doable.

"Good," she said, signing the check for the two glasses of wine. "I'm sure you'll still make a nice profit. You might want to think about getting implants; you're not tall enough to carry off that non-figure of yours."

Chapter 31

April

Tough Times

Now that Wanda was back at work full time, we met for lunch where she took a couple of verbal swings at me. We decided on Sazio's on Atlantic Avenue because they had a nice people-watching patio and scrumptious sandwiches.

"Dina, I know you're doing Gaby's party," she said, as soon as we were seated. "You didn't think you could keep it a secret, did you?"

"I'm sorry. I wanted you to hear it from me, but you were so upset the day I visited and Linz was angry…"

"Forget all that. I'm going to suggest something to help you out because despite your lying to me I still love you and don't want you to get creamed. Turn Gaby's party over to me. I'll ask Platinum to match your price even if it means losing my commission and I'll try to throw you some cash. Even with a new menu and everyone you're hiring, there's just no way you can do it. You don't have the experience of managing all that food and help. Who'd you even come up with for that weekend?" she said.

I ran through my options before answering her:

1. Turn it over to her?

2. Maybe before the new menu was accepted I would have.

3. It was all under control now.

4. I was no jackass off the street.

5. I knew what I was doing.

"I called that new agency down on Palmetto, and they're sending me six servers plus two bartenders. (I wanted eight, but they only had six signed on so far and the manager swore they were top-notch.) It'll do just fine. It's a buffet, not a sit-down. I know you use one per ten, but frankly, I think you're bamboozling your clients for a few extra bucks," I said, taking a chance that she wouldn't blow up at my accusation.

"You think I would pad my quote to a client? Listen, Platinum has been around for twenty years, and I've been with them for ten. Do you think they've built their solid reputation on overcharging? We make our profit on food. If a meal costs twenty, we bill it out at sixty, which covers buying, cooking and other expenses. We pay chefs, servers and rentals separately. If we didn't do it that way we'd go bankrupt, the way you probably will with this deal, but, on the other hand, if she's paying you eight, you'll probably break even if you don't self-destruct," said Wanda, motioning for the waiter to approach.

"Six," I said, waiting for the roof to cave in had we been sitting inside.

"Yes, you said six servers; I was talking about your price."

"Six thousand dollars," I said, just as our server appeared with menus.

Wanda waved him away.

"I guess you just don't care that you're killing the business for the rest of us. While you and Dex trot off to the Carolinas, your discounted rate will be all over town and we'll have to fight for every booking or lose money. I never thought I'd say this, but I'm glad you're going to be leaving. You have no idea of what you're getting yourself into. Have you even seen Platinum's kitchens? Do you know that we set up ovens and grills in the client's garage to finish off the pre-cooked food? Did you think you were going to do all that in Gaby's kitchen?" she said. "And the worst part is that you have no respect for my opinion or advice or our friendship, and that's what hurts the most."

I didn't answer for a minute, but I think it was pretty clear that I hadn't considered any of what she just mentioned. Normally, I prepped at home and finished the meals in the client's kitchen, but a hundred guests was a lot different than thirty.

"Wanda, I do respect you, but I hoped you'd be happy for me and not so discouraging. I didn't mean to say you were cheating your clients; I'm just doing it my way and so far it's working. If I leave Boca, which is ninety-nine percent sure, then you and Taste can go on charging your outrageous prices and the clients won't have a choice. Now, before the waiter gets dizzy from going back and forth I'd like to order," I said, putting an end to the unpleasant conversation.

"Go ahead. I'll get mine at the counter to go. Good luck. Just remember, what goes around can come back and bite you in the ass," she said, her expression misused but stinging nonetheless.

I just didn't understand her reasoning:

1. How could Wanda be upset at my success even though I might lose money on the deal?

2. Was Wanda being just a little selfish and maybe even jealous that I'd scored this party?

3. Taste was her major competition, not me.

4. By the time my big gig was over I'd be packing to leave.

5. I'd let Wanda cool off and then straighten it all out.

Gaby agreed to meet with me one morning at the Bagel Oasis to go over the final plans.

"Dina, I didn't mean to give you a hard time when we first booked the party. I'm really looking out for your own good. You know, there are lots of singles moving into Forest, you could stay here even if your husband doesn't come back. What do you hear from him these days," she asked.

"Well, we're in touch, but no decisions just yet," I said, hoping to end the discussion about my personal life. "I do love Forest and I've gotten to know more women in the past six months than during the ten years Mark and I lived here. I guess I could stay on by myself now that I'm making my own money." I wasn't ready to share my plans about making the break from the country club scene.

I could make it on my own, but not here. When we sold the house and split the proceeds, I'd have enough to start a new life, especially with Dex. I'd no longer have to depend on Mark's monthly checks, or do his bidding.

All those years I cooked for my husband's clients seemed so second nature at the time:

1. I was his helpmate even if others felt he was taking advantage of me.

2. Mark was the controlling factor in our marriage, but hadn't he given me love and nurturing during our time together?

3. Was I rationalizing our former relationship?

4. Maybe most things looked better in retrospect.

5. Like my marriage.

Being with Dex made me realize how happy I could be with someone who was truly an equal partner. When we cooked together it was for love – love of creating something that people would enjoy, and sheer appreciation of each other's skills and willingness to learn.

I finally made friends at Forest and even though we might not keep in touch, I was pleased to know that people really did care about me, and not just the free dinners they used to have when Mark was around. The general feeling was that Mark had used me to gain financially, and even though I'd done it willingly, maybe they had a point. Now even Gaby seemed concerned about my welfare and because she accepted the changes to the menu I was fully confident that I could pull it off.

"Dina, there you go again," said Gaby, snapping her fingers two inches from my nose. "Stop thinking about your boyfriend and pay attention. Now, for the money I'm paying you I expect the proper amount of help. I don't want my guests slicing that filet themselves," she said, with just a trace of hostility.

"No worries, I already hired a sous-chef, two bartenders and six servers." I said.

"Six? I thought I told you Platinum uses one per ten guests. Why are you skimping on help?"

"It's not skimping. Do you really think you need one server for ten people? Isn't that a bit over the top? Why do you think Platinum's quote was so high?" I said taking a shot at Wanda's M.O.

"Maybe you're right about that; just make sure they're well trained."

"Oh, don't worry. There's a brand new agency down in east Boca and they only deal with top employees," I said, not really making it up; I was just paraphrasing the agency's manager. There was no reason not to trust someone who just opened a new business in South Florida. The manager had even accepted a cash deposit when I told him my business checks weren't ready yet. Imagine that.

"I know we didn't discuss this before, but we're going to need rentals; long tables for the buffet, cloths, china, dinner and dessert napkins (thank you, Sammy) plates – all that stuff. I can also get extra seating and small bistro tables from Acorn so your guests won't have to be standing all night. Do you mind if I ask Sammy to meet with us? Once he sees the space he'll know exactly what to order."

"Good idea, but tell him to shove his lame fifties-style pick up lines," said Gaby.

"Well, I can't deny that he likes the ladies, but he keeps it above board. I'll tell him no funny stuff. He's a good egg," I said, trying not to laugh because Gaby was definitely not his type. Although there was no denying her beauty even with the spread-out hips, she had none of the sweetness that Marcy or Mary Lou did.

"Marty is about all I can handle; Sammy is so barking up the wrong tree if he tries anything with me," she said flipping aside her streaked and straightened hair that might have had extensions woven in.

"Not a problem, he'll be on his best behavior. I'd like to set up a meeting as soon as possible because it's going to be a busy weekend all around and I need to put in reserves. Would Tuesday around ten in the morning work?"

"That's fine and the rentals are included in your price, right?"

"Honestly? No. I forgot about it when you first asked me to do your party," I said, hoping she'd rise to the occasion. She didn't. I had a small cushion when she was paying me eight; now I'd be in a hole with Wanda shoveling in dirt.

"I don't want people eating on my sofas, or even standing on my Persian rugs, so I guess we better order plenty of seating. We can set up those small tables and chairs – the ones like you did for Marcy – in the rotunda, and some on the patio if the weather is nice. So, plan on about ten tables in all with four chairs at each. I have plenty of room outside and the tables I have out there can mix in with the bistro sets," Gaby said.

"Okay, I'll set it up for Tuesday morning. You'll have a beautiful party, I promise," I said, with a heavy touch of sadness to my voice.

"Oh please, I can't stand that hang-dog (puppy dog!) look of yours. I'll give you another thousand for the rentals when I pay the balance," she said.

Gaby ate the second half of her bagel piled high with cream cheese. I could just imagine Portia, who was sitting on the other side of the room, saying how that was headed directly to her hips. Portia told me to turn down the party and not get involved in the holiday weekend date for Gaby, but I had to make my own decisions, even if I was losing money on the deal.

Gaby was cordial to me this morning. She could have gotten away without paying the extra thousand, but I think she enjoyed her role as the generous doyenne of Forest. Mark had tried for years to procure their business, but Gaby and her husband were tied into their own financial guy who'd done so well for them that they had no reason to change although that didn't stop them from accepting dinner invitations to our home.

Marty and Gaby were perceived as the power couple, and were revered by almost every resident, as well as the executive staff. They'd made an arrangement when they turned the club over to the homeowners that their golf, tennis and social equities were to be gratis. Although they paid dues for our amenities, no one ever questioned the tens of thousands the Lofts saved by not purchasing the equities that were required by anyone else moving into Forest.

Most country clubs in Boca call for residents to buy into the social membership, but tennis and golf are usually optional. You had to credit the Forest developers with their foresight of making the three equities a requirement. In order to keep the course and courts in top condition we all paid a shockingly high amount of dues. The state-of-the art gym and spa were part of the social buy-in, as was the use of the restaurants.

Under the guidance of Chuck Wilkins, our general manager, residents were proud to say they lived in the best country club South Florida had to offer.

Was the snob appeal worth the expense for me? At one time it was.

"Dina back to earth please," said Gaby, in her domineering voice. "I've got to get going, but let me just say how happy I am that we're going to be working together."

Another long pause, but not a dismissive one, alerted me that there was more coming.

"You've become very popular with the girls and, of course, the men love the food and the fact that they're using the homes they overbuilt. Not that I'm complaining, mind you. Marty and I made a fortune off people's need to impress with their five bedroom homes when they didn't even have kids yet, but who am I to talk. You could fit a small army in our upstairs guest quarters, but that was all Marty's idea. I would have been happier with something like yours, cozy and just big enough for two."

I took the left-handed compliment with a grin not bothering to mention that Mark and I had been thinking about raising a family in our cozy house.

"Well, luckily, the kitchen is great. Otherwise, there'd be no party for you or anyone else," I said, getting into the swing of things.

"That remains to be seen, but I'm sure you never would have accepted the assignment to do my snowbird party if you couldn't handle it," she said. Was she really oblivious to the frightful conditions she'd set forth? "I had to invite some of the year-rounders, so now everyone's talking about the party, and some of the girls practically worship you," said Gaby, her last words filled with false geniality.

So that was it.

1. Gaby had gotten on track because her gang liked me, and not just for lowering their golf scores, or dropping off freebies as I still occasionally did for good clients.

2. Her friends made it their business to get to know me and somehow our friendships affected Gaby.

3. Now she was the one who'd be left out instead of me if she continued to talk smack.

4. Did she give me the shot at her party to please the others even with intimidating the hell out of me?

5. I needed to find out.

"Gaby, before you take off, and I really want to thank you for the extra thousand, I'm curious about something. Why did you ask me to bid on the party? Everyone knows that Platinum and Taste specialize in big events and you can certainly afford them. Was it someone here who influenced you?" I said, immediately wishing I'd said suggested instead of influenced.

"Nobody, but nobody, influences me to do anything especially for some dumb-ass party for people who only want to see my house and drink my booze. Marty and I never entertain, we're the ones who are invited, and if we do have to take clients out Marty would never make me slave over a stove to try to lure them in. We take them to the club where I don't have to be jumping up and down every other minute. Face it, Dina, you had a real shit-heel for a husband," said Gaby, true to form, but not wrong.

"But I must say," she continued, "Marcy and the Chans mentioned I might want to give you a try because you did such a brilliant job for them. Now, of course, we weren't at the Chans, but Bailey told me her family went nuts for the food. And you know them, they think their you-know-what doesn't stink, all that Hong Kong money, but their families are in the luxury hotel business so I guess that qualifies them as food experts."

"Did you know their Uncle Tai used to be the head chef at the Peninsula Hotel in Hong Kong?" I said, trying out my own version of the Impressing Gaby Game.

"Uncle Tai? You mean that place down in Boca Center? Their uncle works there? And that's a big deal to you?" she said, misconstruing my statement.

"No, I said he worked at the Peninsula Hotel. Uncle Tai's restaurant here is great, but I doubt the Chan's uncle is doing stir-fries there," I said, hoping to pull a laugh out of my tablemate. I didn't.

"Anyway, I can't wait to tell Wanda that she's not the only game in town, and that her company better be more careful in the future with their crazy prices," said Gaby as I felt my stomach sink. "Ten servers; what a rip-off."

"I'd appreciate it if you wouldn't mention any specifics to Wanda," I said.

"Oh, for Christ sakes! You'd think this was the inauguration or something. Fine, I won't say anything to Wanda.

She's never even around here anymore. I guess you stole all her business at Forest."

"I doubt that, and she still gets lots of other bookings."

"Your friend better take off some of that weight in the meanwhile or she won't even be able to carry around her menu book. I only gained sixteen pounds with each of my pregnancies, and Rebecca and Emma are perfect, but, of course, I had them in my twenties."

Rebecca and Emma were thirteen and fifteen year old clones of their mother complete with highlights and Tory Burch flats, the kind that were never on sale.

"I don't know why you girls wait so long to have kids. Anyway, when Wanda was here to bid on the party she was already as big as a house, well maybe not my house, but you know what I mean. Your friend has a tendency to be heavy and if she doesn't watch it now, she'll balloon up," Gaby said.

Oh, how I wanted to mention those wide hips of hers. I'd known Wanda since grade school, and if she ever carried more than one thirty on her tall lithe frame, except for her pregnancy, it was news to me. I decided it was a good time to end our meeting before I said something I'd regret.

"Gaby, this has been really nice and I'm very grateful to you for understanding my circumstances," I said.

"Hey, sugar, take some advice from me; your husband's not coming back and if he does, it'll be to sell the house. His girlfriend's the only person I know who's richer than we are."

"Gaby, hold it a minute, just one more thing. Would you really have fired Chuck if I refused your party? I mean I'm glad the way it's all working out, but I did lose some sleep over that. Would you have?" I said.

"In a Boca minute, but you're doing the party so you don't have to worry about that anymore. Now, see that Sammy and you aren't late next week, and send me a reminder email later, and call right before you come," said her highness, picking up her monstrously large designer handbag and exiting the bagel room, but not before grabbing a few bagels from the buffet table on her way out.

Portia caught my eye and made a "so big" sign with her hands watching Gaby waddle out of the room. My one true laugh of the morning.

Chapter 32

April

Turning Point

Could things have been going any better for me? As luck would have it Gaby's party was called for a Sunday, so Dex and I had all day Saturday to prep. I did most of the shopping during the week and arranged all the pots, pans, racks and grills by the time Dex arrived Saturday morning.

Not wanting to make waves and because news travels faster than the speed of light (or sound?) throughout country clubs in South Florida, Dex never spent the night. There was plenty of love-making going on during the day whenever he had time in between deliveries, and every night we shared several hours in the hottest, most passionate embraces. I guess I was getting back at my husband by having sex in our marriage bed, but that was more for practical reasons rather than revenge.

The guest room was filled with everything Mark no longer needed from his office; now five stainless carts and two standing racks rested comfortably in his former business space.

By eleven in the morning Dex had seared the chicken, and rolled and tied the filets, which would be roasted the day of the party. I made all the accompanying sauces and assembled the vegetable lasagnas. I don't like preparing fish the day before it's to be served, so I left it wrapped in the coldest part of the fridge. What I hadn't realized was how much prep was left for the day of the party. Sliced vegetables would turn brown and salads would wilt if made ahead of time. Even the paella had to be put on hold because of all the shellfish (no oysters) I would add.

"Let's go to Publix, at least we can pick up the breads; they'll hold a day and you can always warm them up," Dex said.

"I ordered them for tomorrow; I thought we'd be done with everything else today so I left it plus they're never the same the next day," I said, becoming alarmed at my non-progress.

What was I thinking?

1. Why the hell did I suggest a seafood paella? Did I really think it would be any less messy than the original lobster tails Gaby wanted?

2. Was there enough food?

3. Was there too much food?

4. Would I lose more money than planned?

I assumed those scary thoughts were only in my head, but I'd actually listed them aloud.

"Don't worry! The lasagnas are filling; you have mounds of snack stuff and a lot of desserts. And you're sure about the sous-chef from the club tomorrow, right? And, most important, I'll be here every step of the way. We could start earlier if you let me stay over, but okay, I won't go there now. Come on, the menu is all easy stuff. The paella may take a little time, but nothing is difficult about it," said Dex, picking up my spirits. "What time did you tell the servers to get here tomorrow?"

"They're meeting me at Gaby's at six. That gives them an hour to set up and help us with details before the guests arrive. One bartender can set up inside and the other on the patio near the pool. They're all experienced; it won't take them long and I'm paying them by the hour.

I know Wanda tells them two hours in advance, but her clients believe everything she says and I'm working on a tight budget. And why would it take two hours? Those people are either taking advantage of her, or she's hiring the wrong employees," I said, rationalizing my hostile feelings toward Wanda.

"Well, I guess you have a point, but Wanda's been doing her job for a long time; maybe you shouldn't be penny wise," Dex said.

"Oh please. Now I have to hear advice from you? I think I've learned a thing or two this past year and Gaby's party is going to go off glitch-free and the damn servers better do their job in an hour," I said, practically screaming at Dex.

"Whoa, hold it! It was just a suggestion. You and I should be there by five to orchestrate everything and we'll let the sous-chef set things up in Gaby's kitchen," Dex said.

"I'm sorry, you're right. I didn't mean to take it out on you. It's just that Wanda gave me hell for doing the party; she has no confidence that I can pull it off. Can you imagine this – she asked me to turn the party over to Platinum for whatever the price was and she'd do it as a favor. Not

215

that I'd even consider that, but then when I told her I was getting six thousand she went ballistic. Said I was screwing every professional in the business, and then she picked up and left," I said, almost crying.

"Sshh, baby, you'll make it up with her."

"We haven't spoken since our fight; I figured I'd wait till after the party," I said, my nose up in the air.

"I see, so you can lord it over her how you pulled off the most successful party of the season without her help. That doesn't sound like you," said Dex, "that's not what a friendship is all about. I think you should give her a call."

"Why does everyone think they have to tell me what to do? Don't you think I've been through enough? My parents are driving me nuts, my brother-in-law knows more about my future than I do, and now my best friend hates me and my boyfriend is a royal pain in the ass. Oh, in case I forgot to mention it, my husband left me for a twenty-year old and it doesn't look like he's coming back home," I said.

The silence in my kitchen was deafening.

"So, I'm going to take that to mean that you're still waiting for him and that our plans are tentative and secondary," said Dex, his arms crossed.

"Oh shit! I don't know what I mean. Of course, I'm not waiting for that shit-heel – Gaby's words, not mine – of a husband of mine to return, but I have this party to get through, and Gaby'll fire Chuck if it's not right…"

"What are you talking about? I told you she'll never fire Chuck; that was just some ruse of hers to bulldoze you into doing a cheap party. Chuck knows what you're doing, he and Marty have lunch in the club all the time. So even though she bullied you, you'll have the last laugh because you have me on your team, and if that's not a winning combination I don't know what is."

"Thanks for the pep talk, but as Gaby says: cut the shit," I said.

"So now you're quoting her? I have an idea. Let's go have something to eat and we'll order Bloody Marys and relax a little bit," said Dex, "there's nothing else we can do here today."

"Great idea, only no thanks. If I have a Bloody Mary I won't be able to function for the rest of the day. The only time I have a real drink (not counting the bath-vodka night) is when Wanda and I celebrate our birthdays, and now she'll probably never even share a sandwich with me again," I said, starting to cry because I really felt sorry for myself. "And last time I had a bunch of martinis she had to drive me home and there was a cute young waiter who thought I was hot, and that was the day Wanda told me she was pregnant and we were supposed to have our babies at the same time like the Chans and…"

"Dina, stop! I'd slap you, but I'm afraid you'd slap me back. Snap out of it. What are you going on about? What the hell do you care when the Chans have kids? Okay, so you don't want a drink, but I sure as hell do. Will you please go out for something to eat with me? Maybe your blood sugar is low because I've never seen you like this."

"Low blood sugar? Seriously, you're saying that? Are you psychotic? I'm pouring out my heart to you, and you tell me I have some sort of insulin resistant condition, and that's the right term by the way because I heard it on Dr. Oz," I said, well, actually screeched.

"Okay, I've seen this kind of drama before and it's time for me to get out of Dodge. Oh, don't worry, I'll be back. I'm not going to leave you in the lurch like your husband did. I'll be here early tomorrow morning so you can do the baking and I'll finish up everything else, as planned," Dex said, with a hard edge to his voice.

"Dex, aren't we going to make love?" I said, trying to massage the situation and not wanting to give up the prospect of a few orgasms.

"You've got to be kidding. No thanks, Dina. Why don't you take this time and think about our relationship, and what you'd do if Mark called to say he wanted to reconcile. You need to come to some conclusions. I love you, and we can live in Boca or North Carolina, but I'm not going to hang around while you're on tenterhooks waiting to hear from your ex who dumped you," said Dex. "I'm going over to that flatbread place in the Polo Shoppes, DD something, and that's where I'll be if you care to join me."

He started walking to the front door when I recalled something he'd just let slip.

"Dex, hold it a second. What did you mean before when you said you'd seen this before? Seen what?" I asked.

"The drama. If you must know, when I ended my relationship with Sue-Ellen she went a little crazy, starting yelling her head off about how I wasted the best years of her life and that she told all her friends that we were going to get married; I couldn't get through to her just like I couldn't with you before."

"Well, you were together for years," I said. "I really can't blame her."

"We were never engaged. I never asked her to marry me because I was never in love with her. I told you we met in that support group and helped each other through a hard time. Her fiancé died in a horrific car accident and I guess she was looking for someone to take his place. It was never me, but, well, we became friends with benefits, and I hate to use that term, but that's all it was."

"I guess that it was more for her if she thought you were going to marry her," I said.

"Dina, I swear, I never led her on. I rarely stayed over at her place and even told her to date so she could find the right man. She agreed that we should see other people, but we still ended up in bed a couple of times a week. I stopped it when I started seeing those bridal magazines around her condo, and she had a bunch of pictures of me that she put up on a bulletin board. It was a little freaky so I told her I was moving on and that I'd actually met someone – that was you – who I was falling in love with.

That's when she started another rant against me. I tried to calm her down, but she was beyond listening to reason. I left and haven't spoken to her since."

"But you told me you guys were still friends," I said.

"I lied," said Dex. "You and I were just beginning and I didn't think you needed to hear all that sturm und drang. I take a lot of the blame even though I never made any promises to her; I guess she assumed our relationship was more than it was."

"So whatever happened to her? Are you in touch at all?" I said, my curiosity getting the better of me, and I sort of wanted to find out her cup size.

"I did call her brother because I was concerned that Sue-Ellen had gotten so enraged and almost seemed delusional. I met Ryan a couple of times when the three of us would go out for pizza. It was kind of a strange conversation I had with him because he took my side. I was afraid the guy would defend her honor and beat the crap out of me or whatever guys do these days, but he said that she had a history of psychological problems and that he'd talk to her – you know, spend time together until it blew over. He said he'd get her back into counseling."

"Wow, sounds like a nice guy. I'm sorry, Dex. I promise I'm normal, but you did ask me to marry you, right?" I said, trying to lighten the mood.

"Yes, I did and I meant it, but you have to be sure that I'm the one you want to be with," said my boyfriend, who looked better than ever.

"I'm sure, sweetheart. Let me grab a sweater. I'd be happy to join you – in a glass of Sangria because D.D. Flats doesn't have a full liquor bar – and if you'll come back here afterwards and make love to me," I said in my most alluring post-polyp voice.

"But of course, my dear, and you know, you almost sounded like Lauren Bacall."

Bingo.

Chapter 33

May

Atlantic Avenue

After Saturday's lunch we took a ride to the beach and just hung out most of the day. We walked along downtown Delray's Atlantic Avenue stopping into a few art galleries and then settled in at Couture Cupcake, the latest in cute hotspots where we ordered coffee and red velvet minis. Sitting outside at one of the metal tables I felt so content that when Dex licked off a bit of frosting clinging to my upper lip I wasn't even embarrassed. In a fit of laughter I hopped out of my wrought-iron chair and sat on his lap giving him a big kiss and tousling his hair.

Although sex had always been good between Mark and me, he was never outwardly affectionate. Having grown up in a household without brothers or sisters, and feeling unwanted by his parents he didn't have much practice at being loving. France and I grew up in a happy home with hugs and kisses given out like candy at Halloween. Even our father, who wasn't much on words, never left the house without telling all three of us that he loved us and couldn't wait to get home for dinner. Mom, although more of a worrier, was the same.

I was happy to see that my nephew inherited the love

gene and was so attentive to Priscilla. I'd accepted Mark's standoffish ways holding his parents at fault, and the times I tried to hug him in public just made him uncomfortable. I wondered how Taffie, as part of Gen X, Y or Z, coped with his cool demeanor.

"Come on, let's take a walk up on Pineapple Grove," Dex said pulling me to my feet. "I wanna pick up a few mysteries for the guys."

"The guys who work for you?" I said.

"Yeah, I do that once in a while, just a little extra. They seem to enjoy reading mystery books and I like to support the store."

"Murder on the Beach? I love that place! I took a couple of writing courses after *Gourmet* let me go right before they went out of business. You know, I have their last issue. It was the Thanksgiving one with some terrific recipes. I still make that pumpkin-gingerbread trifle. Funny thing is that no one knew they were going under and the last issue even had subscription cards inside. Actually, it was sad because I loved writing my column even if it wasn't for a lot of money. *Bon Appetit* was our biggest competitor and they're good also, just different."

"So, why didn't you get a job for them? I bet they would have hired you," he said.

"They might have, but by 2009 I was up to my neck with having people coming over for dinner all the time, and Mark wanted me to concentrate on that. I should have kept working, I mean for a salary, because then I wouldn't be in such a tight spot now," I said, trying not to complain.

"Well, I think you should stick to catering and that's a

little selfish of me, but I like doing it together. It's a kind of closeness I never had with anyone else."

"Me neither, sweetheart. Hey, here we are," I said as we reached the intimate mystery bookstore.

"Be right there," we heard someone call out from the stock room.

"That's Joanne, she runs the place," said Dex.

"Hey Dex," said Joanne coming up to the counter. "I had a feeling you'd be stopping by, I put some books aside for you."

"Uh, thanks. Joanne, this is Dina Marshall."

"Hi Dina, nice to meet you. You look familiar. Where do I know you from?" said Joanne.

"Actually from here. I took a couple of your writing workshops."

"Oh, that's right; your hair is shorter now, it looks cute," she said.

"Thanks," I said, admiring her long blond locks. "It's easy for me because I'm in the catering business." I was now so proud of my status that I announced it to anyone who was within range.

"Oh, cool. I have some murder mysteries with a caterer at the helm. Interested in seeing those?" she said.

"Sure, throw the latest one into the mix. The guys know I like to cook; now they can get the scoop. Thanks, Joanne," Dex said, squeezing my hand.

On the way back to the car we took a scenic walking route and passed by a few cute village homes, a far cry from the fancy country club I lived in.

"I was planning to move up here before you came into my life," I said.

"Let's talk about housing another time because someone said something about making love this afternoon," he said.

"Uh huh, that was me," I answered and we took off.

It was close to four by the time Dex pulled his convertible into my driveway. He left the books in the car and followed me into my bedroom where we made love for hours. All thoughts of Mark dissolved and left my body as Dex held me in his arms. For the moment I couldn't even think of moving, but as we hadn't eaten since mid-day, except for the miniscule cupcakes, I suggested a quick bite.

"You stay here, I'll call you when it's ready," I said, kissing his neck.

"Okay, thanks. I'll just close my eyes for a few minutes."

I whipped up a couple of soufflé omelets and tossed together a tomato and green bean salad. The granite table seemed too heavy and serious for people in love, so I set our plates on the counter and pulled up two bar stools.

"I put on this terry robe," Dex said as he came into the kitchen. "Hope that's okay."

"Of course. It's from the spa, one of my previous extravagances. You look cute. Come on, sit down, the omelets will be right out," I said.

"Out of where?"

"The oven. I whipped the whites and folded them into the yolks; added a little cheese, some parsley and then stuck the pans in a hot oven. They'll puff up in a minute," I said.

"Hmm, I can see getting used to this," he said.

We ate side by side and the degree of comfort we had with each other was off the charts.

"Leave the dishes. I'm still hungry," said Dex, as he led me back to the bedroom.

1. We made love until exhaustion set in.

2. Dex got his wish.

3. A sleepover.

Chapter 34

Countdown

Sunday, May 29th, 10:00 am: "Holy shit! Dex! Get up! It's almost ten and we have all that work to do," I said, jumping out of bed.

"Oh my God, how did we sleep so late? I've got to pick up the van and get back here to help you prep. I'll stop for the bread at Publix on my way," he said, pulling on his clothes. "I'd like to stay and take a shower with you, or without you, but I'll do that at home. See ya later, baby, I love you."

"Love you too," I called out after him.

I took a quick shower, washed my hair, which would air dry, and blessed the inches I'd cut off several years ago. I made the bed, threw on some work clothing and headed to the kitchen.

Before I was fully awake I filled the Keurig; we'd be needing it. There seemed to be a funny smell in the kitchen, but it was probably my sinuses acting up. The poor things weren't used to such heavy duty kissing.

I'd get a head start on the prep before Dex returned, and we'd be all ready to go way before five. The phone rang just as I was investigating the odor that permeated the room.

"Hi, Gaby," I said, "you set for tonight? It's going to be knockout!"

"Dina, don't be a cheerleader; just get the food right. I'm calling because Marty wants to know if you can make Swedish meatballs. I told him they were déclassé, but he told me to shove it and call and ask you."

"That shouldn't be a problem," I said, knowing that I had most of the ingredients on hand and could fudge the rest. "If you happen to have a chafing dish, just leave it out and I'll transfer the meatballs when I get to your house."

"Yeah, we have one somewhere. Some stupid wedding present that's never been used. Oh, wait, hold on a minute. What is it, hon? I'm on with Dina, yes, she can make the meatballs. You want what? You are absolutely ridiculous. Wait, Marty wants to speak with you," she said, and handed the phone to her husband.

"Dina, babe, how 'bout cocktail franks? Got any tucked away? Everyone always goes for those little devils even though they pretend it's beneath them to eat that crap," said Marty. You had to like the guy for being so down to earth. You had to love him for putting up with his wife.

Early on in my catering career Wanda told me to always have pigs in blankets available; not to be passed, but just kept in the client's kitchen.

"You'd be surprised how many people will come into the kitchen even though you don't want them there, and they'll all want some of those franks. Trust me, it starts the evening off on the right foot," she said, "it's comfortable food."

I took her advice and made them for the first few parties, but then didn't want the extra work and forgot about it until just now when Marty put in his request. I knew I still

227

had the little franks in the freezer, and I always kept frozen puff pastry on hand.

"No problem, Marty. I'll have them for you," I said, sniffing the air around me, like a hunting dog stalking its prey.

"Hey, thanks, doll. I know it's short notice so don't worry, I'll take care of you," he said before hanging up.

I stored baking sheets in Mark's old office, now my butler's pantry, and pulled out a couple. My convection ovens accommodated up to three trays at a time and because the fan kept the heat circulating, everything was evenly cooked. It was a real time saver and I'd have to remember to take the trays with me to Gaby's to reheat the extra hors d'oeuvres. The microwave would make the crust too soggy.

I began to acknowledge that Wanda had given me cause to rethink my abilities for this party. An extra oven set up in the garage would have been just what I needed to reheat rolls, hors d'oeuvres, and even the lasagnas. I knew Gaby had a double oven in her kitchen and we'd have to make do with that. I'd work on my apology to Wanda after the party.

Before doing anything else, I added the two items Marty requested to a list I'd started on my kitchen's blackboard so as not to forget anything, and so I'd do it all in order. Lists were my salvation.

After setting the trays down on the counter I went to the fridge to get the meatballs and franks out of the way and found the door open about three inches. Damn it, I'd forgotten to call the repairman to fix the gasket that had given me trouble before. I was always careful to slam the heavy door to make sure it was properly sealed, but obviously neglected to do that after taking out last night's dinner fixings.

1. Why didn't I shut it correctly?

2. Probably the same reason I hadn't stuck
   the dishes in the dishwasher.

3. I couldn't wait to get back to bed with
   Dex.

Most of the food was still cold as the door had only been open a couple of inches, so I proceeded as planned. The smell lingered, but at least I'd discovered the cause. It would clear out now that the fridge was shut properly.

Luckily, the freezer was tight as a drum and I pulled out the franks, pastry and some chopped meat. I didn't have the pork that the meatballs called for, but with all the other ingredients, no one would notice the difference.

12 noon: Even though the fridge was sealed shut now, the odor wouldn't give up. I tried to ignore it as I beat eggs for the meatballs, and rolled the pastry around the franks. I cheered up because everything was going according to my schedule, even without Dex. Where was he anyway? It was already noon and his job, for starters, was to chop the salad, slice up fruit and prepare the veggies.

1:00 pm: I grilled the baby rib lamb chops – oh, they were beauties, and would only need a minute to reheat at Gaby's. I worked on all the other appetizers before beginning my routine, but scrumptious, desserts. I stopped for lunch, not worrying about the time because Dex would be here any minute, although he hadn't answered my calls or texts, and we'd finish up together.

The smell wasn't so bad now or maybe my sinuses had gotten used to it.

2:00 pm: I poured my no-fail cheesecake batter into a professional size springform pan and slid it into the oven. I faked the next dessert by using a cake mix as the basis for the Chocolate, Chocolate-Chip Kahlua cake that was an all-time favorite. I prepared three of them and then started on the Key West Lime Pies.

Key West, where Mark and Taffie were wiling away their days on her boat. I hoped:

1. His patches dried up.

2. His wristbands fell off.

3. A shark ate both of them.

Squeezing those damn little limes took forever and I ended up mixing in lemon and orange juice because I was getting nervous about the time.

1. Was there a reason why I hadn't just used the bottled key lime juice from the supermarket?

2. I guess it was the same reason I hadn't ordered the damn pies from TooJays along with their Killer Chocolate Cake.

3. Were mine that much better that they had to be half-home-made? (No.)

4. Did Platinum make their own baked goods or did they farm it out? I never thought

to ask Wanda about that and it was too
late now.

I pulled out several batches of butter cookie dough from the stinky fridge and baked dozens of cookies. They looked so pale when I transferred them to wire racks that I decided to sprinkle on some granulated colored sugar I kept in the pantry. I hadn't used the sugar in a while, and it would add a touch of festivity to the otherwise plain cookies. They looked pretty now, and more importantly, they were ready; all two hundred of them. I transferred the cookies to cardboard boxes and one of my six servers would plate them at Gaby's.

Where was Dex? I called his cell again. No answer. He was supposed to cut up the fruit and arrange it in the watermelon basket.

Wait:

1. Did I buy the watermelon to make the basket out of?

2. No, I did not.

3. What was wrong with me?

4. I never forget easy stuff like that.

5. This was my brain on sex.

2:45 pm: Something was burning. I opened the oven to investigate only to find that the cheesecake batter had leaked out through the bottom of the springform pan, and there was no putting it back. I must have done something wrong with the recipe although it could have been the pan, but there was no time to figure it out. I still had the chocolate cakes going and the Key West Lime Pies only needed to bake for ten minutes. I always kept an assortment of loaf cakes in the freezer and I could dress those up.

1. Always.

2. Except for today.

I sent Dex another text asking him to pick up a couple of Tiramisus, cheesecakes and some petit fours at Publix when he got the bread.

3:15 pm: The off smell from the refrigerator had been replaced by the burnt-on smell of cheesecake batter, which I had to say was an improvement. I was moving right along, but I desperately needed help.

1. Could I call Wanda?

2. No, that was such a last resort it was unthinkable.

3. I could judge my level of panic by the amount of lists I was making.

4. High alert.

Even though my mother didn't have any of the cooking skills I needed, she would have helped organize the platters and trays, but she and Dad were already up at their Asheville condo for the season. She also would have questioned me about why there was no meat in the lasagna, ("What? No sausage? No chopped meat? Who calls that a lasagna?") and why was it that the kitchen didn't smell so good.

For a very brief moment I thought about putting out an S.O.S. call to Frosty who had the energy of a pack of preschoolers, but with her four-inch nails and six-inch stilettos, she'd be more of a terminator than an assistant.

Speaking of nails, I cursed my own pink and white acrylics. They looked like hell because I hadn't kept up with my fills, and now I had definite ridges between the nail bed and where the fake ones began. A couple of the tips were starting to lift so I grabbed some glue which Frosty told me had to be kept in the fridge and stuck them back down. There was that smell again...

Although I had urgent matters to attend to, the question on my mind at that particular moment was how did Frosty always manage to look so perfect? The only natural thing about her was the shock of snow-white hair fluffed up like meringue sitting on top of her head. Her face was pulled so tightly you could have danced the Flamenco on it. The end result wasn't bad, mind you; I just couldn't figure out how she kept it all going. At seventy-five, Frosty, the knockout, had already buried five husbands as she was fond of saying. I thought it sounded morbid, but Mom told me a lot of widows used that terminology.

I had the veggies sliced and oiled and they'd go into the top oven to roast for ten or fifteen minutes on a high heat. They could be served at room temperature with just a squeeze of lemon, a dash of balsamic and a sprinkle of sea salt at the last minute. I sent another text to Dex. Zip.

3:30 pm: A light bulb went on (did people say on or off?) above my head. Why didn't this idea occur to me four hours ago? I'd call my sous-chef, Maximilian, and ask him to come over this instant. It meant extra hours of pay, but I was becoming frantic and he was my last hope unless Dex made an immediate appearance.

Whoever was manning the desk in the club's dining room must have been as busy as I was because the phone rang and rang before someone picked up.

"Winners Club, I mean Circle," said a harried employee. "This is Noah, may I help you?"

"Hello, Noah. This is Mrs. Marshall. I need to speak to Chef André right away. It's an emergency."

"Yeah, we've had plenty of those today. I'll try to patch you through, but we have a sold-out dinner crowd and Chef André's in a shitty mood, even worse than usual," said a very scared sounding Noah.

Did Chuck Wilkins know that his employees cursed into the phone when people were calling with emergencies?

"Patch me through to him, please," I said, picking up on his Jack Bauer "24" lingo.

I waited for what seemed an eternity before Chef André picked up.

"Yes, what is it?" he said as a greeting.

"Chef André, this is Mrs. Marshall and unfortunately, I never got Maximilian's cell number and I need to speak with him right away."

"What for? Max is here, but he can't talk to you. We're full up tonight and there's beaucoup work to do," said the head chef as my stomach sunk to the granite floor.

In my most polite tone I asked if he remembered that Max was supposed to be my sous-chef for this evening.

"Oh, yes, I do remember something like that, but it was only if I didn't need him here, and I do. Sorry honey," he said in his phony French accent before dropping the other shoe. "You see dear, we all know what you've been doing and it might be best to tell Mrs. Loft to book her parties at the club in the future like she's always done. That way nothing will go wrong."

"You son of a bitch," I said into an empty line because Chef André had hung up on me. And he'd call me honey. And dear.

4:00 pm: Now I was officially in a frenzy. No Dex, no Max, and I had to start the salmon and the paella or I'd be behind schedule. I called the employment agency to see if they could move up the starting time from six to five for the servers I'd hired, but of course, being a holiday, they were closed.

I had no choice. I called my BFF.

"Linz, hi it's me," I said, knowing I'd have to get through his interrogation before reaching Wanda. "I'm sort of in a pickle here; is Wanda around?"

"Nope, just me and Hailey doing some father-daughter bonding. Wanda's doing two barbeques over at Boca Grove. Luckily they're only a few blocks apart, but she'll be gone the rest of the day and night. You know, I think we need to talk," said Linz, the every-man's analyst.

"I'd love to, but right now I'm preparing for a big party and just don't have the time," I said, itching to get off the phone.

"That's what we need to discuss – your competitive nature and thinking you can ignore professional advice by taking on challenges you know little about. Think about it honey, and make an appointment with me when you have time," he said.

There was that "honey" again. Dammit! Had my polyps grown back?

"Yep, Linz, I'll do just that. You go bond; I gotta go. Bye," I said and hung up before Boca/Delray's own Lucy Van Pelt could dispense any more psychiatric advice.

As I pulled the salmon package out of the bottom drawer of the fridge another light bulb went off or on.

The fish was the origin of the smell:

1. Was it totally spoiled or just a little off?

2. Would it kill people or just make them a little sick?

3. It probably wouldn't kill anyone since I just bought it...oh shit, I bought it on Friday instead of yesterday, which was Saturday, and it had just spent overnight in the open-door motel.

4. Was there a salmon hot line?

5. A salmon whisperer?

6. Did I want to find out that I had to ditch the fish?

7. I probably shouldn't take a chance, but if I grilled it before smothering it with barbeque sauce at least no one would know they were being poisoned.

Just as I was turning on the grill, the phone rang. It had to be Dex coming to my rescue. If I saw anyone else's name on that caller I.D. I wouldn't pick up, even it was Marty with a request for bologna and Velveeta on Ritz crackers.

It wasn't Dex, but I picked up the phone. It was Sammy.

"Hi, I only have a minute – what's up? All the stuff set up at Gaby's?" I said.

"Yeah, hi, Mrs. M. Uh, that's what I wanted to talk to you about. You know those five long buffet tables you needed? I only had one for Mrs. Loft's party," said Sammy, without his usual magnetism. "I'm really sorry, but at the last minute I needed to get your other four over to another country club for our biggest clients and I had no choice. The others we had were already booked."

"Wanda. Boca Grove. Two barbeques," I said, in short-speak.

"Yeah, how'd you guess?" said Sammy the innocent.

"Just lucky. We'll make do. Thanks for letting me know, Sammy, I know it's not your fault."

"Thanks, Mrs. M. I gotta run. You'll never guess, or maybe you will, but Mary Lou fixed me up with her sister and we're going hot and heavy. And I hear you finally got a guy. Maybe we can double sometime," he said.

"I'm very happy for you, Sammy, but I'm rushed. I'll talk to you next week," I said and hung up ready to stick my head in the oven.

The salmon was grilling on the back patio, and at least the smell was out of the house. It's going to be fine I told myself as I whipped up a large batch of barbeque sauce, extra hot. Maybe it would kill any leftover bacteria still loitering in the fish.

4:15 pm: Paella time:

1. Why had I waited until the last minute to start it?

2. Why had I stopped for lunch?

3. I steamed clams, mussels and shrimp in boiling salted water for three minutes then set the cooked stuff aside. I figured boiling would get rid of any off-taste.

4. All the shellfish had been on ice in the fridge so the likeliness of it going bad was slight.

5. Not that slight. The ice had melted.

I basted a few scrawny lobster tails and crab claws with butter, wrapped them in foil and baked them for about ten minutes in my toaster oven, the only available cooking spot.

I did the following:

1. Sautéed onions, tomatoes and garlic in a giant paella pan.

2. Added saffron threads with salt and pepper.

3. Threw in red pepper flakes for good measure.

4. Tossed in raw rice and stirred for a few minutes before adding broth and wine.

5. Simmered for twenty minutes.

6. Added frozen green peas and cooked it for a few minutes more.

7. Steamed clams and mussels in a separate pot to be added later.

Luckily the paella pan was red enamel, which afforded an impressive presentation so I wouldn't have to transfer the contents to a platter. The colors would look amazing. Plain old rice heightened to a bright yellow by the saffron topped with shiny black mussels and tomato-red lobster tails, all pretty enough to be photographed. What a splash I'd make with this dish if only eight people wanted some.

I took time out for a sigh before realizing I had exactly forty-five minutes to get to Gaby's.

1. Where was Dex?

2. How was I going to get all this food over to Gaby's without his van?

3. Where was Mark's hugely inappropriate Hummer when I needed it?

4. I'd have to manage in my sedan.

5:00 pm: Everything was ready. I jumped into a decent outfit and made three trips to Gaby's with most of the provisions except for the cakes, pies, fruit, and one of the lasagnas. Once the party was going strong I'd run back and pick those up. The servers and bartenders could take over and keep the people happy with food and drink.

I had two hours to finish the food, and set up before the guests arrived. The servers and bartenders were scheduled to arrive at six, which would give them plenty of time to do whatever extras needed to be attended to.

I'd done it and I'd done it on my own, even with the negatives:

1. No Wanda to tell me I was doing it wrong.

2. No Maximilian, thanks to André the Gangster.

3. No Mark wondering what the hell I was even doing.

4. No Dex. The only person I truly needed wasn't by my side.

Just as I was leaving, my cell rang. I reached into my pocket and saw the caller I.D. It was Dex.

"Dex! Where the hell have you been? My sous-chef canceled and I had to do everything by myself. I'm just headed out now," I said, trying not to be shrill, but what choice did I have? Was he just another man who was going to disappoint me?

"Honey, listen to me. First of all, I'm on my way. Do

you want to wait for me and transfer the stuff into my van?" he said.

"No, I have to be at Gaby's now. They wanted a couple of extras and I need time to arrange everything once I get there. Just meet me at her house. Listen, when you stop at Publix for the bread I need you to pick up five or six big desserts – I'll explain later. Just get whatever looks good. And maybe if it's not too much trouble you can explain exactly why you didn't show up all day," I said and clicked off before he had a chance to answer.

5:30pm: A half hour later, most of the food was in Gaby's kitchen ready to finish. Something seemed out of order when I eyeballed the rotunda and living room areas. Then it hit me: no bistro tables with chairs. The one measly six-foot table was set up in the dining room covered with a crazy looking cloth.

Enter Gaby.

"What the fuck is going on, Dina? Sammy was supposed to deliver the rest of the rentals today. Have you seen them? He dropped off this one ridiculous table with the picnic cloth yesterday and we're supposed to have five. Where are my bistro tables and those ballroom chairs?" said Gaby, not bothering to control her temper.

I yanked out my phone and called Sammy before answering my client. It went directly to voice mail. I knew it was too late but for Gaby's sake left a message in my most authoritative tone.

"Gaby, I don't know what happened; Acorn's never let me down before," I said.

"Oh, I can tell you exactly what happened because I had a call this afternoon from my cousin over at Boca Grove who's going to one of Platinum's party and you can bet they stole my rentals out from under your nose," she said. "You're small potatoes for Acorn. Who do you think they're going to service? Some kitchen-cook, or the top party planner from Platinum?"

Wanda had two parties going at Boca Grove.

1. On her worst day she wouldn't do that to me.

2. Would she?

"That's not how they operate. I'm sure it was just a mistake in their loading area. Gaby, there's nothing we can do about it now," I said, keeping my calm, "so let's deal as best we can. I'm going to tell you something and you can believe me or not, but if you ask anyone in the business they'll tell you the same thing. The kiss of death for this kind of party is for everyone to be seated. You want your guests to walk around and mingle. (I had to hope that she'd forgotten my advice about how people didn't like to stand while they ate.)

Also, once they're at a table, they won't get up for seconds and thirds of all the beautiful food we planned," I continued on, certain that I didn't have enough food for even one serving a piece.

"You still have several patio tables, let's put some napkins in your baskets and that'll encourage those who want to sit to do it outside. I know you don't want people at your dining room table, but it's wood – nothing's going to happen to it. Why don't you let me set it up for you," I said, making my best play for Gaby's approval.

Silence.

"Okay. Do it," she snarled, and swept out of the room passing Marty as he came into the kitchen.

"Hey Dina, what's up? Gaby doesn't look too happy," he said. Then as an aside, whispered to me, "so what else is new?"

"Well, the rental place let me down; I know she's upset, but honestly, all those little tables are a pain in the neck."

"That's what I told her! Everyone will be hanging out at the bar or outside. Don't worry about it. We got plenty of room. Hey, what about those pigs in blankets?" said a very jovial husband.

"Got 'em right here. I'll just fire them up and bring you some in a few minutes. Maybe you should go talk to Gaby and smooth things over," I said, really just needing him to exit my space.

I opened the double oven to clear out any broiler pans and got the shock of my life. There was crud stuck onto the top, bottom and all sides of the double ovens. When did Gaby cook enough for this stuff to accumulate? There was no way I could turn on the self-cleaning device because aside from not having enough time, it would set off the smoke alarm.

"What are you doing?" said the lady of the house, entering in yet another Missoni.

"Uh, I need your ovens to heat up the hors d'oeuvres and later to finish the lasagnas – I mean they're par-baked, but they'll need twenty minutes in the oven. The rest of the stuff is fine at room temp," I explained.

"You're using my ovens in the kitchen? Are you insane? Why wouldn't you set up in the garage? Wanda told me her chefs bring an oven with them plus a grill for the lamb chops. I gave you all that information when you took the menu. Why didn't you just follow everything on the plan?"

Why indeed.

True or False:

1. Gaby never would have gotten rid of Chuck.

2. He was too valuable to the club's stellar reputation.

3. She was bluffing all along.

4. Had she hired me just to get a lower price?

5. Did she hire me to keep her status as The Boss with the girls?

6. True to all the above.

Whatever her reasoning was, I was just as guilty. I accepted the job, in spite of all her bad intentions and my lack of enough catering experience, to boost my wounded ego, which was going down the tubes along with the salmon that I'd probably have to scrap.

"Dina! What's wrong with you? Get moving. It's almost six and your help should be here already. Where's Dex? I hope you have a plan because we're not off to a great start. You'll have to make do with these ovens, but they might not be the cleanest. Our housekeeper used to cook for us when we first moved in, now we just go to the club," said Gaby.

Why hadn't the housekeeper cleaned the oven? That fossil-food had been in there for over a decade. At least it would cover up the fishy smell wafting up from the platters of cooked salmon. I turned on both ovens and was met with greasy smoke from each. I threw in the franks so that Marty could have a little nibble, and would add the beef and other items later on.

I thrust two pans of lasagna in the lower oven and didn't let her see me setting the timer for an hour. Since Gaby didn't have a convection oven I'd have to wait for these to be done before adding the third.

I lied to Gaby by saying I par-baked the pastas.

1. I meant to.

2. Dex's plan of action in bed took precedence.

"It'll all turn out fine, Gaby. We caterers are used to last minute trivialities. Uh, your dress is very pretty, Missoni?" I said, pulling out all the stops.

"First of all, Dina, don't call yourself a caterer. You're a cook who better pull off this party. Secondly, congratulations for recognizing a designer outfit. This one's from Saks, but I hear Target is carrying the line also. I mean, it's not the same, but for fifty bucks you can get yourself something decent," said the fashion expert. "Listen, you do whatever's necessary to make this night a success. I want to give the snowbirds something to talk about all summer in their Hampton homes.

I'm going upstairs now to pop in my lenses and where the hell is Dex? Why is he so late?" she said, glancing at her diamond-beveled Rolex. Maybe I could find one of those in Target along with the Missoni.

"Dex had to stop at Publix to pick up the bread and some desserts," I said, mentally kicking myself for indicating that these items weren't at my house.

"Picking up? From Publix?"

"Is that what I said? (Tut, tut.) No, no, everything is homemade, as promised. I couldn't fit it all in my car," I said, nicely skirting the whole truth or any part of it. "Now you go do your lenses and please don't worry. I promised you a fabulous party and that's exactly what you're going to get."

Gaby took a few steps toward me until we were practically nose to nose.

"It better be," she said, flinging back her long swingy hair before making a grand exit.

I smiled and almost dialed Portia to report the best gossip ever:

1. Gaby's eyes were brown.

2. Her contacts made them blue.

6:30 pm: Where was Dex? Only one bartender, Ashton, arrived and threatened to leave when I demanded he remove his nose ring. They both stayed. Three out of the hired and paid for six servers showed up. Jason, Jake and Josh. The J men: late and disheveled.

"Didn't I ask you guys to wear khakis and white knit collared shirts?" I said, smiling through gritted teeth. God forbid I should insult them. The bartender was already looking at me with a sneer as he wiped down Gaby's Italian marble counter with a grimy rag.

"Jason, didn't the agency give you the dress code?"

"I'm Josh, and whaddya think this is?" he said pointing to his beige cut-offs and white tank top.

The other two musketeers were more presentable; I'd keep Josh in the kitchen where he could assist me and stay out of sight.

"Excuse me, Ashton, but I'm sure Mrs. Loft has some clean rags in the laundry room. Would you mind checking?" I said. He didn't acknowledge me so either he was hard of hearing or didn't recognize the name that he probably made up. Rather than start an argument I found a few rags and brought them over to him.

"Here you go, why don't you use these," I said in my syrupy voice. I couldn't afford to offend my only bartender who'd have to serve a hundred people if Dex didn't materialize.

"Listen lady, why don't you go back to the kitchen and leave me to my job. I know what I'm doing which is more than I can say for you. Who the hell runs a party like this? No tables? No chairs? Only one buffet table? No chefs in the garage? Did you even think about a signature cocktail? You're clueless, but I'll tell you what, for an extra hundred I'll help you out. Just stay out of my way," he said.

"Okay, Ashton. That's a deal. Thank you for your help," I said, practically genuflecting before leaving the rags on the counter in the hopes he'd throw out his present one that looked like it had last been used to clean out a car engine.

"I gotta say though, that Gaby dame is some vintage piece of ass. She's built for action," he said.

"Ashton, I'm going into the kitchen now. The guests will be arriving soon and I have to instruct the servers as to their duties. I really want to thank you for your help," I said, playing it to the hilt. Please let him stay away from Gaby I prayed on my way back to the kitchen with the filthy ovens and the sloppy boys.

The three young lads who would pass as my servers had eaten half a tray of franks, and one of them was guzzling a beer he'd helped himself to.

"Guys, please! No drinking on the job! I need your attention because only three out of six of you showed up so you'll be doing double duty. And stop eating those franks."

"Double duty?" said the cleverest of the J men. "So, that means we get double pay, right?"

"Yeah," the other two chimed in.

Apparently all three had gone to the Ashton School of Shaking Down the Boss, but they had a point so I agreed.

"You're correct," I said. "I'll pay you all double, but you have to do what you're told."

"You will?" said the ringleader. "Thanks, Mrs. Marshall. We're gonna be the best servers you ever hired. But, I gotta tell you one thing and this is for your own good. There's something wrong with these franks. I mean, they're okay, but they have a funny smell."

I reached for one and on its way to my mouth I realized that the pastry had absorbed the greasy oven odor from whatever the housekeeper had cooked ten years ago. They didn't taste awful if you could get them passed your nose.

"Hey, there's some strong mustard here," said Jake, reaching for a second beer. "Take it from me – you stick those pigs in mustard and no one'll notice."

"Thanks, Jake," I said, my confidence coming back. "I'll do that, but please put the beer away. With the extra money I'm paying, you can pick up a six-pack on the way home and drink it once you get there. I can't have you drinking and driving."

"Hey, who are you," piped in Jason, "our mother? I'll tell you one thing; you're a real MILF, except for the butch hair. You're not gay, are you?"

"No, I'm not. Now, let's go over what's to be served first," I said, ignoring the MILF remark.

"You gonna grill these lamp chops somewhere?" said one of the three. I'd taken to calling all of them J by this time.

"I've already done that at home, they just have to reheated. Mrs. Loft has some kind of a fancy grill on the stovetop so we'll use that. She won't want us grilling in the backyard."

"It doesn't work; already tried it. Thought I'd preheat it for you," said one of my helpers.

"What do you mean it doesn't work? This kitchen costs more than most people make in a year, it has to work."

"Dina, do you mind if I call you Dina?" said Josh or Jason, sidling up to me. "This stove is a piece of shit. Believe me, we know."

"How 'bout a beer now?" said whichever J hadn't spoken in the last thirty seconds.

6:45 pm: The first guests arrived. No one had the decency to be fashionably late. Marty volunteered to play host leaving his wife to berate me in front of the help. Who was I kidding? I was the help and the three guys were my only support system.

"Dina, this is a disaster. I have six couples in the foyer and nothing to eat. Marty took them to the makeshift bar in the dining room where your bartender is ruining my Italian marble. Where the hell is Dex? And what are you three standing around for? Get to work!" she screamed at my helpers, "and what's that smell?"

"Uh, it's from the oven. It really needed to be cleaned," I said, shifting the blame to her lazy housekeeper.

"If you knew you weren't bringing an extra oven, why didn't you check this one when you were here with Sammy? Oh, never mind, just light those candles on the table, they're supposed to absorb kitchen odors. I have to greet my guests. You three! Look alive!" she said and headed back to turn on the charm.

"Wow, what a bitch," said one of my henchmen. "Who's Dex?"

"That would be me," said Dex, entering the kitchen with paper bags filled to the brim with my Publix order. "Hi guys, we'll do proper intros later, in the meanwhile, can you warm up these rolls – they're a little stale. Hey, what's that smell," he said, wrinkling up his nose.

"Fuck the smell! Just unpack those bags!" I said, scaring the four men into taking a step away from me. "And why is the bread stale? It was ordered for today. Publix doesn't screw up like that."

"No, Publix didn't screw up," said Mr. Calm. "You placed the order on Friday and told them you'd pick it up the next day. I guess you got Saturday and Sunday mixed up. They were all out of fresh stuff, so I had to take your order," Dex said, in a tone you'd use for a five year old. "Who knew it would get stale so quickly?"

"Yeah, Dina, shit happens," said Josh. "They'll be okay 'cause I have a great trick for stale bread. Leave it to me. You better light those candles like that cunt told you to do. Oh, sorry 'bout the language, but if the shoe fits."

"The chops are ready. I nuked 'em on high for five

minutes; they should be just right," said Jason.

"You microwaved those teeny-tiny rib chops for five minutes? They were already cooked. I was just going to warm them up," I said, not believing the theatre of the absurd being performed in Gaby's kitchen.

"Yeah, we've already been through that, the grill's kaput."

"I know, but we could have just thrown them into a hot skillet for thirty seconds. Too late now, let me have a look," I said, flirting with disaster.

What I saw was over a hundred dollars worth of beautiful little Frenched lamb chops looking like dull gray lollipops.

"Holy shit, Dina! No way you can serve those," said Jason. "Gee, who knew five minutes would kill them."

Everyone on the planet knew. Except Jason.

At least I had a gigantic arsenal of Swedish meatballs, and I'd be able to refill the chafing dish several times during the evening.

Ashton made his entrance just in time to hear the bad news, with some of his own.

"Hey, Dina, I'm running out of ice and no one switched on the ice maker in the bar. You do have extra ice, right?"

"Of course I do. It's right here in the cooler," I said, looking down at the non-existent ice container. "Take some from the freezer for now; I have plenty of bags at home. I didn't have room in my car because Dex here was supposed to pick me up with his van. So Dex, please run back to my house and get it along with whatever else I had to leave."

"Got it, and I'll check your fridge for some kind of sauce to bring those chops back to life," said Dex, shaking hands with Ashton on his way out.

"Cool, Dex. You hitting that?" I heard Ashton say as he pointed my way.

"Probably never again," Dex said. Hilarious. "Ash, you get back out there and I'll bring over the ice. I can give you a hand at the bar unless the boss has other stuff for me to do. She's in charge today," he said, trying to butter me up.

When Ashton stopped laughing he headed back to the bar.

7:15 pm: Dex came back with the ice and desserts.

"Hey, Dina, something smells really bad in your kitchen."

8:00 pm: Ashton needed Dex at the bar so the three guys, now my closest allies, worked together to salvage what we could. We smothered the lamb chops in a port wine reduction that I heated up and aside from being a little chewy, at least they were tasty. Jake dressed the platter with parsley and when he reentered the kitchen all the chops were gone.

"See, Dina, it worked out!" said an ebullient Jason, still feeling guilty for cremating them in the microwave.

Ten minutes later Dex came in with a platter of half eaten chops.

"Throw the rest away. I actually saw people spitting them out and we need more plates. We're down to serving stuff on napkins."

I opened one of Gaby's cabinets to find a bottle of scotch beckoning me. Dex could drive me home. I drank a few ounces straight from the bottle.

"Uh, Dina," Josh said, "can you take a look at the cookies? They're moving."

"Josh, how can cookies move?" I said, stumbling over to where he was keeping an eye on them in case they were thinking about taking a trip somewhere. The cookies themselves weren't moving, but the granulated sugar sure was. Apparently, some sort of little bug had gotten into the container and laid eggs, which had now hatched on top of dozens of cookies.

"I think maybe we should throw them out?" he said, more as a question than a statement, not wanting to incur further rage from the crazy lady who was once a MILF.

"Throw them out. They were an afterthought anyway," I said even though there were pounds of butter being wasted or enjoyed by the bugs. "Good catch, Josh, and not to worry, because we have loads of delicious desserts."

10:00 pm: Looking back I can only recollect part of what happened that evening. By nine o'clock, the party was in full swing and things couldn't have gone worse. I told myself that every caterer stumbles now and then; the beef can be a shade too rare, the salad overdressed, the vegetables chewy, but flaws like those are usually considered minor within the overall success of an evening. I couldn't fault the three servers or Ashton, all of whom pitched in to control the free-for-all that the party became.

Dex and I were everywhere; cooking, reheating, serving, pouring wine, and cleaning up the Swedish meatball sauce that dripped unmercifully onto Gaby's Persian rugs. We ran out of hors d'oeuvres after the first half hour, which worked out well because we also ran out of ice. The beef was totally overcooked, the chicken underdone, and the salmon almost caused a revolution. If the smell didn't get them, the degree of fire in the barbeque sauce did.

The lasagna was runny, and the gummy-rice paella had an overpowering taste of iodine. The only desserts Publix had left by the time Dex got there were cupcakes with blue frosting.

1. What happened to my go-to standby chocolate cakes?

2. Why did they taste gummier than the rice?

3. Did I add pudding to the cake mix with the pudding already in it that I bought by mistake?

4. Did adding orange juice to Key Lime pies always cause them to turn to slop?

The salad looked withered and dry; the lettuce never recovered from the open-door refrigerator policy even after being drenched in a cold-water bath. There was no earthly reason why the grilled vegetables should have been a disaster, but they were tough and inedible.

And everything smelled fishy.

The evening was a catastrophe. There was no choice now.

1. After selling the house and getting divorced I'd move to North Carolina and find a job.

2. I couldn't ask my parents for a loan.

3. I'd stay with France and Redmond.

4. I'd lost my best friend.

5. As for Dex? If I couldn't count on him to help me when I needed him the most how could we ever advance our relationship?

Dex asked Jake to drive me home. I was forced to leave early, but couldn't recall exactly why. I did know that Gaby hadn't said a word to me since the meatball and lamb chop debacle.

I figured Dex would come over after the party; he had all my cooking equipment. For sure he tossed the leftovers that tasted like they'd been leftover from the time Gaby's house-keeper last cooked. I sobered up and although I didn't need a party post-mortem, I would demand a detailed explanation of why Dex had deserted me up until the last minute.

With or without Dex, I failed. There was no other way to put it. I screwed up royally, and had no one to fault except myself. If I'd listened to Wanda and at least partnered with her we would have made it work.

Had my former best friend deceived me? Did she book those Boca Grove parties just to get back at me? I doubted Wanda would behave so treacherously, but there had to be an explanation of all the missing rentals. Of course, Acorn would remain loyal to their biggest account, but I was still disappointed in Sammy not coming through although it was probably out of his hands.

I took too many short cuts and had been careless. If I hadn't been in such a hurry to get back in bed with Dex, the refrigerator, which I should have called the repairman for, would have closed properly and the salmon would have been fine.

1. if

2. if

3. if

I could rationalize all night long, but I knew the failure was due to my inflated ego and my need to show everyone I could make it on my own.

It was sort of fun having a pity party even though I had mountains of problems facing me. It looked like it was over between Dex and me, which was the saddest part, because I was truly in love with the man. I wouldn't let our relationship go forward unless he had one hell of a life and death explanation for his absence. I couldn't have another man walk all over me.

I heard Dex's truck pull up a couple of hours later. I gathered my strength and put on some water. I owed him one last cup of tea because he knocked himself out once he finally showed up. When Dex saw that I'd been hitting the scotch (Scotch? Who am I, Winston Churchill?), he took over supervising the servers and they snapped into action. Ashton even created a signature cocktail, which he called The Gorgeous Gaby. I found out later it was only white wine with some cassis and a dash of bitters. It was basically a Kir, but Gaby was quite impressed and Marty had to tear her away from the bar to mingle with the guests.

That was the last thing I remember, oh, except Gaby telling me to get the hell out and that I was finished. Right. That.

Chapter 35

May

Et Tu, Dex?

Midnight: "Hey Dina, it's me," Dex said, "the guys parked your car in the garage and forgot to close it. You okay?"

"I've had better days," I said, attempting to lighten the situation, which was bound to get heavy very shortly.

"Wait, let me talk you down off that ledge because it didn't end up so badly," he said, opening the fridge to get some cream. "Mind if I make decaf instead of tea?"

"Help yourself. You should know where the K-Cups are by now," I said, trying to show how cool and standoffish I could be. I'd pounce after he made himself comfortable.

"Ah, here's a good one. Listen, it wasn't your finest hour, but a lot of the guests really felt bad for you. No one could have pulled off that party with so little help, even Wanda, so don't blame yourself for that."

I could blame him, however, for not showing up until almost seven, but I'd include that later on when I gave him the lambasting he deserved. And the nerve! Not even mentioning his disappearing act on the most important day of my career. I was getting worked up when he brought over a mug of tea for me and sat down.

"First let me tell you the good stuff. Ashton, and by the way, that is his real name, and your three servers, all of whom are in love with you, rose to the occasion. I asked Marty for a golf shirt for Josh so that he'd look respectable to work the living room where we needed him."

"Oh no, I forgot about Ashton. I promised I'd give him a hundred dollars extra because the other bartender didn't show up. I told the three J's I'd pay them double and I'll get that to them somehow."

"Don't worry about the guys. Ashton said to forget the extra bucks; he knew you were in over your head plus he picked up a few jobs from the Chans and some of the others. He wants to look for a better agency because he said the one you used was undependable. No kidding," said Dex as cheery as ever, unaware of my innards boiling away.

"But that's not even the best part. You were pretty wasted when Gaby kicked you out, but you got in a good parting shot."

"I did? I'm drawing a blank. What'd I say?"

"Seriously, you don't remember? You yelled, 'Fuck you, Gertrude, and the broom you flew in on!' You might have been mixing metaphors, but you got your point across," he said. "The folks who've had good luck with you felt really terrible that the evening was so…so," he said, searching for the right word that wouldn't hurt my feelings.

"Shitty?" I said helping him out.

"Yeah, I guess, but I saw Marcy pull Gaby aside to calm her down because she was a little hammered herself with all those cocktails Ashton was plying her with."

"Did she succeed?"

"Uh, no. Gaby started screaming that you'd probably poisoned everyone with that salmon, and that the lamb chops tasted like old shoes and on and on."

"And that's the good news you had for me?" I said.

"Well, the bad news, as far as I can tell, is you won't be able to continue doing business in the club as long as you're still here. Even though your fans stuck up for you, I doubt they'll take a chance again," he said.

"No shit, Sherlock, what was your first clue? The raw chicken or the soggy rolls? Oh, by the way, Josh is going to have to find a new technique for reheating bread," I said, getting even more steamed.

"Hey! Hold it a minute. Yes, the food was bad. All of it except the Swedish meatballs and you had a slew of those, and the lasagna wasn't totally inedible."

"What about the Persian rugs? I'm going to have to pay to get those cleaned."

"I doubt it because Ashton cleaned most of it up with club soda. The guy really knows his trade. I wonder if Wanda could use him?" he mused.

Dex was in such hot water by this time, completely ignoring his part or non-part in today's fiasco, and now he was going to give a referral to Wanda who I still wasn't sure hadn't sabotaged me.

"And here's the clinker, and I mean that in a good way – Marty gave me a check for the balance. Didn't ask any questions, just said you shouldn't worry about a thing. He also tipped the guys because he knew they did their best. Gaby saw him writing the check and screamed that she was going to stop payment on it and sue you for the deposit. Marty's a great guy; she's tough, but who knows what people go through in life or what makes them that way," said Dex, giving me a perfect opening.

"I'm not going to cash the check and I'll return their

deposit. That was generous of Marty to offer, but it wouldn't be fair of me to take it. Dex, enough about tonight. What I need to know is where you were all day. You left here at ten in the morning and then not a word from you for hours. I don't know why all the food turned out so poorly, and leaving the fridge door open overnight probably didn't help, but for you to leave me stranded – how could you do that and pretend nothing's wrong?" I said, cold sober and angry.

"The door was open? How'd that happen, but I guess it explains a lot. Dina, obviously I've been avoiding the issue of my disappearance, and I wanted to get the other stuff out of the way first because this part's going to take a little time," he said.

"Go on," I said, like an old schoolmarm ready to smack her pupil with a ruler.

"I was with Sue-Ellen," he said.

If I'd been eating a poached oyster I would have spit it in his face.

"How could you! Your fuck buddy took precedence over a party I was already losing money on? You left me here with all the food to finish while trying to find extra help not to mention losing my sous-chef because that prick of our club chef, André, wanted to eke out his revenge on me, then make three trips over to Gaby's by myself and take her bullets? That's what you're telling me?"

"Hold on, you're not listening," he said, trying to grab my hand.

I was about to tell him not to waste his breath when my cell rang. Who could be calling at this hour except Gaby to finish her diatribe against me. Force of habit had me check the caller I.D. There was no name, but the area code was from Key West.

So Mark had finally made it official and changed his cell number. Dex could stew while I took the call.

"Hello, Mark," I said, wanting my husband's name to register with Dex.

All I heard on the other end was uncontrollable sobbing and it wasn't coming from my husband.

"Who is this?" I said.

"It's me, Taffie, is he there yet?"

"Is who where yet?" I said, confusion setting in. Maybe I was still under the influence of the two or three or eight slugs of scotch I swallowed in Gaby's kitchen.

"Mark! He left me," said Taffie, now in an all-out wail.

"What? He left you? Where'd he go?" I said, obviously not getting it.

"He said he missed what was really important in his life and was going back where he belonged. Is he there yet? He left around ten. I told him to call me from the road just to make sure he was safe, but I haven't heard anything. I'm so worried even though I totally hate him for leaving me," she continued which brought about a new round of sobs.

"Taffie, I'm sorry. He's not here yet, but I'm sure he's okay. It takes several hours from Key West to Boca and he may have stopped off for coffee somewhere."

"Yeah, that could be 'cause he said he was hungry and I didn't have anything in the house to eat, which wasn't even true because we had some really awesome leftovers. I wanted him to stay, but he said he'd already made up his mind. How could he do this to me? We were having so much fun," she said, livening up thinking about the fun that she'd had with my husband.

"Taffie, you might as well learn this now, some men don't know when they have it good, but listen for a minute –

261

Mark never called to say he was coming. Are you sure about this?" I asked, suddenly concerned for the poor girl.

"He said he'd call from the road," Taffie said. "Good bye Dina. Could you just please tell him to call me when he gets there so I know he's okay."

"Yes, I'll make sure he does. Bye, Taffie, and please don't be sad. You're young; you have plenty of time to meet the right one," I said.

"I thought Mark was the right one. He said we were soul mates," she said.

"Taffie, that's an overused term. My advice? Go out with your girlfriends and have some more fun and forget about Mark."

"I already called the girls; they're here now. They've been awesome bringing champagne and stuff. Thanks, Dina, you sound nice. If Mark had to leave me I'm glad he's going back to you," she said, and we hung up.

Dex, who'd been in and out of the house unloading my kitchen supplies from his van, had only heard a few snippets of the conversation.

When he saw me back at the table sipping tea he felt that was his cue to explain why he'd left me high and dry.

"Kinda late for a phone call, was it Gaby?" he said.

"No. I want you to leave now. My husband is coming home."

"What? Mark?"

"That's the one," I said.

"I don't know what that's about, but I owe you an explanation about today. Please let me tell you what went on, then, if you still want me to go, I will."

"I don't care what happened. Maybe you didn't hear what I just said: Mark is going to be here soon. You and I are done. Leave," I said, enjoying the upper hand.

"And you're throwing out what we have for some jerk who walked out on you? You're not even giving me two minutes of your time?"

"I don't have two minutes; I have to change the sheets. Get out," I said.

"You're going to regret this because I'm not crawling back; I've had enough drama for one day. Good luck because you're going to need it, and for your information, the meatballs sucked!" he said, slamming the front door behind him.

Chapter 36

Husband and Wife

If Mark left Key West at ten like Taffie said, he'd be here soon. I really did change the sheets as Dex's musk was still present and that wouldn't do as a welcome home greeting, although I doubted we'd spend the first night in the same bed.

Before straightening up the kitchen I rearranged Mark's office and rolled the carts into the garage. We'd have time to go over my activities in the last year after he settled back in.

My husband still loved me, and missed me and our home life. He was returning to the fold and family. His attachment to my folks and sister ran deep, and I was grateful for their kindness throughout the years. Compared to his parents, we were practically The Brady Bunch. Even though they thought Mark's behavior about leaving me was despicable, it was in their nature to be forgiving, especially if it made me happy.

By the time I cleared most of the counters it was after two, and I was exhausted. Taffie sent me three texts and I finally turned off my cell phone. Mark could always reach me on the landline if necessary.

I crawled into bed made up with our best sheets and fell asleep. Mark would have to wake me when he arrived. We'd talk, go to counseling, and be a couple again. I loved him for all those years and I'd make it happen again, Dex be damned.

Perfect timing I thought right before drifting off:

1. Girl loses husband.

2. Girl finds boyfriend and career.

3. Girl loses boyfriend and career.

4. Girl gets husband back and puts career on hold.

May 30th, 9:00 am: Mark! Where was he? Maybe he'd gotten in so late that he didn't want to disturb me.

I jumped out of bed, stubbing my toe on the night table and hobbled toward the guest room. The bed was still covered with the extra roasters and cake pans I forgot to pack away last night. I threw on my robe and ran outside hoping to find Mark asleep in the Hummer, but all I found was the newspaper thrown in the middle of our driveway. There was no way he could have eked out any space in our garage loaded with carts for his hulk of a car, but I checked anyway.

When I walked back inside I turned my cell on and booted up the laptop; maybe he stopped overnight and decided to give me notice of his return after all. There were three more texts from Taffie and a slew of email. I scanned the list and not seeing anything from Mark's email address, opened one from Chuck Wilkins.

Dear Mrs. Marshall:
Please don't do any more catering here.

I guess Gaby had gotten to him earlier this morning with news of my services.

I opened a few from some of the guests and they were kind of nice. Belle simply wrote that she was sorry things didn't turn out well. There were others with similar sentiments and I'd reply as soon as I located my husband. I was now as worried as Taffie and although I didn't call her, I felt a responsibility to alleviate her anxiety. I was just about to send her a temporizing text when I noticed an email address that wasn't familiar. The subject line had one word: Mark.

Dear Dina:
Mark has asked us to let you know that he flew to Mexico last night and will be living with us. I'm sorry we haven't been in touch, especially after your separation. Our son is distraught about a lot in his life, but said he was making all the divorce arrangements with Ted. Part of the agreement is, with your concurrence, for you to take care of selling the house, splitting the proceeds with him after reimbursing your parents for the down payment and the equities. Mark has no money to pay alimony, but Dan and I would be happy to send you a check to help out. Mark called us from Miami and we arranged to pick him up at the airport. We were surprised that he decided to come to Mexico although we're very happy he's with us under any circumstances. He said he needed his family.

All the best, Erica Marshall

Part Two

...to Another

Chapter 37

June

Moving On

After the divorce I listed the house with Frosty and our phone conversation went something like this:

Frosty: "Hey, cutie, if you want a quick sale, price it to sell. You have a great kitchen, but you gotta repaint it. Get that crap out of Mark's office, and let's get it on the market. You paid bupkis for it so you'll make out okay. You don't have a mortgage, and your delusional husband is actually giving you the money your parents paid for the down payment – who do you think they're going to leave it to? Whatever; after my commish, you'll have a nice chunk of change and you deserve it for what he put you through. Listen, I don't want to get into your personal life; your mother already gave me a brief outline, so now honey, it's your time. Go to North Carolina, be with your sister, Frannie, (Frosty was the exception – I'm telling you, this woman could get away with anything.) your mom and dad are there half a year anyway and you can always come back down and stay in their guest house."

Me: "I'm ready. How much do you think we can get?"

Frosty: "Half a mil, more or less."

Me: Nothing, because I was flabbergasted at the figure.

Frosty: "Yeah, you don't have to say anything, I know we probably could do a little better if we wait till December, you know, start of the season, but the market's pretty good right now and why take a chance that it'll dip lower. Forest is hot – take my word. That price seem okay to you?"

Me: "You're saying that I'll get a hundred thousand over what we paid?"

Frosty: "Yep, that's what I'm saying, and if you roll it over into something nice in North Carolina you won't have to pay the taxes. I have plenty of clients up north who I'll get in touch with. They'll put the word out; everyone in the Hamptons wants a place in Boca. I'll advertise in the local papers up there also. If I have the right house it's nothing for them to hop a flight down here. You gotta do a few things – I mean the house is in great shape, except for the office and that's a major selling point because you only have the two real bedrooms. Last time I was there it was a total mess – what the hell were you doing with all those steel carts? Looked like a morgue."

Me: "They're gone; I left them for the garbage men." I could have sent Dex a text to pick them up, but I'd cut off all lines of communication, ingoing and outgoing, and that's how it was going to stay. The first few days, despite the drama he didn't want, he called every hour on the hour with no response from me; then gave up.

Frosty: "If you can paint the kitchen and front door that'd help; other than that just have it looking spic and span 24/7. You never know when I'll show up with clients. You wanna give me a key or what?"

Me: "Of course, and I'll try to be out of the house when you show it."

Frosty: "Good, 'cause that way folks can talk openly and you won't get your feelings hurt if they don't like your taste. So, let's get started. I can bring the papers over today if you're around. Then once I have the listing I'll go to work."

Me: "Sure, come on by. I'm home anyway cleaning out closets. Frosty, how can I ever thank you. I need to be free of this house and Boca." My short-lived hopes of reconstructing my life with Mark and/or starting a new one with Dex were gone. I'd been wrong about both men. Silly me.

Frosty: "I'll tell you how you can say thanks; how about baking me some of those cherry-macadamia scones."

Me: "I'm putting on my apron as we speak."

Frosty: "Great, I'll be there around three and if they're ready I'll try one out with coffee. Ya know, you could sell them, oh sorry, doll – you've already been down that road. Bye sweetie."

A week after signing the listing papers Frosty called me from her car.

"Hey girlfriend. (From Frosty I could take the expression.) Got a nice young couple who'd like to see your house. We're just coming through the gate; okay with you?" she said.

"Now's fine. I'll put on some coffee and defrost a cinnamon strudel that'll make the house smell yummy," I said, already knowing the drill when Frosty had a prospective buyer.

"Be right there, hon."

271

"Dina, say hello to Lou and Leslie Gates. Ha! No relation to Bill," Frosty said sending the Gates into a fit of laughter. Wanting to appear affable, I chuckled along with them.

"Please come in, I was just about to take a walk, but Frosty's familiar with the house. Oh, I put on some coffee if you have time and there's cake on the table," I said, starting to leave, "just help yourselves."

"Don't let us throw you out," Leslie said, "we may have some questions and our time is limited, so if you can hang around we'd appreciate it."

"Sure, no problem, just don't want to be in your way. Let me get the coffee."

"Thanks," said Lou, studying the granite floors. "Nice stone."

"Yes, it's beautiful and totally durable," I said before leading them into the kitchen, and yet to more granite.

"Oh, my god! I love this kitchen – it's got everything," said Leslie.

"That's my wife, the great haggler," Lou said. "That's her special way of getting the price down. Listen, you three gab while I take a look at the rest of the house. Hon, find me when you're finished in the kitchen."

"There's a home office with built-ins, Leslie, and you said something about an online business you have?" said Frosty, pouring coffee into my wedding china that I planned to sell on eBay once I finished sucking up to prospective buyers.

"Yeah, but I'm never leaving this kitchen. See how Dina has her laptop on the desk here? That's exactly what I want. Our kitchen in the city is too small for that, and our place out in the Hamptons, well, we try not to work on the weekends. I better see what Lou is up to and I'll tell him he can have the office, but I'll let him think it's his idea."

Did women still do that?

As soon as Leslie ventured down the hallway I arched a brow in Frosty's direction to which she responded with a wink and a positive nod.

"Okay, Dina," said Lou, reentering the kitchen with his wife. "Like Leslie says, we're only here for the day and we gotta get to the airport by five. I know the normal way is for us to act so-so about the house, and then give Frosty here a low-ball offer and we dicker around for weeks, but I'm not like that and neither is my wife. We love the house and we'll make a fair offer on the way to the airport. Frosty'll call you and you can take it or leave it, no counter offers."

"Thanks, Lou," I said, "that makes it easier all around. Do you have time for some coffee, a little cake?"

"Yeah, sit down, we're only twenty minutes from the airport and your bags are in the car, and Dina here's a first class cook and baker," said my promoter.

"I can't wait to have our first dinner party here," Leslie said, as I choked on my coffee.

An hour later Frosty called me from the car with an offer of just under our asking price. They weren't in a rush to close, but I was, so they agreed to have their attorney close for them on July 2nd, a little over a year since Mark's departure.

My nephew offered to fly down so we could drive back to North Carolina together, but I welcomed that time in the car to plot out the next phase of my life. Aside from a few more emails from my ex mother-in-law, and a check for ten thousand dollars, which I returned, I had no further communication with the Marshalls.

What I didn't expect was a going away party that Marcy threw, catered by Platinum. Gaby and Marty were there; I guess she wasn't willing to abdicate the throne just yet. Marty gave me a hug and Gaby inclined her head, a groundbreaking move for her, to acknowledge my presence.

For the few remaining weeks in Boca I made a colossal effort to restore my relationship with Wanda:

1. I arranged a weekend away for Wanda and Linz, and took care of Hailey.

2. I groveled at Wanda's feet until she forgave me.

3. I didn't question her about the missing rentals and there was no explanation forthcoming. I knew she screwed me on that but it no longer mattered.

4. We were still BFF.

We had lunch a week before I left and reminisced about our years together through school, Manhattan and Boca.

"You and Linz and Hailey must come visit once I'm settled," I said. "I'm going to miss you so much. And I'll have plenty of room for you because I was supposed to stay with my sister for a while, but France said she found a great house for me to rent so my furniture is being shipped directly there. I already sent my deposit."

"You took it sight-unforeseen?" said my wonderful

friend. I could have corrected her, but instead said, "let's order dessert. We'll split."

I traded in my sedan for a brand new station wagon. With the profitable sale of my house, and some of the catering money I still had, I felt financially secure although far from independently wealthy.

Because Mark was such a major part of my life for so many years, I would always feel a certain type of love for him, but as for being in love? No.

I wasn't over Dex, but there was no way I'd be willing to share my life with a man who went back to his old girlfriend on the day he knew I was counting on him. I saw him driving the PPS delivery truck through Forest every so often before I left, which meant he was still in business in Boca and not in North Carolina. Maybe he decided that Florida life with Sue-Ellen was more suitable than a major move to Greensboro. Just as well. I didn't need him living twenty minutes away from me.

June came and went, and a few days after the closing I left for Winston-Salem.

Chapter 38

July

Arrival

I allowed myself the luxury of a three-day journey to North Carolina, listening to audio books or Elvis CD's, but mainly I reflected on places I'd been and where I was headed. It was a short list even though there'd been more ingredients in the past year of my life than the most complicated recipe from Julia Child's original French cookbook.

1. My husband left me.

2. I started a catering business that did well until it bombed.

3. Fell in love and got dumped again even though technically, I was the dumper and not the dumpee.

4. Life in Boca Raton was finished.

I arrived at my sister's house late in the afternoon, and Redmond took my bags upstairs to their guestroom. We sat down for an aperitif, some homemade (although not in their home) cheese straws and marinated olives.

"All your furniture and cartons are over at the house because Wesley took care of accepting delivery and Pris had a couple of her guys arrange it, but you can move everything around once you're settled, and you'll stay here in the meanwhile, and I forgot to tell you, the kids went away for the weekend, but they'll be back tomorrow night," said my sister, combining three or four sentences into one.

"Tell me a little more about the house," I said, sipping my drink.

"Now, don't take a fit because Redmond and I know it's perfect for you and it's only a rental for a year and if you hate it after that, we'll find something else," said my big sister, who seemed strangely unnerved. Anyone who legally changes her name to France before she's of drinking age shouldn't have been jumpy now.

"What's up, France?" I said.

A pause.

"Well, Dina," said my sweet bear of a brother-in-law, "France here knows a good deal when she sees it, but we didn't want to spook you."

A giant pause.

"A chef owns the house," said France in the fewest words possible.

"Oh shit," I said. "Don't tell me he was a friggin' caterer."

"No, nothing like that. Ronnie tried to start a cooking show from home, but he had such a miserable personality on the air that the station couldn't get sponsors, and the ratings were down in the dumps, and poor Wesley, you know he works for the station and the show was his idea, well, he had to fire poor Ronnie and we were all afraid Wes was going to lose his job also, but the head of the station liked the idea; just not the chef."

"Where is Ronnie?" I said, decoding France's last bla-therings.

She explained further. "Ronnie moved to California and asked Wesley, because there weren't any hard feelings between them and because Ronnie knew he wasn't cut out for TV, to try to find a responsible renter. He wants to sell eventually so he needed someone who'd take care of the house and that's when we did the deal. Ronnie's out in California and emailed Wesley that he likes L.A., just doesn't understand all those vegans."

Although I hadn't wanted the responsibility of a house again, with my family nearby it didn't seem so off-putting. The next morning Redmond, France and I drove the two miles to my new home.

"No granite, I love it," I said as soon as we were in-side. The floors were laid with deep ebony-stained wide-planked wood, which flowed throughout the main area of the house. "And the kids did a great job with the furniture. I'm not moving a thing."

"Dina, like we said, the house is perfect for you. Now, honey, the bedrooms are carpeted; we'll look upstairs in a minute, but don't you want to see the kitchen?" Redmond said.

"Not particularly. There might be granite on the coun-ter tops," I said, only half kidding.

"Now, Dina, let's not have any negativity. You moved here to get away from Boca and that guy you were in love with and I'm not even going to question you about that, but you simply cannot get away from everything made out of stone," said France.

"Alright, let's get it over with," I said, hopping around the twenty or so cartons making up an obstacle course in the living room.

"Oh, my god!" I said as we walked through the butler's pantry into the kitchen. "I've never seen anything like this."

"This" turned out to be a multitude of cabinets wrought from bleached white oak with ceiling beams of the same wood, and counter tops that were almost pure white marble, not terribly practical compared with granite, but I wasn't complaining. The large island with a second sink had a butcher-block top, perfect for the slicing and dicing Ronnie must have done. Stainless steel appliances including three ovens were top-grade and perfectly situated for a real cook. The specialized refrigerator with glass doors had an automatic closing feature. (Did Ronnie install that after leaving the old one open all night while he had sex in the bedroom?)

"We knew you'd like it. I think one of the magazines did a spread on it a few years back," said Redmond. "Come on, let's go see the bedrooms. France has a surprise for you, right honey?"

The staircase off the foyer led to the master and two other bedrooms.

"We'll look at the guest rooms in a minute, but let me show you your room because even though I'm sure you have all your own sheets and stuff, Wesley and Priscilla wanted to give you a housewarming gift, so she fixed up the master with linens from Blum's," said France, barely needing to draw a breath. "They had all the carpets cleaned because we all know how fussy you are about those things with your special Brazilian housekeeper twice a week."

Add to list:

1. Mention to sister that I could only afford Valentina once a month after Mark left.

2. Paid her double to clean the house on my last day there.

3. Valentina probably dreams in English by now.

My niece-to-be had real flair; the bedroom was spectacular. Bronze floor to ceiling draperies covered the casement windows, and light peach-colored sheets, pillows and a down duvet looked stunning on my king-sized bed. Even though I'd be sleeping alone, it'd be in luxury. There were thick white and peach Egyptian cotton towels in the adjoining bathroom, and the tile floor looked like it belonged in a Mediterranean villa.

"It's beautiful. I'll thank Priscilla and Wesley tomorrow night," I said and gave my sister a big hug.

France and Redmond helped me sort out the cartons, but when it came to setting up the kitchen I sent them home. Before his betrayal, I'd been hoping to do that with Dex.

"You two have done enough. I need a lot of time in the kitchen. Thanks for everything. I love you guys," I said, sniffling.

"It's our pleasure to have you near us," said Redmond, looking a little weepy himself. "We'll pick you up for dinner around seven, something simple. How does pizza and beer over at Brixx sound?"

After they left I sat on the kitchen floor and cried my

eyes out. I'd so wanted to begin my new life with Dex and that was not to be.

Even with the sale of my house, I knew I'd have to work. Ronnie's kitchen was a caterer's dream, but the thought of going back into that business without Dex would have been a constant reminder of how much I missed him in spite of his actions. There were plenty of good restaurants in Winston; someone would hire me as a sous-chef or a line cook, and working in the evenings would fill my loneliest times.

Redmond stocked the wine closet with a varied selection, and France had filled the enormous refrigerator with enough food to last a week. I called my parents to let them know I was settling in. They wanted to take a ride down over the weekend to see us and my new digs. I opened the most important cartons, took a nap and was ready for dinner when my sister picked me up.

Chapter 39

July

Catering, Seriously?

After making my luxurious bed the next morning I continued unpacking. When the landline in the kitchen rang I almost dropped my vintage Rosenthal platter jumping over three cartons to answer it hoping without reason that Dex might be calling. Although I deleted his previous voice mails without listening, I was still too proud and hurt to make the next move. For all I knew he and Sue-Ellen were back together, but from what he'd told me that didn't seem likely.

Maybe I should have given him the benefit of the doubt and let him explain before he left my house the night of Gaby's party. All men can't possibly behave as badly as my ex-husband, and I knew if I hadn't fought with Dex, I wouldn't have even considered letting Mark back into my life whether he wanted to or not.

1. I played one against the other and ended up with neither.

2. I only wanted one - Dex.

3. How could I possibly tell Dex I still loved

him after I demanded he leave because
my husband was coming back to me?

It was France on the line, which I should have figured because no one else had that number yet.

"Hi sweetie," she said, "you up?"

"Only since six; I'm putting the kitchen together."

"How's the house? You feel comfy yet?"

"You know, I really do. Those sheets are heavenly, slept straight through."

"Good. Now, I want to tell you about this idea I had about planning a casual cocktail party in your honor and to introduce you to all our friends, and it'd be an ideal opportunity to promote your catering abilities with all your specialties. Actually, I've already called everyone and they're just dying to meet you so it's for next Saturday at five and do you think you could do a nice heavy hors d'oeuvres buffet for about fifty?"

"France, I told you I was out of the catering business and now you're asking me to cook for fifty people I've never even met? I'd love to get acquainted with your friends, but couldn't we start by going to lunch with a few at a time?"

"Well, we could, but that leaves Redmond and the men out, and Wes and Pris want to be here to help and you won't have to make everything because I'll bring in a bunch of stuff like cheese biscuits from Dewey's 'cause there's really no need to make those from scratch and Redmond's got the wines covered because we won't serve hard liquor, so honestly, I simply don't understand why you should have any objections." she said.

"What men," I said, ignoring the rest.

"Don't get in a snit. Just some very nice single men

who live in Winston and we invite them to a lot of parties all the time because we like to have a good mix when we entertain."

1. It's possible France could've made that up on the spot.

2. She was pretty good at improvisation also.

3. They'd done so much for me already.

4. I couldn't beg off.

"Okay, I'll behave."

"See that you do," my older sister said, and we ended the conversation as we usually did – with her telling me what to do. (Did Bailey always listen to Belle who was only a minute older?)

The evening of the cocktail party arrived and every guest showed up just as France predicted. We had a spread that could have made headlines in the Boca Forest Newsletter. France brought in a few southern specialties, and most of Dina's Dinners finest canapés made their debut. Redmond attended to the wine while Wesley and Priscilla arranged the food and insisted on cleaning up.

France's table displayed Dewey's biscuits, cherry tomatoes stuffed with herbed goat cheese, mini-crabcakes with remoulade, and turkey salad with bits of dried cranberry and toasted pignoli nuts served on pumpernickel rounds. There were endive leaves filled with egg salad topped with (non-Beluga) caviar, grilled baby lamb chops that steered clear of the microwave, miniature egg rolls, bite-sized potato pancakes topped with smoked salmon and sour cream, and oodles of freshly cut vegetables with a tangy blue cheese dip.

The weather cooperated and Redmond's flower garden was in full bloom. France introduced her little sister as the foremost caterer from Boca Raton, and mentioned the special hors d'oeuvres I prepared for the evening.

Redmond had his own agenda.

The Dating Game:

Bachelor Number One: Steve Mulliins. Steve was drinking white Zinfandel, my least favorite wine, so even though I wasn't a wine snob, I dismissed him as a serious candidate. He was perfectly pleasant and good looking, and I spent a half hour listening to more than I ever needed to know about the candy industry before my brother-in-law came along with the next guy on the hit parade.

Bachelor Number Two: George Cain. I gave him a big smile because he reminded me of Dex.

"You make these crab cakes?" he said, holding one up.

"I sure did, George, hope you like them," I said, still smiling.

"You think France has any catsup?" he said. I lost the smile and moved on after finding the catsup for him because no way could I connect with someone who was at the opposite end of the food chain.

There were three or four more perfectly suitable single men, but I found fault with each. I'd moved on from Mark and Boca, but not from Dex.

The party lasted for a couple of hours, and by eight o'clock the house emptied out and France brewed a pot of coffee.

"Aunt Dina, I don't believe anyone left here hungry. You saved them all the cost of dinner," said Wesley.

I laughed and shared the Bar None scenario with them.

"I loved doing this, but I just can't go back into the catering business. I'll find something else," I said, and no one questioned me.

1. Why had I bought a station wagon if I wasn't going to be a caterer?

2. Why did I cry in the Saab showroom when the salesman showed me a white convertible?

"Dina, how about I come over next week and plant an herb garden for you; there's an ideal sunny spot for it. Wes and I did it at our townhouse and we love it. How about next Friday? I'm taking the day off anyway," said Priscilla. "France, would you like to help?" she added, wanting to be sure to include her future mother-in-law.

"I would like that very much if Dina makes lunch for us and then afterwards, I'll treat for manicures over at Dream Nails," she said.

"Deal," Priscilla and I said at the same moment. My acrylics were long gone, and I was sure the white crunchy stuff Gaby found in her otherwise soggy chopped salad were some of the tips.

My cell rang on the way home and although I didn't recognize the number, I knew the area code was from Boca.

"Hello," I said, walking from the car to the house.

"Dina, my name is Ryan Franklin. I'm Sue-Ellen's brother."

The conversation was so painful I had to sit on the front porch to take it all in. The hours I'd been expecting Dex to show up to help with Gaby's party were spent at Sue-Ellen's side – in the Intensive Care Unit of West Boca Hospital. Her problems were more severe than anyone realized and she attempted to take her own life by overdosing on pills she'd been stockpiling. She must have had a change of heart at the last minute because she called her brother who in turn sent Dex a text.

Ryan raced over to Sue-Ellen's apartment while Dex called 911 before meeting them at the hospital. The paramedics were able to keep her going before settling her into the ICU. Ryan and Dex sat with her all day until the doctors told them she was out of the woods, although they were keeping her for observation and medical attention.

Ryan went on to explain why Dex wouldn't leave her side. She'd been calling and texting him for days saying she couldn't live without him and if he didn't hold to his promise of marriage, she threatened to commit suicide. Dex ignored it knowing he'd never asked her to marry him, and she'd had similar tantrums before. The only promise he made was to be there if she ever got sick or really needed him in an emergency. Dex and Ryan had always been open and honest with each other about Sue-Ellen's fantasies and Ryan had no reason to doubt his friend's veracity.

"Dina, I was so grateful that Dex was there in the hospital waiting with me. He felt terrible about letting you down, but Nurse Ratchet in the ICU made us give her our cell phones and there was no way he could have contacted you. He tried to get you on the way to the hospital, but couldn't reach you. (I'd left the phone in the car during one of my trips to and from Gaby's.) He said you'd make out okay because of all the extra people you hired.

Dex called me every day to find out how Sue-Ellen was doing, and when I asked if he squared everything with you, he told me what happened. He said he tried to explain, but that you wouldn't listen and he didn't even blame you for that, but when you wouldn't take his calls he figured it was over and that you and your husband were getting back together."

"Ryan, I'm divorced, but why didn't Dex explain all that at the party? We were there for hours together."

"He said he didn't want to bring you down while you were working, particularly when he saw the trouble you were having, and then you guys had that big fight and all. I just felt I had to tell you what you should know even though I promised Dex I wouldn't. He's a good guy and he loves you, did I forget to say that?"

Chapter 40

July

Show Business

Frances, Priscilla and I were digging out the place for my new herb garden, even finding room for some tomatoes plants, when Wesley stopped by. His television network was presenting a panel of home professionals and offered me a spot.

"Aunt Dina, we need someone who has experience in the food business, but not from a restaurant or a big company. I gave the higher-ups your background and they said fine. Now, you'll be on television and it's live, so you're going to have to ham it up a bit. Think you can do it?" Wesley said. "When Ronnie's show tanked, I knew I'd need to come up with a hit and I think this is it."

Had I been too hasty giving up on my catering career? I was in a new town with new people (and a new station wagon) and maybe this show was just the spark I needed to rekindle my love of preparing food. Frances said she had loads of compliments on the party and Ronnie's kitchen couldn't have been more suitable for the profession. With all the connections my sister and Redmond had, I was sure to find an assistant.

Dex wasn't the only person who could cook.

1. And serve.

2. And tend bar.

3. And clean up.

4. And make the most beautiful love to me.

"Dina! I'll need an answer this century, how about it? We have an open time slot a week from today. We'll do a couple of quick rehearsals, but it'll be unscripted – you guys have to sound natural," my nephew said.

Summoning up what I thought was a good Emmy-acceptance speech, I said, "I'd be honored, and thank you so much for the opportunity and I'll try to drop a few pounds by the air date because a caterer should be in great shape to make people think that she uses healthy ingredients, which I do, and then…"

"Hey Dina, you taking after Mom now with those run-ons?" Wesley said. "Now, let me explain the show. Well, the title is sort of self-explanatory; we're calling it 'Flops and Failures.'"

I guess the news of Gaby's disastrous party had traveled over a thousand miles to North Carolina. If I agreed to do the show then every local would find out about my event malfunction (that's what I was calling it now). Who'd hire me then?

"I'll do it, Wesley," I said. Then I'd look for a job.

Four self-employed professionals appeared on Flops and Failures: an interior designer, a landscape architect, a personal shopper and me. The format was for each of us to relay our tale of woe, beefing it up when necessary, although my segment didn't need much exaggeration, and then we were to give details for our future plans.

The interior designer, Missy Deschamp, started off the show by recounting stories of ordering two matching sofas that didn't match, wallpaper that bled through the paint, which according to the painter had never happened before even though she'd been warned by several colleagues that it was a major probability. Just when she was explaining the mishap, the irate client's cat (the client and the cat were both irate) scratched Missy so severely that she had to be rushed to the emergency room for massive doses of antibiotics and seven stitches.

The client sued Missy and refused to pay the medical bills. Missy admitted to our studio audience that she'd taken a short cut, and had the job redone correctly at great personal cost. It was the only way she could attempt to resurrect her reputation. The client eventually dropped the lawsuit when she saw her beautiful new living room, but still didn't pay a penny toward either the paint or the hospital charges. She did, however, take the cat to an animal psychologist to stop him from clawing people. It worked.

The landscape architect, Mac Epstein, had a pool built for his clients that immediately caved in and while he was assessing the situation with the contractor, the client's dog climbed into Mac's truck and ate some flowers that were slated for his next job. It turned out the flowers were poisonous to animals and old Yeller died.

Rosie Leigh, the personal shopper, purchased an entire wardrobe in size sixteen from a manufacturer's showroom sale and was fired as soon as she presented it to her new client. The client said the size fours that her last personal shopper bought fit perfectly and where did Rosie come up with a size sixteen for her?

The previous shopper had sewn size four labels into the older garments, unbeknownst to her client. The clothing, which would have fit the client had she not been so vain, couldn't be returned and as Rosie was new in the business, she gave all the garments to a consignment shop, where she recouped about ten percent of her cost. Rosie, eager for the wealthy client's business, took the hit because she hadn't bothered to seek out a reference from the retired shopper.

(Note to self: Find out where that consignment shop is.)

I went into just enough detail about Gaby's dinner party (deleting my expletive to the hostess) to have the entire studio, including my three stage buddies and crew, laughing at what amounted to the end of my career in Boca. It was another one of those situations that looked better in retrospect.

By the end of the show there was a common thread pulling the four of us together:

1. We had each made costly mistakes.

2. We paid dearly for having done so.

3. We tried to go on with our careers.

4. Except me. I knew I was finished.

Amazingly, the phone boards lit up with callers wanting to know how to hire us; they appreciated our honesty and humility.

The next surprise was when Wesley and his boss offered me an opportunity to do a cooking show, which would be broadcast live from Ronnie's home. They wanted a family dinner hour complete with healthy foods, informal and unscripted. Here's what they suggested and I swear I would have made up the exact same list:

1. Dina: Run the show with France helping out as needed.

2. France: Listen to your sister.

3. Redmond: Suggest appropriate wines for the meal.

4. Wesley: Create salads from my organic garden.

5. Priscilla: Demonstrate different table settings from Blum's, one of our sponsors.

The show was a success from the first episode. Our audience loved the informal banter that ran throughout the hour, and the five of us sitting down together for dinner at the close of the program seemed normal and comfortable.

Chapter 41

July

A Good Place

North Carolina was beginning to feel like home to me. I was content in the house, and Ronnie agreed to sell it to me for an attractive price. The show was doing so well that Wesley received a promotion and a raise. He and Priscilla decided to get married on August 11th in my sister's backyard. Frosty was invited and attended the service with husband #6, a younger man she met on a singles cruise. His name is Judah.

My mother produced and directed the kids' wedding and I didn't have to cook a thing.

We continued working on the show and at the end of one segment, Mitch, our cameraman yelled out, "Hey Dina, some guy in a van here for you. Says he's your 'soul mate.'"

And so he was.

Epilogue

1. Dex and I got married.

2. We adopted a kitten.

3. I got pregnant.

4. We had a boy.

5. We named him Wyatt (for Wanda).

6. His middle name is Jay.

7. The Chan sisters each had a set of twins.

8. Marcy became a C.P.A. and developed a computer program for tax attorneys.

9. Gaby began to call herself Gertrude after her stylist at Saks told her the name was all the rage in Paris. (France says not true at all.) Not to be left out of anything, Gaby donated $10,000 to Gilda's Club and attends Portia's breakfasts and dinners.

10. Wanda and Linz had two more baby girls and moved to Greensboro.

11. Valentina opened her own bi-lingual house keeping service with a loan from Portia.

12. Taffie and Sammy got married. It's a long story.

13. My hair and nails are short and natural, and I run two miles a day with my sister.

14. I'm in the right place at last.

Readers' Group Guide

Questions and Topics for Discussion:

1. What insight do you have into Dina's nature from the first chapter?

2. Have you even been with a group of contemporaries and felt you weren't really an insider?

3. Before Mark leaves her, does Dina cook and entertain to help her husband's career or to advance her own popularity?

4. Does Dina feel inferior only because she and her husband are on the low end of the financial strata at their country club?

5. Why didn't Dina pay more attention to her failing marriage? Have you been in a situation where leaving (husband or wife) came as a surprise to the other spouse? Do we overlook signs on purpose?

6. Dex is Dina's white knight, but he's not perfect. In what ways do you think he could have been more supportive?

7. When Dina and Wanda come to verbal blows, whose side were you on? Are some friendships irreparable? Do you think Wanda deceived Dina with Acorn Rentals, or was it just a coincidence?

8. In many ways the villain, Gabriela, gives Dina a hard time. In what areas was Gabriela on the right track?

9. In the two scenes ending Part One, we see Dina going crazy trying to stay on schedule organizing the largest event of her career. Have you ever geared up for something where everything went wrong? Were you able to fix it and go on?

10. At the end of Part One were you more forgiving toward Mark and Taffie?

11. How does Dina relate to her parents, sister and nephew? Do they overpower her?

12. Finally, doesn't everyone know someone like Frosty?